Linh Ly
Is Doing Just Fine

Linh Ly Is Doing Just Fine

♦ *A NOVEL* ♦

THAO VOTANG

alcove
press

Copyright © 2024 by Thao Votang

Published in the United States by Alcove Press, an imprint of The Quick Brown Fox & Company LLC.

Alcove Press and its logo are trademarks of The Quick Brown Fox & Company LLC.

Library of Congress Catalog-in-Publication data available upon request.

ISBN (hardcover): 978-1-63910-789-6
ISBN (ebook): 978-1-63910-790-2

Cover design by Rebecca Nelson

Printed in the United States.

www.alcovepress.com

Alcove Press
34 West 27th St., 10th Floor
New York, NY 10001

First Edition: July 2024

10 9 8 7 6 5 4 3 2 1

cho mẹ

◆ 1 ◆

I DIDN'T KNOW EXACTLY how my mother met her men. By *her men*, I mean the men she dated after she divorced my father. At first, she sent me pictures and names. I spotted a wedding ring in the first photo I received and asked her about it. She didn't reply, and I didn't bother asking about that man again. My mom didn't make dating profiles, but many of the men did. I read their likes and dislikes. I looked up the value of their properties. I studied their children's social media platforms.

But I'm getting ahead of myself.

In February, aptly around the Lunar New Year, my mom emailed the final divorce decree to me as an attachment. She never wrote in the body of her emails. Sometimes she added a question formed as a statement in the subject line. Usually, she followed her emails with a torrent of text messages. I couldn't explain why one form of communication made more sense to her than the other. I only knew what I expected from her.

By April, she was getting settled in her new house. I had come over to help her move a table. The house was a modest building with two bedrooms and one bathroom. It had a light brown brick facade, wood cladding along the sides and back, and fake shutters. There was a small front yard with a larger backyard surrounded by a wooden fence. A place under her own name and no trace of my father. No trace of me. But that didn't really matter. I was twenty-seven, old enough to no longer need the physical mementos of my childhood.

"Leave your cup. I'll wash it later," Mom said. She set a key on the table in front of me. "Here. This is for you."

"But this is your house." I got up to wash my glass, setting it in the dishwasher where she put dishes to dry.

"You need a key. We're still a family."

The key was shiny with sharp teeth, so sharp they felt like they could break skin. With the old house—my childhood home—gone, the only things that were left were my mom, my father, and me.

I let myself out so my mom could get ready for her first date after almost thirty years of marriage. I had done everything I could to be there for my mom through the divorce. And now, she would start on the path of finding herself, something she hadn't been able to do when she'd married at twenty. Would she go through the same things I had at that age? I frowned at the memory of drunk nights and hungover days throughout college. I cringed at the memories of seeking acceptance in all the wrong places. Would my mom's experience be as messy? Would she be able to bounce back without getting hurt?

As the questions swirled in my mind, I took my foot off the gas pedal. At a honk from behind me, I circled around the block and parked two lots away from Mom's house. I could see her front door while the other cars parked on the street blocked me from view. I pushed my seat back so that I could rest my head and still see just above the dashboard.

There was only an hour before her date was supposed to pick her up. An hour wasn't a long time to wait, so I waited. It seemed perfectly normal to make sure my mom's date started off without any bumps. Perfectly normal to make sure she didn't get stood up. As I waited, I let myself drift to sleep. As if to prove I wasn't really spying on my mom. Every time another car drove by, I woke up.

Finally, a beige Honda slowed to a stop in front of her house. It was five minutes before the hour. He was early like I always was. A promising sign. Mom had told me that her date's name was Peter, and he worked in another department at her company. He wore the polo shirt and khaki pants ubiquitous to people who lived in the suburbs that made up most of the metroplex. The metroplex was made of Dallas, Fort Worth, and the vast spread of suburbs around the two cities. The highways that stitched all of them together were so thick, like an ivy swallowing a tree, that it became the metroplex.

It occurred to me that Mom should have met her date at the restaurant. I made a mental note to talk about that with her. She shouldn't be giving out her address.

As I watched Mom walk out of her house, I tried to see her as a stranger would. She kept her straight, black hair short, cut just below her jaw, and always wore makeup. She wore a dress with leggings underneath for the date, probably because she was perpetually cold. Despite that, I could see that she hadn't zipped up her jacket. The corners flapped in the wind. I wanted to run out and zip it up for her as if she were my daughter and not the other way around.

What did people think of her if they did not know her? When they met her as a woman, not a mother, not a wife. If they had not witnessed so many of the bad moments of her life as I had? With her quick laughter and fast smile, would they think nothing terrible had ever happened to her?

The setting sun was blotted out by a cloudy sky that cast a soft blue-gray over everything. Peter opened the car door for my mom and then quickly ran around to the driver's side like he didn't want to keep her waiting. When they drove off, I swear I intended to head home. But then, the errant thought that he could murder my mother skittered through my mind.

It wasn't an unusual thought. What kind of woman didn't constantly gauge her surroundings for danger and death? That morning in the news, the body of a woman had been found on the shore of one of the metroplex's lakes. She'd gone missing a week prior. I'd thought about how I wasn't shocked because it felt like women went missing or were found dead every day. You only had to pay attention to the headlines farther down the fold to see it. The headlines about the dead women didn't even warrant the largest font size. I worked in the public relations department at a university. I knew how priorities manifest themselves in newsreels.

Peter looked harmless. Peter looked like someone who didn't have secrets. He looked completely and utterly normal. *Maybe that should be a red flag,* I thought. But my mother and Peter worked at the same place. He probably wouldn't murder her, I told myself over and over. And yet I still went to the restaurant.

I was able to find his car because I remembered he had one of those red tasseled lanyards hanging from his rearview mirror. I was lucky that the decoration made his car stand out in this particular part of town. Still, the red tassel and gaudy gold plastic made me nostalgic for things I didn't think I could have in my own life. I didn't have the cultural knowledge of what it meant. Had my parents ever told me? Maybe it was only red and gold bling to hang on your car. Maybe it was for luck. Maybe it was nothing but a trend.

I couldn't see them inside the restaurant, and there wasn't a parking space open. So, I got onto the highway toward home and thought about how I would need to make sure my mother couldn't recognize me next time. I would have to be more prepared next time, maybe have binoculars and a disguise. Wear something I would never usually wear. Next time.

◆ 2 ◆

ONLY FOR TENNIS WOULD I agree to be anywhere at seven thirty in the morning on a Saturday. It felt like the wine I'd drunk the night before while binge-watching a Korean drama-comedy-horror series was still coursing through my veins. It smelled like everyone in my league was off-gassing alcohol. In contrast, our coach, Nesbitt, looked hydrated and fresh.

"I have a treat for you ladies," Nesbitt said, bouncing on the balls of her feet. The movement was making me queasy. "We are playing a men's team today."

I looked over at Lauren, who was the only person on our team that I talked to on a regular basis. It wasn't that I thought the others weren't good enough. Lauren was the only one who pushed through all my monosyllabic responses and still talked to me. She raised an eyebrow.

"Of course, I know you won't admit that you're becoming complacent. But you are. And this will be a fun way to shake you out of it." Nesbitt clapped her hands in excitement. "I did try to make it a bit easier. The team is a men's group in their fifties and up."

"They're going to kick our asses," Lauren said. "They've been playing for decades longer than we have."

"Yes, but you'll play up, and they'll play down. They agreed to it, so have fun!" With one more bounce, Nesbitt walked away from us.

"What, they agreed to show some young women how it's done?" Lauren asked, squinting up at the sky. "I'm hungover as fuck."

"Me also." I rolled my ankles. I always stretched from my feet up and then back down. The others were half-heartedly making the movements of stretching. The blonde twins in our group, Jessica and Tiffany, went through their routine together as if they were doing a choreographed dance. They had on their tennis whites, and I knew they were feeling something because I saw them taking pills before leaving their car. They were the best players on our team in large part because they started playing when they were three. I wasn't sure why they bothered with our league.

Elana sat on the ground to stretch her legs. Her long braids were gathered in a ponytail that slipped down her back. Some strands were almost long enough to touch the ground. Elana was the next best player, and if she were only five inches taller, I thought she'd be able to beat Tiffany and Jessica without breaking a sweat. But then again, maybe she was just holding back.

Becka sprawled on the cement next to Elana but wasn't even trying to look like she was stretching. Ann-Marie and Jan hooked their fingers in the chain-linked fence as they swung their legs to loosen their hips. We were all in our late twenties. Even though we competed in league tournaments together, we weren't really friends. I usually stayed in my car until the last minute, to avoid having to chat. Tennis wasn't a team sport, after all. I tried to look around the corner at the bleachers where the men were probably gathered.

"Let's make a bet, ladies," Lauren said, pulling us all together like she always did. "The first person who pukes gets treated to breakfast as a thanks for ending this torture quickly."

"All ready?" Nesbitt came back to us. "All right, hands all in. Show them what you've got!"

We put our hands in, and Nesbitt shouted, "One, two, three!"

"Drinks!" I said, our traditional cheer, along with the rest of the players.

Nesbitt assigned me to court eight. The person I was supposed to play wasn't here yet, so I stretched and hoped they wouldn't show. That would be lucky. Then I could go home. I let my teammates file to their courts first. The team we were playing looked vaguely familiar. I played at these courts enough that I probably had seen most everyone who also played here on a regular basis. Of course, that didn't mean there was any sort of community. Tennis was still the sort of sport that was heavy with class baggage, which meant people didn't even acknowledge one another when changing courts.

The sun was up, but it was still chilly. I kept my jacket on and didn't sit down on the bench. If I sat, I didn't think I'd be able to get up again. The courts were painted blue and had a rubberized texture that still felt decadent. I learned tennis on hard cement courts. Running on a rubberized court made me feel like I had climbed up a level, and I never took it for granted. What would it be like to play on the fake clay at one of those fancy clubs?

The other players were beginning to hit, and the familiar sound of the racquets striking the ball in their sweet spot calmed me. I resisted the urge to pull out my phone. I had wanted to message my mom immediately this morning, but I didn't want to do it too early. I didn't want her to think I'd sat around thinking about her date. I'd told myself I'd wait until after tennis, but the phone's presence in the pocket of my bag tempted me with every second.

After a few minutes, I noticed someone making their way to my court. He was jogging, and I could only see his black jacket and hair through the green tarp that was zip-tied to the chain-link fence to reduce wind. The shape of his body was familiar, just as his teammates were.

When he came through the gate, I recognized Peter. I had run a search on his name last night. The first photo of him I found was his sterile headshot on the company website. He had worn a white shirt, black suit jacket, and blue tie for the photo. Dressed in quick-dry polyester for tennis, he looked slightly less like your ubiquitous MBA grad.

"I'm sorry I'm late," Peter said, holding out his hand. Up close, his headshot was surprisingly accurate. "I'm Peter."

"Linh," I said, shaking his hand firmly. "Out late last night?"

"Oh no. My alarm didn't go off this morning."

"I'd still be asleep if mine did that," I said. *Did my mom invite you inside?* I wanted to ask.

"You look familiar." Peter was stretching hurriedly. "These courts are the best in the area, don't you think?"

"Our team practices here." I shrugged. I'd picked these courts randomly years ago. "We don't usually play matches this early."

"We have an advantage then. We're usually halfway done with drills by now."

"I'm sure," I said, drinking a tiny sip of water. Nesbitt had done this on purpose. She was more malicious than her sunny disposition let on. What was her point in making us play when she knew we would all be so hungover?

"Should we start?" Peter asked, popping open a new can of balls, then peeling back the metal top.

I inhaled the fresh scent of the rubber balls and nodded. We hit gently at half court, the traditional warm-up, for a few minutes before moving to the baseline to hit across the full court.

Peter hit his balls cleanly, with a little bit of spin. I assumed he could do more but that he was reserving himself. I watched his feet move to try to catch any hint of injury or favoring that I could exploit. The ibuprofen I had taken this morning would probably last an hour before whatever headache was left came creeping back. I ground my teeth together as a cold sweat swept through my body. Alcohol didn't go down as easily as it used to, and I channeled the annoyance I felt into my strokes.

Tennis is a game that requires strategy and concentration, but to play well, players must learn to play without thinking. The body needed to be trained to know what to do in microseconds and without thought. But even with all the training in the world, some days the perfect timing could be gone. It was hard to watch when that happened to someone. Being hungover typically made that magic timing disappear.

Peter motioned for us to come to the net. He spun his racquet, and I won the spin. I chose to serve first, and he picked the side of the court. My stomach was churning. Would I be the first to vomit? When I hit my serve, I felt exactly when my body faltered and altered my movement—only slightly, but enough to take off the force of my serve. With every step and swing, I could tell I was moving too slowly. I played defensively even while I was serving. I wished someone would puke to end this, and I hated Nesbitt for scheduling this challenge match. She was chatting with the other team's coach. I could see her through the fences. As I tossed my ball up in the air, I saw Nesbitt laugh. Was that the real purpose of this match-up?

Our points flowed past me quickly until we were one–four and switching sides.

"Are you okay?" Peter asked.

"Fine." I felt like I might vomit. I sipped from my bottle of water slowly.

As we started to our opposite baselines, I heard the clatter of a tennis racquet. The sound made me cringe, and everyone on the courts looked toward the source. It was Becka. She had dropped her racquet and made a run for the wastebasket hung from the fence. I was too far away to hear her but could see her leaning over the bin. I felt sorry for the court staff. They never put bags in those bins. Why would you when it was usually only filled with tennis ball containers?

"I should go check on her, I think," I said to Peter, relieved to excuse myself from a match I was going to lose.

When I got to Becka, someone had brought her a towel. Nesbitt was rubbing Becka's back, and our team had gathered around. The other coach was already breaking his team into pairs, to use up the courts. No one wasted court time.

"Were you beating him, Becka?" asked Jessica.

"My head feels like there is a groundhog rolling around in it," Becka said.

"Really?" Lauren bent down to look into Becka's eyes.

"Of course, she wasn't beating him," Tiffany said. "They were all kicking our asses."

"They're fives, aren't they?" Jessica asked, looking at Nesbitt. Skill level was measured on a seven-point scale, sevens being professionals.

"Fourish to fives," Nesbitt said.

Elana laughed. "I'm leaving."

Jessica and Tiffany followed Elana off the court. Lauren helped Becka with her bag, and they headed to the bathrooms in the shop. I looked around for Ann-Marie and Jan but didn't see them. They'd probably left as soon as Becka puked and everyone abandoned their game. Nesbitt had already stopped paying attention to all of us and was watching the other coach with his team.

"Is that coach any good?" I asked, walking to Nesbitt's side.

"Oh yes, he's wonderful," Nesbitt said.

"Maybe I should take some private lessons."

Nesbitt was startled until she looked at me and laughed. "I always knew you were a jokester. The quiet ones always are."

"See you Monday, Nesbitt," I said.

The teenager in charge of managing reservations had already given my court away. I pointed at my things before I walked onto the court. Out of the corner of my eye, I watched the players hit. They were probably my age but seemed so much younger in the way they moved about with their chests puffed in self-importance. They acted annoyed that I was on the court, breaking tennis protocol, even though my bag had been there before them.

As I walked through the courts, I snuck glances at Peter playing, like I would be able to see all his secrets through his tennis form. My phone buzzed, and my racquets vibrated against each other. Lauren had messaged me an address where the group was getting breakfast, and she insisted that I come. I weighed my options. I had planned to drive home to Lollipop, my cat, and read in bed while waiting for the right time to message my mom. Usually, I would make up something to say to Lauren and skip the team outing, but I decided a distraction might be good. Besides, a heavy and greasy breakfast would help stabilize my body.

★　★　★

When we were settled in our booth, Lauren snapped her menu shut and said, "They have some rule and won't serve mimosas until after ten."

"I thought that was only on Sundays." Jan said.

"God bless Texas," Tiffany said.

I looked at Tiffany. I hadn't known she could be so sarcastic.

"Maybe that's for the best?" Becka asked.

We ordered, and I finished two cups of coffee by the time our platters of eggs, toast, and pancakes covered the table. The quiet of food descended upon our table, broken only by the scrape of silverware on the ceramic plates.

"So," Lauren said as she leaned back and rubbed her stomach, "what's going on with you these days, Linh?"

I felt seven pairs of eyes on me, and I could feel nervous sweat in my armpits. "Not much."

"There's got to be something," Tiffany said. "You never come out with us."

"Oh, I'm just very busy," I said.

"You play tennis twice a week, sometimes three times a week as part of this team," Jan said.

"We are your 'busy,'" Ann-Marie said, finishing Jan's thought.

"I feel like I'm going to be sick again," Becka said.

"Sit at the end of the booth, Becka," Jessica said, waving her hands. Half the table got out of the booth, then slid back in, with Becka at the end.

"We're ready," Lauren said, pointing at me. "Let's hear it."

"Well," I said. They all waited. All seven played tennis like me, and they were probably all better players than me. They could all be patient and wait for their opponent to make a mistake first. They watched for past injuries, muscles being favored, and how their opponents might signal the direction of their serve. "My parents got a divorce this year, and my mom went on her first date last night."

"What did she wear?" Tiffany asked.

"Did he open the car door for her?" Jessica inquired.

"How expensive was the restaurant he took her to?" Ann-Marie asked.

"What is he like?" Elana wanted to know.

"Well, it's weird," I said, sipping from my coffee mug. "He was the person I played with today."

The group gasped, then everyone talked at once. When they had calmed down, I gave them a small smile.

"What a coincidence," Lauren said. "Were you beating him? Did he know?"

Their questions overlapped. They broke into sub-conversations, and I could hear them go through various versions of hypothetical situations that had been bouncing through my own mind. I'd eaten everything on my plate, my coffee cup was empty, and the server was nowhere in sight. I felt around in my bag for my wallet.

"Well, breakfast was nice," I said when their voices lulled. "But I have to get going."

I could feel the seven pairs of eyes on me as I left. My bag hit the door as I went through, my racquets clattered, and I rushed to my car without looking back at the table. I could still feel their eyes and hated the idea that they would keep talking about me after I left. I shouldn't have gone to breakfast with them. I didn't know them. They didn't know me. I liked it that way. That kept me out of situations where I had to pretend to feel happy. Pretend to be cheerful. Pretend to care about the thousand little things that happened in their lives.

Once I was parked in front of my home, I messaged Mom, asking how her date went, and waited as the three dots bounced.

Mom: *It was fun! Getting mani-pedi can't talk.*

My mom was getting her nails done, and I had been about to get my ass kicked in tennis by my maybe new father. Did you even call them that when your mom remarried when you were an adult? Lugging my tennis bag into my apartment, I dropped it next to my shoes and flopped onto the couch. Lollipop meowed and sat on my stomach. I petted her absently as she "made biscuits," kneading my belly with her paws.

The couch was set across from the sliding door that led out to the patio. I didn't own a television, so I spent most of my time watching the birds outside, with Lollipop. I'd gotten a three-person couch specifically so that I could nap on it comfortably. With my head on one armrest, my feet weren't even close to touching the other end. There was a rectangular coffee table made of real wood planks that I'd gotten from a vintage store. A circular dining table with two chairs separated my living area from the kitchen. A short hallway led off to my bedroom and bathroom. The walls were the beige of most rental properties.

Though I had lived there for years, I hadn't put up decorations. The emptiness of the walls calmed me. The lack of objects assured me that the rooms could belong to anyone—that my presence and absence would go unnoticed. I watched the ceiling fan whirl and wondered where my mom was and how she was going to spend the rest of her weekend. I couldn't picture what she would do with her spare time, and found that alarming.

How could I know so little about the person who had given me life?

♦ 3 ♦

THE DOG AND HOUND was a restaurant bar with upholstered wood chairs, green walls, and low light. It would have been better if smoking were still allowed inside, except for the unshakable miasma that came with that. I overlooked that it was a chain business with at least twenty-five locations within the metroplex. I ignored how the wood of the tables and counters was cut to look worn by age when they were not. I ignored how the kitchen was spotless, the floors never sticky, and how all the bathroom stall doors were perfectly straight. This was the metroplex, after all. Everything had a certain level of polish.

Hoa would never admit to it, but I knew she thought it was a silly place for us to meet at first. But eventually, Dog and Hound had won her over. She always made concessions like this for me. She was sweet where I was a curmudgeon. Hoa was taller, paler, and had a heart-shaped face. It wasn't just that she was prettier. She was also more kind, and people were drawn to her. Even I couldn't resist her. We made quite a strange pair through school. In junior high, we were the only Asians in our class, so I suppose our friendship made sense to everyone. But even in high school, when the number of Asians in our class swelled to five, Hoa stayed friends with me. But then she went down to the university in Austin while I went to one of the commuter colleges in the metroplex.

"This place is starting to remind me of a bar that closed in Austin," Hoa said as she slipped into the booth seat across from me. "Yes, I can see it if I squint. Close to campus. The underlying scent of vomit."

"Are you thinking about going back?" I turned all the bottles of condiments on the table, so their labels were facing the wall.

"I don't think about Austin much anymore," Hoa said, flipping through the menu even though we always ordered the same thing. "The last time I went to visit, it was starting to feel like the metroplex anyway. Except the buildings have the tiniest bit of design flair."

"You don't think you'll ever want to move back?"

Hoa closed the menu in front of her. "I don't think so. It's changed. I've changed. There's something satisfying about that. Time and place and who you become when you go somewhere new. Time goes by so fast too. I can't believe it. Maybe that's the years talking."

"We'll turn that dreaded thirty soon."

"We still have three years. Plenty of time."

"For?"

"Marriage and babies. Isn't your mom always bothering you about that? How is she doing, anyway?"

"Fine. She's excited. She's always excited and cheery. The divorce has distracted her from my single and childless state."

"Is she seeing a therapist?"

"She says she can't afford it. I can only suggest it so many times. She doesn't listen to me. Do you have a therapist? Do therapists have therapists?"

"Therapists should always have a therapist. So, yeah, I do. You're doing a lot for her. You've done a lot for her. It's good

of you." Hoa smiled at the server, Daylon, as he came up to our
table with glasses of water.

We always sat at one of his tables because Hoa adored him.
Or she thought he was really hot. But she would never say anything or do anything. I didn't know why I contributed to whatever their relationship was. Hoa made a good salary. I didn't like
what I imagined dating between the two would be. He would
attach himself to her and let her pay for everything. Would he
move into her condo, expect her to always have food ready for
him to eat, and let her clean the bathroom every week without
lifting a finger to help?

"The usual for you two tonight?" Daylon asked, looking
only at Hoa.

"Yes," I said.

"Please," Hoa said.

"Coming up." Daylon smiled and bounced a bit before
walking away.

I turned to the window to give Hoa time to watch him.
A car was parking, and its headlights glared against the glass.
Could the driver see me through the window? Did their head-
lights make me look as white as a ghost?

"I'd suggest giving him your number, but you never would,"
I said as Hoa took a sip of water from her glass.

"I'm not dating right now."

"Oh, I wasn't suggesting dating. A date. A night. Not even
the entire night." I shrugged. "It doesn't have to be serious."

"I don't really enjoy that. Besides, it would ruin your favorite place."

"Maybe we should find a real sports bar anyway. This place
only has three TVs."

"So?" Hoa knocked on the table, as if calling us to an
agenda. "How does it feel to have your mom out dating?"

"I don't know," I said, putting my head in my hands for a moment. "They worry me. It all makes me worried."

"Why? Who do you mean, 'they'?"

"She's older now and doing something I don't think she did before. I mean the men. Do you think she went on a lot of dates during the war, when she was growing up? Before she met my dad and they came here?"

"Ask."

"My parents don't talk about that. Ever."

Daylon brought our drinks, and the jolt of electricity he brought with him to our table annoyed me.

"She's going to get hurt by them. By the men," I said when I thought Daylon might linger. He turned and left.

Hoa reached out to squeeze my arm. "If she does, she'll recover. We all go through this."

"She's older now than when we started dating. What if the men who are all single now are all damaged or even more fucked up than we were as teenagers?"

"What if their wives died in an accident? What if they grew, but their partner did not, and they decided they needed someone who wanted to grow with them? Have you talked to your dad recently? Has she?"

"I haven't. I don't know about her. He hasn't reached out to me in at least two years. I'd be surprised if he kept my phone number, much less knows where I live."

"Do you have his phone number?"

"I have the last one I had. I don't know if it works. What would I say to him?"

The last time I had seen and talked to my father was more than a year ago now. Mom had moved out but needed me to pick up the rest of her belongings. I had gone when he would be at work. It had taken me longer than I anticipated to pack Mom's things, or he had come home early. All I remember was the panic of being caught. I didn't know which version of my father I would get. The public or private version of himself. It was still early in the afternoon, and so I quelled my flight instinct. It was too early for him to be drunk. My father asked me about the divorce, looking at me like I was nothing. As if the divorce meant the severing of his responsibility to me. I still remembered the derision in his voice. I could have been a stranger. I was just another girl who was there to clean up for him.

"Maybe start with a 'How are you?'" Hoa said.

"How has your work been?" I asked.

"Or that. Oh, really?" Hoa rolled her eyes, but let me change the subject. "My work is fine. It's the same."

Hoa couldn't say all that much about her job. She was a therapist at an assisted living facility. It was an extremely posh facility, so she was paid exceptionally well to make sympathetic noises as the residents complained about how their children were spending the millions of dollars they had spent their lives hoarding. Then, in her spare time, she did the same work for free at a facility where residents didn't have much money at all.

"I'm sorry. I didn't mean to make you provide counseling for me too," I said.

"It's not. We're friends. I'm here for you."

Hoa put her hand on my forehand, and I counted to three before I sat back and looked out at the restaurant. The glow of the televisions and neon beer signs reflected off people's faces. Hoa put her chin on her hands and looked up at the nearest TV, which was playing a basketball game. This is what I loved about our friendship. Silences didn't have to be filled. Nights out weren't some kind of performance where I had to be interesting all the time. I didn't have to worry about saying something astute or amusing. I could just be me.

When Daylon came up to our table then with our baskets of fried fish and fries, I didn't say anything, and he struck up a conversation with Hoa. As they talked, I watched a couple get into their car. I thought about my mother's date with Peter and wondered how it had gone, exactly. Had they lingered over dessert and drinks after dinner? Had they gone somewhere else for another round of drinks to stretch the night out? Mom would make him laugh. They would have a good time. My mom was too cheerful to sink into sulky silence. I must have inherited that from my father. I attributed all of my difficult characteristics to my father. Had my mom invited Peter into her house at the end of the night? Surely she knew that she should not. That was an international sign for sex, wasn't it? Would I have to review the rules of dating with my mom, as if I had all the experience in the world?

Again, I tried to see my mom as a stranger. It was impossible. So then, I tried to imagine how I would feel if I had been married when I was so young and was now single after thirty years. How would those years that didn't pan out the way they were supposed to change me? What was it like to have a child, spend years working, and then work two jobs to escape your unloving husband? What was it like to have the man you married turn out to be nothing you had wished for?

"What have you been up to?" Hoa asked as she squirted ketchup into her basket.

"Tennis and work, like usual," I said.

"It would be fun to see you play sometime. Do friends come to watch?"

"For tournaments, I guess. Not for practice or anything like that."

"I'd like to see you play sometime."

"Sure," I said, even though I knew Hoa knew I'd never invite her to a match.

"Do you still never play doubles? Isn't it lonely to play by yourself?"

"It's less complicated. Mistakes are only yours when you play alone."

"I see," Hoa said and waited for me to say more. I pretended not to notice.

There was a loud crash as someone knocked a pint of beer off their table. I glared in the direction of the offending group and saw five college kids. One of the girls had spread out her arms to emphasize something and knocked the glass four feet away. She'd pulled her arms across her chest in embarrassment and now looked like she was performing some sort of incantation.

Like me, students from the university frequented this place because they could walk to get to it. I usually liked being around them because they came from all over the country and kept the neighborhood from being saturated with the kind of people who jogged pushing double-wide strollers. But tonight, their inexperienced youth reminded me of years I didn't want my mother to relive again.

"Does it make you feel older or wiser being around the students?" asked Hoa.

"Both," I said. "I like the reminder of how stupid you are when you're twenty-one."

The university that these kids attended paid my bills. I thought about the boring marketing copy I had to write and edit to entice high school students who would become these college students.

"You know, at that age the brain isn't done forming yet," Hoa said.

"I'm not sure it fully forms for a large swath of people."

"You're becoming jaded."

"Becoming? And shouldn't that be some form of good luck?"

"I doubt that is what our ancestors had in mind."

"I doubt they expected us to be transplanted clear across the planet."

"No?"

Daylon brought us another round without our asking, and I watched Hoa blush at his mere presence.

"What's his story?" I asked.

"Who?"

"Daylon—what's his story?"

"He works here at night and takes care of his mom, who's sick."

"Oh. Is that what he wanted to do?"

"It's not usually what someone wants to do, is it? He had just graduated college when his mom was diagnosed. His older sister had a good full-time job she couldn't leave. So, he takes care of his mom during the day, and she takes care of her through the night. You know, we've been going here for years, and he's worked here for at least a year. You ought to talk to people more. They're not scary."

"I say hi. I'm shy."

Hoa laughed, and I smiled. She knew the truth about me. I hated small talk.

"You never know when you might make another friend, Linh."

I let out a long breath slowly. Did she know that I didn't have any other friends but her?

"What do you have planned for this weekend?" I asked.

"I have to go to a baby shower. Do you remember Helen Madison from high school? We all had calculus together?"

"Sure, but I didn't know you kept up with her."

"We struck up a conversation on social media, and I guess we got close enough for a baby shower invite."

"Do you think she invited you to make sure she got everything on her registry purchased?"

"Well, it paid off because I purchased the most expensive item."

"You did not!"

"Of course, I didn't. I bought all the safety fixtures they had on the registry. You know, people like to buy new families cute toys and all of that, but what they need are the locks, diapers, and child gates. The toys are only going to get saturated in drool."

"How is it to be around people from high school?"

"That's what we are."

"Yeah, but we're—" I waved at us. "We have known each other since junior high. Obviously different. They're all . . ."

"It's the same, Linh. We're all just older now. You make more out of it than there is."

"Is everyone there going to be from high school?"

"I'll report back. I didn't look at the guest list."

Hoa took everything in stride like that. If I had been invited, which I was not because I avoided talking to anyone I knew from the past, I would have looked at everyone who had RSVPed "yes," and decided whether or not I would go, based on that.

We had a third drink and talked until the last call. I waited with Hoa until her rideshare came, and declined her offer of a ride home. After she left, I heard footsteps and grabbed the pepper spray I kept on my keychain.

I made out Daylon's figure and relaxed my hand slightly.

"Hi," said Daylon.

"Hoa just left." I took a step back.

"Oh." Daylon fidgeted with his keys. "I'd wanted to say bye."

"She's not dating anyone else. Just so you know."

"Oh, okay." Daylon ran his hand through his hair, and in the dark, I could see why Hoa thought he was cute. His motions were gentle, and I knew he was friendly, like Hoa. He probably found me ugly in all of my rudeness.

"See you next time," I said, turning away.

When I heard a car door open, I looked back at Daylon. He had gotten into a Toyota Camry. I wasn't sure what I expected. It was in good shape, even though it didn't seem that new. What did a car tell you about a person? Daylon and Peter were both men who drove reliable cars. Sensible sedans. Better a sedan than an SUV. Better an SUV than a truck.

I shrugged and turned toward home. A car wasn't going to tell me what I wanted to know. I looked up at the dark sky. The light pollution from the city blotted out any possible trace of starlight. The cold air broke through my alcohol fog, and I looked behind me. Tree shadows moved at the insistence of the wind. I heard leaves crunch and looked behind me again. Maybe I should have let Hoa take me home. This was how women disappeared, wasn't it? And it would be my fault for walking outside at night alone. Was my mom home safe right now? And would I get home without harm? I knew that if I could, I would trade my own safety for hers.

★　★　★

I slept in on Sundays. On Sundays, everyone rushed around, busy with church. Hoa had an open invitation for me to join her, but I could never get my head around the priests. Catholicism was too full of bad men. The same ruler could be used to cross out most of my life, but I had to draw the line somewhere.

I didn't hold her church against Hoa. I understood how rituals were a comfort.

My own Sunday routine involved cleaning. As others went to wash their souls of their sins or whatever, I cleaned my apartment. I convinced myself that I had been born a very neat person who didn't like disorder, but what kind of ten-year-old naturally decides to spend their weekend cleaning the house? A clean house meant that there wasn't anything for my father to shout about when he came home drunk, at least before I hit puberty. After my body changed, my father found plenty of accusations to scream at me. It didn't matter how clean I kept the house for him.

I always started with the bathroom, then vacuumed and mopped the floors of the kitchen and bathroom. The kitchen never took a long time because I rarely bothered to cook complicated meals for myself. Dishes were washed after each use, so I never even opened the dishwasher. My lack of decorations meant there wasn't much to dust. Sometimes, I wished I had more to clean so it would take longer. So then I wouldn't have hours and hours of time to fill on Sundays.

The vastness of Sundays had never bothered me before, and now I tried to think of how my mom was spending her time. Was she out shopping? Was she working on the garden she had mentioned? She'd never grown anything before. Of course, she'd never had time to do something for herself and only herself before.

I was parking in front of her house before I realized that maybe I should have messaged her first. But no, she was my mom. Not a friend. Our lives didn't have the same rules as social acquaintances. We were family, and it was different. I knocked, even though I had a key.

"Just come in," Mom said. "Did you already lose your key?"

She had her gardening gloves in one hand and was dressed in an old shirt and shorts.

"I was just driving near here." I followed her into the backyard.

"I wouldn't have heard your knock out here. You should use your key. Do you want to help?"

She was being nice. Mom always invited people to help with whatever she was doing. It was her way of making everyone feel included.

"I don't know anything about gardening," I said. There was no place to sit, so I stood, resting my weight on one leg and then switching to the other.

"I don't really either. I've been reading, and the people at the nursery gave me directions."

"Did you have a garden in Vietnam?" I didn't usually bring up Vietnam. The few times I had in the past, the overwhelming sadness that seemed to come over my mom was too much. I learned to avoid it, so we didn't drown in the feeling.

"When we could. But everything is different here, so I have to learn." Mom smiled up at me. I nodded. My dark hair was absorbing the sun's heat, as were my black pants and black shirt. Sweat trickled down my back. There was no breeze, and I could feel my body heat get trapped between my skin and clothes.

"Do you want to go inside and watch TV? It's too hot if you're not going to help."

As far as I could tell, Mom was just moving around dirt.

"Okay, yeah, I'll be inside," I said.

She had moved around some furniture since we'd unpacked together. I noticed a new lamp in her bedroom from the open door, but I didn't go look. Her room felt private, but I also knew she wouldn't care. Maybe it was something about her from growing up without ever having her own room. Maybe that was a very American thing, to have things that are only yours. All that ownership and individuality.

I settled on the sofa in the living room and turned on the TV. Mom had a cable subscription, and I started flipping channels. The couch was new and smelled only of her. It was a strange smell to me. Her smell had always been my parent's smell or our smell.

I inhaled her scent deeply.

Mom eventually came in from the garden and joined me. I heard a sniffle and watched her yank a tissue from the box on the side table. I had chosen a romantic drama, and it was nearing its end. Someone much loved was dead, and dead after some terrible misunderstanding or missed connection. My mom was crying so hard I didn't think she would be able to notice that I wasn't crying. Except I was crying, very much against my will. I didn't like crying. I certainly didn't like crying around other people.

We let the credits play so we could regain our composure. Our relationship had softened to the point where we could cry around each other, but we mustn't watch each other cry. As I was leaving, she gave me a sideways hug. I stilled at the rush of warmth. My parents never hugged me. It wasn't so strange to be touched by my mom, though. She must have held me countless times when I was a child, but the thought of my father comforting me was impossible to imagine.

"I love you," Mom said as she shut the door.

I stared at the door, and she turned off the porch light while I was still there. Those three little words. How casually she said them. Had she ever said that to me before? My parents had never said things like that to me as I was growing up. I'd always thought the saying of them was an American thing my parents couldn't bring themselves to do. It wasn't as easy as getting a

Christmas tree and hanging lights. I didn't know which was worse: that I'd never told my mom that I loved her, or that I'd never said those words to anyone, period. I drove home, mouthing those three little words silently, as if muscle memory could make me feel something. What was love supposed to feel like? What was it supposed to look like? I had no idea.

♦ 4 ♦

ALL I NEEDED FOR work was a computer with a word pro-
cessor and an internet connection. I didn't often meet with
colleagues, and yet I was expected to sit in my cubicle for forty
hours a week. Forty-five if I counted our mandatory lunch
breaks. What I hated most, though, were our Monday morning
department meetings. I would sit, with my laptop open on my
thighs, and sip coffee over it, hoping someone would bump me
and cause me to spill all over the machine so I could have an
excuse to leave.

This morning, I took my usual seat next to the window.
There were too many people for the conference room table, so
chairs lined the back wall. People from marketing, design, and
media relations teams were all required to attend. Though we
all worked in the same realm, it was like bringing a group of
snakes, cats, and flamingoes into a room together. I stayed on
the outskirts, trying to take up as little space as possible. It was
easy to be overlooked.

Chad, the chief of communications for the university, sat at
the head of the table. His shirt sleeves were already rolled to his
elbows as if he were proving to us how hard he'd worked by ten
in the morning. His tie was loosened, as if his typing had made

him work up a sweat. Chad's directors and assistant directors sat in the rolling chairs at the table. Those seated at the table were all inadvertently men. The men were the type who leaned back in chairs with all their weight, as if daring them to break. What would happen if the chairs were adjusted so they didn't lean back? Perhaps one of them would give themselves a hernia trying to force it?

These men and the staff who wanted to be like them were always "shooting emails" or "taking a stab at things." They were obsessed with violence. They worked with words and yet paid so little attention to their own usage. Would they have felt more accomplished in the military? But instead, and instead of making it as journalists, they were here doing communications for a university. Instead of saving the world through their writing, they were swindling parents and young people with dreams of climbing the ladder to success.

"All right, guys," Chad said. "As you know, building renovations will start this summer. We will need to shuffle people around. Possibly share spaces or work from home. The directors will start some high-level conversations in the coming weeks and share them with you after that."

When someone addressed a group of people as guys, I took it as a cue to stop paying attention. I started a game of solitaire on my laptop.

"We can't do our work from home," said Nancy, our business officer. She sat in the stackable chair closest to Chad. I could imagine her killing for a seat at the table, and I watched her three employees stare anywhere but at her as she talked.

"We'll discuss this with all managers to see how we can make this work," said Chad. He never responded directly to a woman's comment. "Like I said, we're just starting some high-level conversations to think about options. Let's do check-ins."

I looked at my calendar as the directors went around the table. It fell into the usual attempts to brag about their own work. Round robins were a waste of time. The rest of us were held hostage as the managers preened and paraded accomplishments, and I was thankful I could stare at my computer screen. When the meeting ended, I had to squeeze past the group of people who had gathered around Chad for another word, as if he were a celebrity.

My cubicle was like my home. I only needed a pad of paper, two pens, one black, the other blue, and a green highlighter. Decorating at work seemed like a strange thing to do. Why decorate a place I didn't even want to be in?

Since my office was in the most prominent historic building on campus, everything was slightly off-kilter. Low ceilings, creaky floors, ungrounded electrical outlets, non-ADA hallways, and tiny windows, some of which were stuck slightly open and others painted shut. My cubicle was one of four crammed into a room that used to be a single office. I could touch all three dividing walls without stretching.

After the meeting, I packed my computer, notepad, and lunch into my bag. My next appointment was across campus, so I hoped to find someplace pleasant to eat before coming back.

I had completed my undergraduate degree at this university. What would it feel like if I worked here until retirement? They'd never feature me in one of those alumni spotlights, that's for sure. I hadn't even done all four years here, instead opting to start at a community college. No, they used students like me as numbers to brag about, but not for website homepages.

Still, I preferred the environment. I would never be able to swallow the Kool-Aid of a for-profit. Here I got my fill of oldish buildings with Doric columns that were purely aesthetic. It was easy to write copy to sell the school to parents with the backdrop of campus beauty shots. The prospective students only really cared about the football team.

My appointment wasn't really a meeting. I had been asked to attend an admissions tour of the art department to help write a brochure for them. It seemed like it should be fun, but I knew it wouldn't. They would want drippy sentences enticing students to answer their artistic calling. Manipulations that sounded like they were worth thousands of dollars to the parents. The teenagers didn't care. They wanted to go somewhere cool, and they wouldn't learn that from a glossy brochure.

A student currently majoring in studio art led the tour. They were clean-cut but had a tattoo peeking out from under their shirt sleeve. Just edgy enough. I bet their supervisor told them to be sure to only let a little bit of their tattoo show to demonstrate what the high schoolers' futures held. As we walked through the studios, I couldn't help but see only how paint drops covered everything, the dirty baseboards, and the chipped wall panels. Rolls of one-ply brown paper towels sat next to the sink instead of inside the dispensers, and broken lockers hung open. How would any parent who saw this decaying building want to let their child study here?

I suppose there was a certain charm in the fumes of oil paint, the disheveled studio spaces, and the bathrooms still operating with their original fixtures from the sixties. I inhaled the odor of tarnish and printmaker's ink. Did each breath shorten my life despite the guarantees of low volatile organic compounds? Did young people decide to be artists to excuse their dirty fingernails?

A professor leaned over a student in the lithography studio as she worked. His stomach billowed out toward her as he spoke at her. If he moved a centimeter more, he could smother her. As if she knew it, she responded without looking at him.

It was the middle of the semester, and the students in the room looked exhausted from late nights studying for midterms on top of their partying. The professor wore a faded cotton T-shirt with holes, and his gray hair was uncombed and disheveled. His eyes looked bloodshot, and he was old enough to be retired. But who would give up tenure, health benefits, an easy schedule, and young women around you all day long? I turned my focus back to the tour.

The largest program in the department was studio art, though they offered programs in art education and art history. The prospective students were still primarily white. I'd hoped that had changed from my time. The students of the global majority still only wanted to go to the business school. Maybe they were right. Make the money that was kept out of reach from our parents. Take from the world what had been denied.

Many students on tour today probably didn't have the grades to be admitted into their first choice and were looking for any way into the university. These parents could provide everything for their children. I could tell by the manicured nails, the leather of their purses, and the glow of their skin.

I fell to the back of the tour group. I had only gone to get away from my coworkers, who stomped their feet when they walked and wore too many fragrances. To write the copy I'd been assigned, I'd simply pull up old text and update the adjectives with this year's trending words.

The hallway swelled with people around me as classes were released, and I drifted to the edge until I could stop out of anyone's way. When the hall was empty, a sign on a locker caught my attention. Three numbers that I assumed were the numbers of the combination. Inside, someone had installed a faux wood floor, painted the interior of the locker white, and taped up miniature works of art. It was as if I were a giant who had ripped off the side of a museum gallery. There were tiny benches that were painstakingly made in miniature. I thought I could see individual metal nail heads against the small pieces of balsa wood.

I could barely make out some of the tiny paintings, and then others were clear. As I moved closer or away, different images came into focus. A sculpture made of paper clips was set in the middle of the locker, as if to remind you of the trick the artist was playing on you.

The entire floor had emptied out by the time I was done looking, so I decided to wander around one of the studios. A low stage was placed in the back of the room for life drawing lessons. Did the models change in the room, and what kind of person might do that kind of work? How did it feel to have so many people studying the shape of your naked body? What was it like when your most intimate odors drifted throughout the room, to be inhaled by strangers?

There were open shelves on one side of the studio, vertically oriented so that canvases could slide in and rest sitting upright. Empty easels were scattered around the stage like mannequins waiting for clothing.

Muffled words played over the PA system, and the emergency lights flickered. I knew it wasn't the day for the university's monthly warning system test, but I couldn't hear what the voice said; and furthermore, couldn't remember which announcement meant what. They'd updated them recently, and there were three different warnings. I froze at the burst of adrenaline in my system. The recording played over the speakers again, but it sounded even worse, like the static of a low-quality radio.

My phone buzzed, and I only read the words *active shooter* before slipping the phone back into my pocket. I was alone and on an unfamiliar side of campus. Walking to the door, I listened for sounds in the hallway but only heard silence. I opened it an inch so I could press the button that would lock the exterior doorknob, and then shut the door as quietly as possible. Turning off the lights made no difference to the brightness of the room. There were no tables to get under or closets to hide in. Only shelves. I grabbed a blanket from the stage, squeezed past a canvas, wet paint smearing over my arm and clothes, and propped up the blanket so I could sit in the dark recess.

I felt warmer under the blanket immediately. Sweat and body odor from the nude models had seeped into the fibers, and it smelled musty and intimate. The blanket blocked out most of the light, and I shut my eyes. Someone ran down the hallway, and then I heard a door slam shut. All my muscles seized up. How many shooters were on campus? The siren had stopped, and no more information was being played over the PA system, not that I could make out the words. What were we supposed to do? They made it easy so you could remember the instructions when it happened. You were supposed to practice, which I clearly had not done enough between my projects of writing copy to entice children to come here for college. Run, that was the first, I remembered. There was nowhere to run. Then hide, which I had done. My breath came in short wheezes, and I started feeling light-headed. The last one was fight, and there was no way I could do that. I knew my instincts. There would never be that rising to the occasion that *heroes* did. I would never fight.

Pulling my knees into my chest, I tried to block out everything. If someone came into the room, I would not hear them. If someone broke down the door, I would not hear them. I would be safe and alone. I slowed my breathing until I believed it was silent. I tried to empty my mind so no human could perceive that another consciousness was present. An exercise I had not done in years. An exercise I had perfected as a child.

It would be unspeakable now, but as soon as my parents thought I was old enough, they left me home alone. I was probably eight or nine. My dad worked as an AC repair technician, and some calls would go far into the evenings. My mom worked two jobs to help make ends meet, or so she always told me. She cooked in a school cafeteria and then sewed clothes at a warehouse when I was very young. That was all before she finally made her way into banking. Mom was always the one who picked me up from school and dropped me off at home between the two jobs. Dinner would be in a bowl in the refrigerator. I was afraid of setting a fire with the microwave, so I often ate it cold.

When I was a child and alone, I imagined monsters breaking into the apartment, chasing me, capturing me, and smashing me to death. The dishes would settle in their rack, but the unexpected sound would send me into my closet, where I kept a blanket to hide under. I feared every creak, step, and murmur around me. The strange logic of childhood compelled me to protect myself by hiding in the darkness. If someone broke into the house, I would be hidden and safe—just a pile of blankets on the floor. I would stay hunkered in the dark until I heard one of my parents come home. I could identify the way they kicked their shoes off at the door. Only then would I creep out.

And so I stayed under the dank blanket and drifted to sleep as if sleep could protect me from bullets. When I woke back up, my entire body tingled with numbness. I scooted out of the cubby. Every movement sent spikes of pain through me until I could spread out on the floor, letting blood circulate through my limbs. When I could move again, I pulled out my phone. The messages were displayed on my lock screen. Shooter. Shelter in place. Stay away from windows. Emergency. Emergency. Emergency.

I could hear sirens again, and I looked online to find information about the shooter's location. The main building. The building where I spent every weekday. Where I had been just this morning. At lunchtime, the plaza in front of the building would have been packed. How many shooters were there? Typically, there was only one. Was this a typical school shooting? A kid that would act out on their own and follow the script that had been templated for them throughout the years? Or was this something new? Were kids who did this always trying to win something in life, like it was some video game?

I was standing in the center of the room, trying to consider what to do. There were no messages from my team. None of them would ever bother to put my cell phone number into theirs. And yet, I worried what was happening to them. Had the shooter run through the hallway that led to our offices?

And what should I do now? I didn't know anyone in the building. If I knocked on any doors, they wouldn't answer. I wasn't close enough to the edge of campus to leave, and that would be risky with cops everywhere. We had been told to shelter in place, so I sat down on the floor next to the stage, where I wouldn't be visible through the door window. I was gasping for air again, and I stretched out on the ground, hoping it would help me breathe. Then the sirens went off again.

I could hear the static voice over the PA system. I rolled onto my side and pressed myself against the stage. My phone buzzed, and "Emergency! Emergency! Emergency!" flashed on the screen. Curling into a ball, I thought of a song that used to calm me, a Vietnamese children's song about a butterfly that my mother would sing. It was set to the melody of "Frère Jacques."

Kìa con bướm vàng. Kìa con bướm vàng.
Xòe đôi cánh xòe đôi cánh.

Tung cánh bay năm ba vòng.
Em ngồi xem. Em ngồi xem.

I remembered Mom singing to me while we sat on the car-
peted living room of an apartment. There were hand gestures
that went with it that I could not remember. I made up new
words to calm myself:

There isn't a kid running down the hall.
No one is here, shooting an AR-15.
No one is trying the doorknob.
This is not the day I will die.
I am alone. I am alone.

Somewhere in the cloud of fear, I felt a sharp anger that was
like a fire I had in my body that I could never totally put out. If
my father were here, he would say this was my fault. Everything
was always my fault. My existence caused him irritation and
anger. Had he not wanted children? Or had he not wanted the
obligation to me and Mom? Or was it as simple as him wanting
me to be a boy, and so I had failed him at my very conception?
Or had he planned on using Mom to get to the States, and then
leaving?

Everything bad had always been my fault, and that repeated
injustice in childhood had been like winding steel around my
soul so that I formed in a mangled shape. In the ages when I
was supposed to learn about that foreign thing called love, my
father made sure I knew I was the source of everything that
was wrong with his life. And in that, as much as I was scared, I
also knew I had the same seed in my body that had driven this
student to pick up a gun and roam through the university. The
gun wasn't a difficult thing to acquire. Apparently, getting onto

campus with one was not hard either. The hard part had been done years before: the seed that could only form in the dark terror of a youth's brain had been germinated. I felt sorrow for the student. I felt pity for those who were hurt. I felt despair for all of us caught up in this violent civilization.

I turned until my cheek hit the cold tile. My father. My father owned a gun. My father probably had nothing on a background check that said he should not have a gun. He was a man like any other who went to work every day. Mom had told me he purchased one casually during a phone call. I'd forgotten because soon after that, she told me she was moving out and was going to divorce him. What had happened between them that she did not tell me? To protect me from knowing?

★ ★ ★

I woke up again. It was good I didn't work in any sort of emergency response situation. My emergency response, apparently, was to sleep. Oranges and pinks from the sunset doused the studio in warm evening light. I could see dust whirl in the air. Flecks floated and danced like nothing was wrong. The dust would be here long after me. I found my phone on the stage and checked my alerts and email.

It was a student. Male. Fifth year. Ran through the main building shooting an automatic rifle. Three people were injured and in Intensive Care. No firm number of fatalities. Yet. Then the student went up to the highest floor he could get to. He killed himself there. I felt a drop of water run down my face. Were any of those wounded my colleagues? Would those hurt today die years from now with complications from today's injuries? How much time would pass before their names were forgotten? There were so many gun-related deaths. So many people forgotten.

When I picked up my bag, I smelled fish sauce and discovered my lunch container had leaked. Wiping it up as best as possible with the rough brown paper towels at the paint sink, I studied the food. It was lukewarm from sitting in my bag for hours. The rice wouldn't be so hard that it became mealy in my mouth, like many childhood dinners. I dumped it into a trash can and wondered if the smell of fish sauce would always remain in this room. Maybe for one student, it would be a comfort. The tiniest comfort I could leave.

I opened the classroom door slowly. The hallways were empty. The building was empty. The street was empty. I saw someone in the distance, but they were walking in the same direction as me—off campus. Away from the scene of the violence. It was a long walk back to my car. There were barricades blocking off roads toward the main building. The presence of the police made me uneasy. I'd slept through the exodus from campus. The quiet was strange. The campus was usually noisy. There were always people walking to and from labs and dorms. But not this evening. I hurried to my car and drove home.

5

I TOLD MYSELF THAT everything was fine. I was fine. Things like this happened so often that it wasn't even on the front page of the local news site by the third day after the shooting. It wasn't even the first time I had been on campus for an emergency. There was that bomb threat years before. There was that other shooting when I was a student. All of it was normal now, wasn't it?

It had become normal for people who worked on university campuses. We had fire drills and active shooter drills, and memorized various phrases for different situations every year. There could be chemical dangers, internal or external. Knives and guns were the dangers we might face, and these days we had to be prepared for what we didn't know. I remembered that the university had brought someone in from the military to help with emergency preparedness. How had things escalated to the point that a college campus needed a military man? Were we fighting a war?

Since the shooting, I hadn't seen anyone. I'd told my tennis coach that I was sick. I cringed at loud sounds and wasn't sure what the continuous thwack of a tennis ball would do to me. I felt silly about it all and couldn't bring myself to tell my mom that it had upset me. She'd lived through actual war and the aftermath, hadn't she? I remembered a story she'd told me about dodging bullets while coming home from school. My life was easy in comparison.

Working from home for the rest of the week after the shooting turned into working from home for the rest of the summer. Everyone was assigned a time to pack up their office. I only needed the power charger for my laptop. I hadn't taken it with me when I left for that tour on the day of the shooting, and since then, I had been using the charger from my personal computer. Having to power an object for work with something I'd purchased for myself annoyed me. I figured I ought to take home the entire box of the .07 mm gel pens that I'd made them buy for me. At least, this is what I told myself as I sat in my parked car.

I hadn't been to campus since the shooting. But it had all happened in the building I officed in, so it seemed right that I should visit it again. If I saw it again, maybe the shooting wouldn't be so big in my mind. Maybe it would shrink to the smaller font size the newspapers treated it with now. Perhaps it would help me get to sleep and stop flinching at loud noises. It would stop the dreams I had of blood running over vinyl tiles.

Walking through campus felt like any other day. It felt like nothing had happened. Students were scattered across grass lawns, with their heads on their book bags like pillows. I walked along the main mall, and a blond girl posed for selfies with the tower of the main building behind her. I doubted the influencer selfie would mention the violence. *Maybe the girl wasn't on campus that day,* I thought. Maybe there was a way for a student to be flippant about a shooting. Maybe they had too many exams to bother with anything else. Maybe that was the only way they could cope. The selfie girl was still snapping pictures. Wasn't there an app to turn any photo into a good photo? Was it necessary to take so many? And who wanted to stare at so many versions of themselves?

I looked away from the girl, but it was the same everywhere. Kids were studying. Kids were walking to class. Kids were joking around with friends. Male professors stood out with their unkempt hair, shirts unbuttoned one too many, and their consummate messenger bag slung over their shoulders. I'd never thought about how female professors blended in with the students. They were younger. Maybe they were working in their offices. Was I drawn to the white, receding hairlines out of bias? Grad students stuck out with their haunted looks of exhaustion and bags stuffed with everything they needed to get through another sixteen-hour day crisscrossing campus. It was like nothing had happened.

A bus pulled to the curb, and the sound of its large engine and the pop of its brakes were all that I could hear. Goose bumps sprung up over my arms, and I took a deep breath to keep myself from running. A modified sports car wove through the slowed traffic caused by the bus, and its exhaust gurgled and coughed. I cringed and resisted the urge to put my hands over my ears. Everything on campus sounded louder. I yearned for the quiet of my apartment.

I expected the police to still be milling about like they were when I had last left campus. There wasn't extra security at the doors. There wasn't a uniform in sight. I walked into the building, and—I don't know—I expected it to feel different. Someone had killed himself in this building—shouldn't it be different? Someone had tried to kill so many others. Someone had lashed out in violence. How could a building—how could *we*—be so stoic in the face of such violence? How could people just keep on going as though it was a day like any other?

The only peculiar thing I ran into was that the office door was locked. As I pulled my keys from my pocket, Nancy opened the door. Her perfume hit me like a gust of garbage, and I could feel my sinuses begin to close up.

"Do you need a box?" Nancy asked. She was standing in the doorway, so I couldn't pass, and her cork platform sandals allowed her to look down on me.

"Hi," I said. "No. Thanks?"

"Let me know if you need anything. I'm down the hall."

Nancy turned so quickly that I almost let the door shut and lock. She had gone off in the direction of Cory's office. Her office was—or had been—in the opposite direction. Had she moved? Did she plan to work in the office through the renovations, to prove she would do more than anyone else? I wanted to shake Nancy and tell her she would never get the promotions she wanted. She was a woman in a man's world. She was pale, but her last name was too far from Smith for her to get anywhere. They'd never trust her. She'd never be one of them. But Nancy was trying to play the game. I knew better than to mess with white and light-skinned women who had the privilege to believe they were equal to white men. They were cruel when they finally banged their heads against the white supremacy, patriarchal boundaries.

My cubicle was just as I had left it. The arm of my chair jabbed me in the back as I crawled back out from under my desk with my power charger. I took three packages of the pens I liked and a handful of Post-it Notes for good measure. I shoved them in the tote bag I'd brought and put the charger on top.

I stood for a few minutes at the door before realizing I was waiting for someone to say goodbye. All the doors along the hall that Nancy had gone down were shut, so maybe she'd left. Only half of the fluorescent lights had been switched on, so the suite was spotted with light in a way it never usually was. There wasn't anything to do but leave.

The door shut behind me. The building was desolate. The students paid no attention to me when I walked past. I had spent the last few years on this campus, yet my presence was so easily removed. All I'd left behind were some unattributed brochures.

I had read that one of the people injured by the shooter was a staff person. The other two were students. The students were recovering from minor injuries. Lucy Ramirez was undergoing more surgeries. She had worked for the university longer than I'd been alive, but was paid less. I had looked it up to confirm my suspicions. It wasn't a surprise to me. When I'd overhear managers talking about steady, lifelong staff like her, they would talk about how employees should be so grateful the university paid for their health insurance and ensured them a pension. As if we all didn't know our pensions were based on the salaries that they kept low. Would Lucy not be able to come back to work because of lasting issues with her injury? How much would her insurance cover at the end of the day? How long could she be on family and medical leave, and how much sick leave did she have to use concurrently with it? Would she have enough money saved up to make it through? Was she supporting herself and her children? Was she supporting herself and her parents and cousins and aunts?

Lucy had been treated worse than me by the university, and she was already being forgotten. As the days had gone by, mention of her name had lessened. It reminded me of how little a woman meant if she wasn't part of the right group. As neither student nor white, it turned out she meant very little. But I'd known this already. It shouldn't have surprised me. It shouldn't have kept me up at night, my body burning with fury. It was the way that it was. I knew this all already, so why was it bothering me so much?

As I drove home, I focused on the positives of working from home. It was my responsibility, after all, to reframe the way I looked at the world, to survive. To be able to wake up and exist, day after day. I would never again be able to recognize who had recently passed by in the hallway by their perfume or cologne. I would never have to listen to Nancy stomp through the office on her way to Cory's office, with crucial, very urgent information. I would never have to take a shit in a public stall with too wide gaps between the plastic planks again. I would never have to know when everyone went to get drinks after work and forgot to invite me. I didn't have to pretend to be interested in my colleagues' children or listen to their references about television shows and movies that I didn't watch because, where others found humor, I was offended. Maybe, I wouldn't even be on campus when the next shooting happened. Because there would always be another.

◆ 6 ◆

M OM WAS GOING ON a second date with Peter.
        "Didn't you just go out with him? What's his name
again?" I asked, swirling my glass of wine. I had taken her out
to a nice restaurant. I wanted her to experience nicer things so
she knew what she ought to expect from the men who took her
out.

"That was almost three weeks ago," Mom said. She fussed
with the napkin in her lap, and I smiled to comfort her. She
belonged in fancy restaurants. I wanted this for her. She'd been
through so much in life, moving to another country before she
was even twenty. She deserved the best I could give her.

"Did he call you to ask you out again, or did you call him?
Do you see each other at work?" I asked.

"There are a lot of people at work. We don't see each other
unless we want to."

"But you're going on a second date."

"Yes," she said, adjusting her silverware. "I like him. Do
you eat here a lot?"

"Now and then," I said. "It's the kind of restaurant where
you should go on your dates. Don't you want to be treated?"

"If they can afford it."

"It's not that expensive. I don't make that much money. Anyway, it's nice. Men should be trying to impress you, don't you think? Do you like it?"

"We haven't eaten yet," Mom said.

"I mean the atmosphere. It's quieter."

Our salads arrived, and I fidgeted in my seat. I went to this restaurant to prove that I could go and belong. I put on bravado for my mom, but there was no way to fake the entitlement of growing up wealthy. I could put on my most expensive clothing and still move in a way that showed my lack of a trust fund. As I watched my mom, happily enjoying her salad, I pushed the worry out of my mind. I doubted she wasted her time thinking about things like that.

Our server soon returned with our entrees and topped off our glasses of wine. The candlelight and alcohol softened the way I saw us, apart from everyone else. We could belong. We did belong. We were here, anyway.

"It is . . ." Mom paused to give her food consideration. "Good."

"Good."

"Do you want to drink this?" she asked, waving to her glass of wine. "I'm driving home. Did you drive?"

"One of us can take the bottle home," I said. I had ordered one that was fifty dollars. More than I'd usually spend, but I'd wanted to impress my mom.

"How is your work?"

"Good. Fine. The building is being renovated, so I can work from home." She didn't ask about the shooting, and I didn't bring it up. There was no reason to worry her. Besides, there had been another shooting at a university in Indiana just this week. Ours was old news, and there was nothing special about my experience. I had simply been on campus. My story did not matter; my experience was normal. I repeated that to myself in order to make the experience smaller and smaller. Eventually I had stopped cringing at loud noises. I stopped waiting for emergency alerts to show up on my phone. It helped that I didn't have to go to campus anymore. I wasn't walking into a possible line of fire.

"That's good. Less money on gas."

"Yes, and I like being around Lollipop."

"Your cat? What about any boyfriends? You need to get married so you can have children before I get too old to pick them up."

"You could have new children with someone else."

Mom laughed. I couldn't remember the last time I'd seen her laugh like that. Like it wasn't planned and from her stomach.

"I mean, one of your boyfriends might come with children who have babies already," I said.

"I still want some from you. I think you'll have an Asian American baby."

"I'm too busy." I had ordered a steak and put a large piece in my mouth that would keep me chewing for a while.

"Doing what? You work and play tennis. Don't you play tennis to meet boys?"

"Tennis is for exercise and fun. Not boys," I said around my food.

"You run around in a short skirt, and it's not for boys?"

"Mom, you don't have to wear a skirt. I wear them because I think they're actually functional. They have shorts underneath where you can tuck your tennis balls. And they're cute. Don't you have things you do just to make yourself feel good?"

"I'm learning."

"Good."

"Peter plays tennis. Do you know a Peter?"

I fidgeted with my napkin in my lap, out of my mom's sight. "There are courts all over the metroplex. Besides, we are a women's team and usually only play women."

"Oh, okay. I saw some tennis balls in his back seat, but I didn't ask."

"And what were you doing in his back seat?"

"I wasn't. I saw them through the window when I was getting into the car," Mom said. I didn't know if she understood me or pretended to misunderstand.

"I think he should have taken you to a nicer place for dinner."

"We are different. I don't need a fancy restaurant. Not on a first date. Maybe for a special occasion. You should only date men who take you out to restaurants you want to go to."

"And your next date with Peter? When is it? Where are you going?"

"We're going to see a movie in a couple of weeks."

"Which theater?"

"The one at Squarehills Mall. Why?"

"I want to know where you are, so I don't have to worry about you," I said.

"I'm an adult and your mom. You don't have to worry about me."

I leaned back, grateful for the interruption of our server with our desserts. We'd finished our meals only a second ago. Was the server rushing us so he could get us out of the restaurant? I imagined Peter taking her to a box restaurant near the mall for dinner. Maybe there the servers wouldn't price out customers by looking at them. It could be charming in its own way, surely. And like my mom said, if it was what you could afford, it was what you had.

I asked about her vegetable garden. Once mom started talking about soils and plants, it was hard to get her to stop. I imagined my mother working on her garden happily for years into the future. An errant image of her in the back seat of Peter's car flashed through my mind.

"You will always use a condom, right?" I asked, interrupting something she was saying about squash blossoms.

"What?" My mom looked at me, and I stared back at her silently, heat prickling my cheeks.

"Condoms," I said. "You have to use them. I don't care what those men say to you."

"Sure. I can't have children anymore anyway." She couldn't meet my eyes.

"It's not just about children."

"I know. Of course. I told you: you don't have to worry about me." Mom fussed with the napkin in her lap and looked away. She was deflecting and playing the submissive part she had been trained to do since childhood. I hated that she felt like she needed to use that with me.

After I paid the check, I watched her drive off before starting my car. I didn't want to go home yet, but no one had contacted me to hang out. There wasn't anyone who would do that. The only person I could call was Hoa, but she was probably busy. Our dates were usually scheduled at least two weeks out. There was always Lollipop and a movie.

Mom never brought up my father, so I didn't either. Still, I wondered who cleaned up after him now. His ideal life was living like some white man in an American movie from the fifties. He must have dreamed that kind of life when he was a teenager, based on what he had seen in old movies that had made their way over the Pacific. Maybe he'd had time to dream a life for himself before the newest war pulled him into its violence. Maybe he had never known peace. Maybe he had never had time to dream at all.

As I drove home, I remembered watching the white lines between lanes dance closer and farther from the car as a child. It had been one of the last times I was out with both my parents at the same time. That night had started out simple enough. Some of their friends across the metroplex were having a party. My parents took me over with them in the late afternoon. An afternoon turned into dinner and then continued late into the night. When we finally left, my dad wouldn't let my mother drive. He was her husband, and so it was his responsibility to drive. Although I was young, I knew enough to be scared. As my father drove us home, the two of them silent in the front seat, I watched the white strip between the highway lanes creep closer to the car and then move away. Was it after that my mother began working two jobs and was at home less and less? My childhood memories were hazy, as if I were contact drunk.

As I got older, I assumed that must have been the last incident of many. As a child hiding in the closet from noises, all I had been sure of was that there was no one to comfort me. No one to show me love. As a child, I had felt abandoned. Mom had left me to deal with my father. To listen to his drunk rages. To be the girl in his life who cleaned up after him once my mom was tired of it. I understood what my mom was staying away from, and I had never asked her about their past. Not even when she told me that she was divorcing my father. The only satisfaction I knew was of her need for me. I thought that if I asked her what she had thought all those years ago, I'd expose myself as truly American and thus as completely different from her. So different that she might decide she didn't need me after all.

My apartment complex was small and secluded. The brick sidewalks, the trimmed hedges, and the vines that grew up the sides of the buildings made me feel like I was someplace more interesting than the metroplex, in a different state from Texas, where racism, covered up with not-quite-Southern hospitality, poisoned everything, like mold spreading from a water leak behind a wall.

I was sure that the apartment complex was on land that used to be part of the neighboring mansion. There was a flatness that indicated farmland. The mansion was now a lawyer's office. Lawyers whose families had built their wealth with enslaved people. They would clarify, the "good" owners and really believe that was possible. On days when I called in sick for no reason other than to use my allotted sick leave, I watched luxury cars drive in and out of the firm's parking lot. I watched, and I thought about all of the ghosts that probably lived in the mansion.

Lollipop was always waiting for me when I opened the door. She sat on the couch armrest and watched as I put my coat and bag on a hook and changed into my house slippers, before meowing at me. It was like she didn't want to dirty herself with the outside. Before I did anything else, I walked around the apartment, holding her like you might when you burped a baby, and told her about my adventures outside the walls of our home. She meowed and jumped out of my arms when she grew impatient with hunger. I imagined it was similar to living with a man.

I could walk to a bar to drink alone, but on the weekend that seemed morbid. It was nice to be able to do so during the week, and even more convenient to be able to walk. It was strange to live in the metroplex and be able to walk to a grocery store. It was why I'd fought so hard for the apartment. I must have called the leasing office every day for months until they had the news I wanted. Finally, a tenant moved into an assisted living home. I wasn't deterred by the lingering smell of potpourri and medicine for the first few months. That was life. It was hard to wash away the existence of another person. You simply had to wait until your presence became stronger than the lingering memory of theirs.

Even though I was near enough to campus for the occasional student to be out walking, in the summers, people driving by would give me pitying looks. No one in the metroplex walked if they could help it. Cars and the oil industry ruled. They looked at me like a sad little refugee: too poor to own a car, must have arrived recently, and only owned a meager two pairs of clothes provided by a white Baptist church. It seemed like all the largest churches here were Baptist. White Texan Baptists were the type to raise children who would tell their friends that their pets were going to go to hell. I opened my laptop. Was this Peter religious? Did he go to a mega-church with its own marketing team?

◆ 7 ◆

Since I'd started working from home, tennis had been easier. I no longer raced from one place to another, fighting rush hour traffic and making the decision between changing clothes in my car or in the bathroom while listening to someone pass gas in the next stall.

One day, I broke my tradition of arriving right on time and went early to watch others play. A spring shower nearly canceled practice. Some courts still required drying, and players were pushing foam rollers that spread the water around so that it would evaporate more quickly. Humidity weighed down the air, and I knew that I would sweat through my clothes in five minutes as soon as we started drills. At least the heat loosened my muscles.

"You're early," said Nesbitt, setting her bag next to me. "Something happened?"

"I wanted to make sure we were still playing," I said, retying my tennis shoes, which had loosened as my body temperature warmed them up.

"You work at the university? Terrible, what happened. Did you know—"

"It's fine now," I said quickly. "I don't work with students."

"It must be—" Nesbitt started to say but stopped suddenly.

I looked up to see a man coming toward us. It was the coach from the barf tournament.

"Hi, Anne. Hello, I'm Karl," he said, smiling at Nesbitt while holding out his hand to me.

I'd never heard Nesbitt called by her first name. I only knew it because it was listed when I'd paid membership fees. Karl's handshake was firm, but not crushing. Of course, he wouldn't have a bad handshake. Tennis players needed to know how firmly to grip their racquets and when to loosen their hold.

"Linh," I said.

"Anne, did you see the notice for the fundraiser? Are you going to participate?" he asked.

When Nesbitt opened her mouth but didn't say anything, I asked, "What kind of fundraiser is it?"

"A fundraiser for renovations here. If we raise enough, we can get our courts resurfaced. It'll be like the Davis Cup, sort of. Four players to a team, a coach and student pairing. I wanted to see if you had already signed up with someone else. One of my students volunteered. Peter. I think he played you for a little, Linh? That day our teams practiced together."

"Oh yeah. I didn't play very well that day," I said. Nesbitt was still not making any words. "I'd be interested. Unless you were planning to ask someone else, Coach?"

"No—I mean, yes," said Nesbitt. "I mean, no, I wasn't sure. And yes, I'd like to. With you. Both."

"Great. Well, I don't want to hold up your class. I'll sign us up now. We'll need to set up a practice time." Karl waved goodbye.

"This will be great," I said. "I wanted to ask you about individual lessons, but this will be better. Two coaches. Maybe Sunday mornings?"

"Yes, sure," Nesbitt said. She was already looking into the distance, dreaming of her crush. Karl had paired off Peter with me when our teams played, without a thought. Maybe it made perfect sense to him that the only two players of Asian descent on the teams should play each other. It annoyed me that I thought about things like that. I hoped it didn't tell me everything I needed to know about Karl. It could be nothing—until it was everything.

As my teammates started to arrive, Nesbitt wandered away to prepare our court. I'd never guessed she would be so shy. On the court, all she did was yell at us. I had imagined she approached her life with the same forcefulness. I followed everyone else to our court on the hour mark, and we lined our bags up on either side of the bench. A net suspended from a cable separated our court from the one beside it. Four people were stretching, getting ready to play a doubles match. I recognized one of the pairs and was surprised that they hadn't asked for another court. They were quite good but unfortunately so serious about their tennis that it was unpleasant to be around them.

A loose network formed through tennis courts, whether you wanted to be part of it or not. People's schedules collided, and you tended to see the same people over and over. I knew this guy was a shouter and high strung. He talked to himself when he missed a ball, so I knew his name was Sean. He was a really good player, which made it worse. He got angry when playing next to people who were learning and flopped balls into his court and ruined his points.

I steered clear of guys like Sean—those young men in their twenties, sometimes early thirties if they were particularly stuck, who exuded aggressive energy. The kind of guy you knew fucked badly and only wanted a girlfriend to organize his social calendar.

Toward the end of our practice, Nesbitt had us do overhead shots. The doubles match on our neighboring court had gotten tense. At least, that is what I thought by the tone of Sean's outbursts. I imagined Sean's head as a target and tried to mishit the ball as many times as I could into his court. By the tone Nesbitt used as she gave me pointers, I knew she'd had us drill overheads on purpose. She didn't like Sean either. The rest of the team caught on, and each one of us would hit an overhead with the rim of our racquet. There was that awful sound the ball makes when it hits metal instead of strings, then Nesbitt shouted, "Ball help!" as the bright yellow sphere sailed over the net that was supposed to protect the other court from ours.

Soon, all of us were hitting balls purposely badly, and the doubles match next to us had taken an extended water break. Poor Sean was running back and forth to keep his muscles warm. He didn't have the power to complain about a coach, and I could see a vein in his forehead jumping from a distance. The team gathered the errant balls as our hour ended. The season would be picking up, and Nesbitt rattled off dates for future games.

"Let's do the same matchups, Linh," Lauren said as we stacked balls on our racquet heads.

"Maybe," I said. "Email the ones you sign up for. I signed up to play with Nesbitt for that fundraiser. Her crush asked her to participate."

"You won't play with Nesbitt. The coaches play together."

"Oh, then I'll be playing with his student. Peter."

"Is that the one your mother went on a date with?"

"Yeah." I dumped the balls I'd balanced on my racquet head into the cart of balls.

"Come get dinner and drinks with us. We must talk about that," Lauren said, clapping her hands and then bringing them together as if praying. "Please, Linh. Please?"

I hesitated. I always had limited team hangouts, but I didn't really want to spend another night drinking alone. I was going to turn thirty soon, and at what point did drinking alone become problematic? Or was it always problematic?

"Okay, sure," I said. I felt as if I were floating above the tennis courts and able to see myself talking to Lauren as Nesbitt rolled her cart of balls away, and Lauren and Tiffany lifted their five-racquet tennis bags elegantly onto their shoulders. Did they do it in unison?

"Brandy Cake?" Lauren asked the group.

"I have an early presentation tomorrow. I should get home," Jan said.

"That means I should make dinner for us," Ann-Marie said.

"No, it's okay if you want to go out." Jan pinched Ann-Marie's elbow lightly.

"It's a Monday night. I'm beat. I'd rather go home. We can make salads with . . ." Ann-Marie waved and walked off as she listed salad ingredients. My stomach rumbled.

"Who do we keep if those two break up?" asked Elana.

"Who says they're breaking up?" Becka said from the ground. She sat with her legs spread out and reached for her toes.

"I like to have a plan. People break up, and that's that." Elana shrugged. "I vote for Ann-Marie."

"I'm not voting. It's possible they'll always be together as much as it's possible they won't. Well, shall we go eat?" Tiffany said.

"I didn't know you were such a romantic," Lauren said as we walked toward the parking lot. Tiffany cackled.

Becka and Elana dropped away, citing early mornings, and I shrugged. I was hungry, and I didn't want to be alone.

★　★　★

Brandy Cake was a popular bar set along a strip mall. The big craft, sports, and clothing stores were closing, and the parking lots were filling with people going to the restaurants and bars that were set closer to the highway, to attract customers. The metroplex was filled with highways, and along the highways were miles and miles of box stores and chain restaurants.

The building was designed to look old. High ceilings and exposed faux brick walls mimicked old warehouses. Wood beams crisscrossed above us. Our server bragged about their freshly squeezed juices and launched into a verbose description of the special brandy cocktail of the week. I ordered the house wine and a burger.

"So, tell us about this fundraiser and you playing doubles with your future dad," Lauren said, changing the subject after our drinks and food had arrived. Lauren, Tiffany, and Jessica all turned to me. Three pairs of sharp eyes were less intimidating than seven.

"There isn't much," I said. "The coach Nesbitt has a crush on, Karl, came before our practice to ask her to play in the fundraiser tournament with him. She didn't say anything, so I offered to play with her."

"So, the fourth is your future dad? The man your mom went on a date with?" asked Tiffany.

"That's right," I said. "He's not my future dad. Do you even have to call them that if you're an adult?"

I didn't tell them how relieved I was to be able to get closer to Peter. To make sure he wasn't an asshole. To watch how he played tennis and see whether he was aggressive toward his opponents.

"He doesn't know, though?" Jessica raised an eyebrow. "That your mom is your mom?"

I shook my head no.

"The blessed man won't know what hit him," Tiffany said, delicately eating a single ketchup-dipped French fry.

"Is that lying by omission?" Lauren tapped her chin.

"I didn't meet him through my mom," I said. "Why should I ask every Peter I meet if he's the one my mother went on a date with?"

Never mind that I'd watched him pick up my mother. Never mind the fact that I'd stared at his headshot and committed his face to my memory. Never mind that I might have spent a few minutes trying to figure out where he lived before I forced myself to stop.

"How do you know it's him, then?" Tiffany asked.

"I knew he worked with my mom, so I looked at the company's staff directory," I said, shrugging. "He had a headshot. You can find everyone on the internet, can't you?"

"You're every person's worst nightmare," Lauren said.

"You should look up the people you date," I said. "For safety. What if they're racist?"

The words came out before I thought about them. The three white women didn't even blink, but I could feel my blood pressure increasing. I was used to being surrounded by white people, from working at a university, but I generally tried not to be the only Asian person in a gathering, if I could help it. I had no desire to be the one that died first, like in horror movies.

"I think it's sweet," Tiffany said. "It's like a background check. I'd do it for you, Sis."

Jessica rolled her eyes and raised her left hand. "Now you don't have to."

"Ooh, congrats," Lauren said, holding out her hand to get a closer look at the giant diamond on Jessica's hand. I'd never seen a stone so big before, and there were more around the main gem.

"You all are invited to the wedding. I'm thinking it will be January first," Jessica said, giving her ring a study. "New year, new start—or whatever they say."

"That seems fast," I said. "Don't weddings take a long time to plan?"

"Our mother has had our weddings partially planned since we were thirteen," Tiffany said. "Jessica wanted a spring-themed winter wedding, and there was no way in hell Mom was going to wait until next winter."

"We have nine months," said Jessica. "Plenty of time to plan."

"Kind of like a pregnancy," Lauren said. "Are you pregnant?"

"No, but that would be a plus." Jessica smiled. "The scandal."

"Well, cheers," I said, making sure my statement ended on a high note. I bared my teeth in what I thought was a passable smile as they brought their drinks up and got into the wedding details. I had trained myself to react in a way people expected when they announced engagements and babies. When people told me about these things, I had a routine. Smile; make a loud, high noise of congratulations; clap; and best of all, hug them so they can't see the alarm in your mind reflected in your eyes.

As a woman, people sincerely expected me to be excited as if someone else's marriage or baby should give me joy. As if I were waiting around for my own moment to come, and someone else's moment brought me closer. As if I didn't enjoy being alone and without the responsibility of keeping another human alive. As if climate catastrophe and war didn't exist. As if I should burden someone else with me when I reached old age, rather than taking care of myself.

Thankfully, Jessica, Tiffany, and Lauren didn't seem to expect me to have much to contribute to wedding discussions.

I ate my burger and hoped a wedding invitation wouldn't lead to bachelorette parties and later baby shower invitations that I'd have to attend. I'd have to purchase something in the registry, even though Jessica could buy it all for herself. I'd have to contribute to the wasteful wedding cycle by buying a dress I might only wear once. I'd have to attend a ceremony and party with a smile frozen on my face. I already dreaded it all. This was one of the many reasons I didn't have friends. Friends meant obligations.

◆ 8 ◆

"AT LEAST TRY THIS on." Hoa shook an orange dress in front of me.

"It's really bright," I said.

"You wanted to try something different, so here this is. No one will see you in it but me."

"I thought maybe some makeup. And some clothes, like, cut differently?" I wanted to buy items that would be my costumes when I followed my mom, but I hadn't imagined them being colorful.

"I never knew black had so many shades until I met you," Hoa said, raising my arm and tossing the dress over it. "And don't worry—we are going to get our makeup."

"What I really was thinking was more like black turtlenecks. You know, different styles or shapes."

"A turtleneck? In Texas? In the summertime? What style are you going for? French literary? That's really not going to get you more dates."

"I'm not looking for dates."

"No?"

"Why, do I need to?"

"I'm wondering why all of this—clothes and makeup—then. And if you want to be single, fine. I just didn't know. It never seemed like you wanted to be single. It always seemed like a comfy armchair you settled into and didn't have the energy to get out of."

"I don't know what I want," I said. "About the clothes, I mean. I guess I wanted something new. I don't know."

"Okay, small steps. No turtlenecks, though. They are a staticky hair disaster anyway. How about scarves?" Hoa hopped in excitement. "Yes, scarves!"

I followed Hoa across the store to a rack full of brightly patterned scarves. She held up something with paisley, and I scrunched up my face at her.

"Summer scarves," Hoa said, laughing. "That was a joke. Paisley. Never wear paisley around me, please."

"Can you wear black to a wedding?" I asked.

"Your own wedding?"

"No, a friend's."

"Which friend?" Hoa asked. "I mean, it depends on the mother, maybe. If you want to care about that sort of thing. I think it's allowed these days. People don't really care about what you're wearing unless you're part of the wedding party. Are you part of a wedding party?"

"It's a person from my tennis team," I said. I caught Hoa's look of surprise before she schooled her face. "I can probably wear black. It'll be in the winter anyway. You didn't think I had other friends, did you?"

"Of course I don't think that, Linh. You're always trying to get a rise out of me. You just don't mention other friends often."

"Well, I suppose she's more of an acquaintance."

"That's how friendships start. Haven't you played tennis with that team for years now?"

"There's no limit to the acquaintance zone."

"I'm sure you're the expert on that," Hoa said as she ran a silk scarf through her fingers. "Speaking of limits. I'm thinking about looking for a new job."

"Is your job getting bad?" I couldn't remember her mentioning more issues at work.

"I'd just like to be more fulfilled, and it's clear that I wouldn't be able to at my current job." Hoa shrugged. "If I find something, it probably won't be in the metroplex."

"Oh," I said, processing the bigness of Hoa's statement.

"Scarves are great accessories. You can wear any of these with your all-black ensembles and dramatically change the way you look."

"You want to leave the metroplex?"

Hoa added another scarf to the clothes she'd draped over her arm for me. "It's time. I don't want to live anymore in the place where I grew up. Everything is familiar, and it feels like I can't grow."

"You don't have to hang out with people we knew from high school."

"I like those people," Hoa said. "I don't mean people can't live where they grew up. I just mean that for me, right now, it feels like I'm stagnating. I don't want to stop here forever."

"That makes sense."

"We'll keep in touch, always. Besides, I've only started looking, and it'll probably take months to find something. Do you like houndstooth?"

"Houndstooth is good. I like this one too." I pointed to a red scarf with tiny white flowers.

"Then we'll take it. Now, let's try some of these things on."

I ended up purchasing the orange dress, a dozen scarves, a light jacket that was almost knee-length, and a few tops in colors my closet had never seen. The tops and jacket were cut unlike anything I'd ever owned. I hoped they hid my shape and thus would hide me from recognition.

We went to the makeup section of a department store, and I followed Hoa as she wove through the stalls and declined entreaties from the sales reps for different brands. Was Hoa trying to escape me? Did she think I was her shadow? Was I what was holding her back from growing? Before my anxiety caused me to make some excuse and leave the mall, Hoa linked arms with me and led me to a makeup station.

"Linh, this is Max," Hoa said, letting my arm go to hug and air-kiss Max. Max was stunning, tall, and looked like she was headed to a photo shoot.

"Are you a model?" I asked. The words were out of my mouth before I could stop them.

"Flatterer," Max said, holding out her hand for me to shake. "A lifetime ago, yes, but there are some things that are simply not meant to be."

"I trust Max with everything," Hoa said. "This line is almost completely organic. What kind of look do you want, Linh?"

"Oh, I hadn't really thought about it. Easy? Is easy possible?" I asked.

"You must believe anything is possible," Max said. "Sit here. We can make it as easy as you like. It's your face. Today you can be formal, tomorrow you can be fun. How much time do you want to spend doing makeup?"

"Five minutes?"

"Perfectly doable. Absolutely. A foundation, some lipstick. Smoky eyeliner. All things you can explore more as you learn. And as you get better at it, you'll get faster. Then you can visit me again to keep filling in those five minutes." Max winked. Hoa nodded encouragingly.

"I've never used makeup. Is that lame?" I barely remembered to tame my eyebrows once a month. But I needed to look different. I wanted Hoa to believe I was turning over a new leaf or having an about-to-turn-thirty crisis. I wanted to become unrecognizable to my mother. It would be easier as the weather cooled. I tucked a note in the back of my mind to get more jackets when fall came around. If my mom was still dating. If I was still watching over her.

"Honey, no. Everyone lives at their own pace. And makeup isn't for everyone," Max said. She had pulled tweezers from some hidden pocket and held my head steady and plucked away. Each pull brought tears to my eyes.

"I think I'd like to get my hair cut too," I said, shutting my eyes.

"You're going all the way," Hoa said. "Are you sure you didn't have a secret boyfriend and are going through a breakup? I wouldn't be angry, you know."

I opened my eyes and found her looking at me closely.

"I told you, I want to try something new. Like you," I said. Max was building a pile of boxes on the table next to me.

"Do you have a hairstylist? I'll put my friend's card in the bag with your purchases. She's an expert with your hair type," Max said, uncapping a tube of lipstick and gently applying it to my lips. "What do you think?

The woman that looked back at me in the mirror was polished. Put together. She would get promotions and not be stuffed into a small room split into four cubicles. She wouldn't be sent off to work from home to be forgotten. Her only friend wouldn't leave her.

"I look good," I said.

"You looked good when you walked up to me," said Max. "But now, you also feel good about the way you look. I put on your 'weekend shopping' color because that's what you're doing now. Here's a good nude color for those work things where you have to look, I don't know, responsible? As you can see, I couldn't survive in an office-type job. That's what you do, though, isn't it? You look like you could use more sun. And here's a light rose color for the boring work meetings where you need to impress, but not be aggressive. And here is a weekend selection. There's one called 'Warrior for Nights' when you want to be fierce. That's the fun in makeup. It's your life, your story."

"Are you a therapist too?" I asked.

Hoa and Max laughed.

"I go to enough therapy to sound like a therapist," said Max. "I have recommendations for that too, if you're looking. Every person needs a good therapist."

"Just a haircut next for me," I said.

After purchasing everything Max recommended, Hoa and I went out for lunch. The mall food court was noisy with families.

"What's really going on?" Hoa asked. "Are you okay?"

"I'm fine. What do you mean?"

"New clothes, makeup, and a haircut? That spells major life change. Usually, those things follow a breakup. But if you're not hiding a secret boyfriend, then I want to make sure you're okay."

"It's really nothing."

"Your parents' divorce, though. Do you want to talk about it more?"

"It's not that big of a deal. I'm an adult. They are adults. Can you imagine my father making the effort to contact me? What would we say to one another?"

"We could talk about it."

I wondered if I would ever see my father again.

"Maybe this is like how you want a new job and city," I said. "I can change here without leaving."

Hoa pulled her glass of water to her. The water cups were giant, and Hoa brought the straw to her lips instead of picking up the glass. The condensation left a trail on the tabletop.

"Okay, Linh," Hoa said. "But you'll tell me if something is the matter? I'm here for you."

"I know," I said. But Hoa had just told me she was going to leave. Her words now were an empty promise. "When are you going to tell Daylon you're leaving?"

"Nothing is for sure yet. I'm only looking. You're worried about Daylon?"

"You will tell him."

"Yeah, sure. I mean, I don't want to disappear on him, but we're not good friends or anything."

"He's just a server?"

"No, it's not that. He's an acquaintance, and . . . I don't know. He has to stay here for his mom. I'm going elsewhere. What was I supposed to do? Date him and drop him? Date him and change all my plans?"

I shrugged.

"Don't tell me you believe in soulmates all of a sudden," Hoa said. "I'll really think you've been replaced by an alien."

"You got me—let me show you my true form," I said. Our number was called, and I stood to pick up our sandwiches before Hoa could.

"Well, do you?" Hoa asked around a bite of her panini.

"Believe in soulmates? Of course not."

"Daylon isn't someone to plan my life around. No guy is. Not right now. Besides, I don't even know Daylon, not really."

"You and he have been flirting for the past, what, year? Ever since he started there. You two could have gotten to know each other."

"I didn't want to spoil our bar for us."

"You knew you were going to leave, didn't you? For that long?" I asked. I ate a chip to let Hoa respond, but the potato was like sand in my mouth.

"Not consciously. I haven't been planning it. Not like that. I had a feeling, that's all. I really cherish our friendship, Linh. It's just the metroplex. It's suffocating. All the highways and cars and cookie-cutter houses."

"What else aren't you telling me?" I could tell Hoa had rehearsed how she would tell me. I could tell by the way she kept clipping the ends of her statements with a quick intake of air that there was more.

"All right." Hoa took a deep breath. "I have an interview in New York in a couple of weeks. I'm taking a bit of a vacation to sightsee while I'm there."

"What will you see?" I asked, because I knew Hoa would go on about all the museum exhibitions she had lined up. A familiar tension of panic was wrapping around my chest. My breaths were short and shallow as I thought about all the times Hoa had mulled this over without telling me.

I nodded and smiled and commented when appropriate. I slipped into someone else. In my mind, I watched us from afar. We smiled and talked. Around us, families and friends split baskets of fries. Servers walked around with trays full of pizzas and sandwiches. If I zoomed out far enough, the food court swelled and spun like a kaleidoscope.

Hoa's news made me second-guess whether we were actually friends. How could she keep her plans from me for a year, at least? Did she spend time with me out of pity? Pity that I never wanted to leave? *"Look at Linh, working her low-level office job and living with her cat."* Did she laugh about my life with her other friends? Was it like that all through high school?

Have I been ignorant of the reality of our relationship all this time?

★   ★   ★

Max's hairstylist, Aida, was also very tall and very beautiful.

"What are you looking for today?" Aida asked. "Your hair is so virginal. I can feel it. Have you ever dyed it?"

"No," I said. My black hair was unbrushed and clumpy, like normal. It was almost halfway down my back and had a kink in it from a hair tie. "I want it short. About my chin."

"Oh, a big change. Would you like to donate the hair? It'll be plenty long enough."

"Sure."

"Have you ever had your hair that short?"

"No," I said. I didn't tell her that I hated getting my hair cut because it involved so much small talk with a stranger.

"Why the change?"

I debated whether saying that it was due to a breakup would make her stop talking. "To do something different."

"One time, I shaved off all my hair," Aida said, looking off into the distance. Her hair was straight and dyed a bright purple, which went well with her black outfit. "Off to wash this gorgeous hair, though. It will make someone very happy."

Aida talked nonstop to me for the next hour without much encouragement. When she was cutting my hair, I shut my eyes and listened to the snip of her scissors. She could slip and stab me in the neck, and I would have no warning. How many people get cut by hair shears every year?

When I got home, I showered to get all the cut hair off my skin. As it air-dried, I put on makeup. The lipstick for tonight was the warrior one. I stuck to my all-black clothes but tried out one of the new jackets that hid the shape of my body. I tied the red scarf around my neck.

Regarding my reflection, I turned my head slowly. My hair was already almost dry, and I thought maybe I could bear the hairdresser's small talk to keep it that length. I looked nothing like my usual self. From a distance, my mother wouldn't know me. She only knew my clumpy hair and bare face.

I filled up a bottle of water to take with me, and checked the time. The sun was setting later and later as spring rushed toward summer. I filled the largest purse I had with a notebook, pens, flashlight, hat, granola bar, sunglasses, and an extra phone battery. I couldn't think of anything else I needed. How does one spy? There was probably a handbook I could buy. There were probably videos on YouTube I could watch. All in good time. Tonight, I would park down my mother's street and follow their car, and on Sunday I would have tennis practice with Peter. It was perfect.

◆ 9 ◆

OF COURSE, I RAN into my father at an Asian market. Of course, I had a basket full of fresh egg noodles and quail eggs. I pushed my hair over my ears so that it was covering the sides of my face, and shoved my entire basket into a refrigerator. I walked into the parking lot and pretended to be talking on the phone as I watched the exit for him. He got into the car I remember him last having. Without a thought, I followed him just like I would have followed my mom. He took his groceries into a first-floor unit.

How much was he drinking these days? Had he ever bothered to read the divorce decree? He hadn't shown up to court. Was he angry that the money from the sale of their house hadn't been split evenly in half? I was afraid to ask because he might not even know. And if that was the case, when he did find out, how angry would he be? Would his anger compel him to pick up the gun he had bought?

I'd cut my hair but was sitting in a car my father could recognize. My sunglasses were oversized, but not large enough to cover my entire face. I quickly backed out of the parking space, and a car honked, then swerved around me. The door to my father's apartment was shut. The blinds did not move, but that did not mean he wasn't in the window, watching me.

I had learned to stay silent and keep still around him at a young age. If my father was sober, he lectured me continuously, imparting the knowledge he had about life. Father always expected perfection. "Never say sorry," he would say; it was a waste of time. "Do it right the next time. It's too late to be sorry," he told me.

If he was drunk, he yelled at me for not making better grades or not having food ready for him, no matter what time of night it was. He yelled at me when I was a teenager for staying out late, as though he could enforce a curfew when he himself had arrived home only moments before. He called my mom and me whores when he was drunk. Whores for not doing exactly what he wanted without him asking. Whores for not always being home, waiting for him. I would stand there silently, as if my lack of defense could lessen the volume and vehemence of his words. I would stand there, trying to be so still and so quiet while this adult, one of two that were supposed to protect me, yelled with such livid rage.

When I heard my parents arguing, I learned that any counterarguments were always twisted by my father to be the wrong thing or incorrect facts. They were rarely home at the same time, but when they were, they fought. Fights about cleaning the house. Fights about money. Fights about who the other person spent time with. When I was in high school, there were days when I would wake up to find all the dishes broken and swept into the trash bin. I assumed it was all normal. Parents were never happy.

*   *   *

Since I knew which movie theater Peter was taking my mom to, I didn't bother keeping Peter's car in sight as I drove. It made me feel like a professional, taking my time in my pursuit. I lost the feeling as I tripped over my words at the ticket counter. I didn't know which movie they were planning to watch, and the teenager was already looking past me to the next person in line.

Mom and Peter stopped to get popcorn, and I ducked behind an arcade game. I kept my sunglasses on and watched their reflection on the glass walls. I had put on a cap that had fallen out of my tennis bag and onto the floor near my passenger seat. I typically never wore hats off the tennis court, so it seemed like another layer to my disguise. With my newly shorn hair, jacket, and cap, my mother might not recognize me.

I lingered around the entrance until they gave their tickets to the person at the gate, and then I hurried through the line after them. The hallway to the theaters was emptier but dark and shadowy. They were going to watch a romantic comedy, and I followed them into the dark theater, sitting five rows behind them.

Advertisements and trailers for other movies played well after the listed start time, reminding me why I hated going to the theaters. I found a piece of candy in my purse and sucked on it as the movie started. If they started making out, what was I going to do? Was my mom the kind of person to make out in a theater? What kind of person did that anyway? A person who had been married for thirty years and was suddenly free? Teenagers? Would Mom pick up where she left off before she got married?

I was cringing at the breakup scene when I saw my mom and Peter get up. The movie wasn't over yet. Did they both have to use the restroom? Pulling my cap back on, I waited until they were halfway down the stairs before I started to make my way out of my row.

Following them in the parking lot was made harder by the fact that the mall was closing, and there were hundreds of people leaving. There was nothing else to do but go to the mall for entertainment in this part of town. This particular one was designed so the stores were in two concentric circles, so shoppers could walk through the mall over and over, like hamsters in a capitalistic wheel. The full moon reflected off windshields in the parking lot but barely added to the light provided by all the lamps throughout the lot. It was almost as bright as daylight.

My car was a couple of rows away from Peter's car, and the flood of people leaving the parking lot made it difficult to keep track of them. If I lost them, I'd go home. But I didn't lose them. Peter took Mom to a restaurant on par with the one they'd gone to on their first date. Not so fancy you needed a reservation, but not a buffet; somewhere in the middle-upper range of those chain restaurants that all ordered their food from the same source.

I ate my dry granola bar slowly as I watched people enter and leave the restaurant in my rearview mirror. There were couples, families, and groups of families. People stood around the entrance to wait for tables. Most of the men wore khaki trousers and polo shirts. The women wore flowery dresses and moved strollers back and forth to keep their babies from crying. Was this why Hoa wanted to leave? The mall industry, restaurants that all tasted the same, cars, husbands, and babies, all on repeat everywhere you went.

The vehicles parked around me turned over, and I watched the moon move across the sky. They had been in the restaurant for an hour and a half. Going in was too risky. Mainly because I would see Peter at tennis. If my mom saw me, she would introduce me to Peter, and I didn't want him to know who I was. Not yet.

My stomach was eating itself in hunger, and I was about to leave when I saw them come out. Mom crossed her arms over her chest. Were they keeping a distance from each other? I frowned as I started my car. Had he said or done something mean to her? I regretted not following them into the restaurant and somehow hiding close enough to eavesdrop. Visions of spilling a pitcher of water over Peter's head, grabbing my mom's hand, and running out of the restaurant with her filled my head as I followed their car.

When I was sure they were headed to Mom's house, I turned down a parallel street so I could park in the opposite direction. As I pulled to the curb, I watched my mom get out of Peter's car and wave goodbye. I bent over and put my head in the passenger seat as he drove past. After a count of ten, I sat up, pulled out my phone, and texted:

Hope your date was good! How was it?
Mom: *Fine. Going to bed. Talk tomorrow.*

Shortest exchange with my mom ever. I resisted the urge to knock on her door. She thought I was at least an hour away, at home with Lollipop, like usual.

10

I COULD ONLY BEAR to take sips of coffee and nibble at an energy bar as I waited for Nesbitt, Karl, and Peter to arrive at the tennis court. Even though I hadn't had a single drink the night before, eight AM was not my best time. Outside of this practice, I had a personal rule about not agreeing to anything that took place before noon on the weekends. But learning more about Peter was more important. I repeated this to myself over and over.

The tennis court facility opened at seven, and the courts were filled with people, primarily people who looked like they were about to or had already retired but were still spry and alert because of tennis. They wouldn't dream of being anywhere else but running after a yellow tennis ball before the rest of the world got up. I covered a yawn and put on my sunglasses. The things I did for my mother.

"Is this going to turn out like our round robin day?" Karl asked as he set his bag down next to mine. "I got us court eight."

"Don't coaches always get whatever court they want?" I asked.

"I can pull strings," Karl said, winking.

I hated men who winked at people. The only worse thing was a woman who winked at you. I'd always felt that it was infantilizing and mocking.

Peter arrived next, and we shook hands, as if to erase the fact that we had been opponents before and were now doubles partners. Nesbitt came running up soon after, and we started a game.

"To get used to our new partner," Karl said, "after a few games, we can do drills."

"When is the fundraiser?" I asked. I hated playing games and then practicing. During the game, I wanted to destroy my opponent. But as soon as it ended, I was supposed to slip back into being friendly. It was difficult for me.

"Saturday, July fourth," Nesbitt said.

"Really?" asked Peter.

"It's all supposed to be part of the celebration," said Karl, shrugging. "I tried to get them to move it. But they want to have a barbecue and kegs."

"Becka started a trend," I joked. Karl and Peter looked at me blankly. "The woman on our team, who threw up? Because she was hungover? Never mind."

"Ah, yes, I remember. That was an exciting practice," Peter said, nodding and smiling. "Shall we start?"

I turned away, frowning at his niceness. Ashamed that I had tried to joke with strangers. He pitied me. I didn't need his pity. I didn't need him to comfort me. I assessed what I knew about Peter as I walked onto the court. The company website told me that Peter worked in marketing. I could imagine him clicking through a slide deck full of graphs and pull quotes. My marketing colleagues were the most odious. Everything had a spin. Everything could be turned into manipulation. Was he the one that made sure every type of person was represented in the stock photographs for a level of diversity that didn't actually exist? Or was he the type to drone on about the latest user-experience best practices?

"Which side of the court do you prefer?" Peter asked.

I motioned to the left side. There I would have more opportunities to hit my backhand. My trusty, two-handed, powerful backhand. The only thing that saved me in a game sometimes. A benefit to this arrangement was that I would be better by the time we finished training for the fundraiser. Tennis players played up. It was imperative to play with people better than you if you wanted to improve. Maybe then I'd be able to beat Jessica and Tiffany. I laughed to myself. No, there was no way to catch up to them.

"That's perfect for me." Peter examined the three balls he had. We were serving first. "How long have you played tennis?"

"Learned in high school. Took a break, then joined Nesbitt's team a couple years ago. I'm a solid three on good days."

"We're even then. Sometimes, I like to believe I'm a three point five, but then Karl decimates us in practice."

I was sure to smile at that before turning my back and getting into the position. Peter was a solid four. The scale wasn't so subjective as that. He was still trying to comfort me. To be friendly. As I bent down to clear the way for his services, I thought about how I would serve at his back for the next three months. If I missed and he wasn't down far enough, I could smack him in the back of his head with the tennis ball. It would hurt, but not injure, him. Not too badly. After all, it was only a rubber ball.

All four of us played quickly, which was a relief. No slow servers who bounced the ball too many times or injected some flair into their game, as if that could make you more like a pro. Nesbitt and Karl won the first set, easily beating us six to one. Once we got into our rhythms, Peter and I didn't talk other than to call the ball if it was bouncing into the gray zone, where either one of us could make the shot.

"Maybe we should mix it up," said Karl. "Linh and I will play Nesbitt and Peter."

The second set was more challenging, and I could tell Nesbitt had fun scoring points off Karl. Tennis made it easier for her to flirt. I hoped he wasn't letting her score points. As we settled into a new beat with our new partners, I watched Peter move on the court. He was an attentive teammate. Picking up balls and passing them to Nesbitt when it was her turn to serve. I could tell by how he grimaced that he was working to change the way he hit his forehand. The transformation of muscle memory was a long, frustrating thing to do in tennis. So, I preyed on his weakness and scored some points.

After Nesbitt and Peter won the second set, Karl and Nesbitt switched into coach mode and broke down our weaknesses.

"Your backhand is how you'll destroy people, Linh," Karl said. "And you'll do better at all the rest after practicing with us. Are you afraid of the net?"

"I like the baseline, and I don't normally play doubles," I said, rolling my ankles as we debriefed.

"Peter, you're rebuilding your forehand?" asked Nesbitt.

"Yes, I have to keep up with the kids and their spin," Peter said. "I was playing too flat. It is too obvious where I'm going to hit the ball."

"How long has it been?" Karl asked. "We must have started that a while ago."

"Six months," Peter said.

"It'll click soon." Nesbitt nodded knowingly. "That's very brave."

Our court reservation was ending, and I could see a pair starting to make their way down from the shop where you paid your court fees. There was a slope of the shoulder and a gait that made my memory prickle. When the two men opened the gate, I picked up my bag.

"Next week, then," I said. I pretended to be digging for something as I passed the pair, who walked onto the court. The brim of my visor hid most of my face. I didn't dare look up and didn't look back all the way off the facility. Not until I was locked in my car did I exhale. Everyone looked the same here, and besides, the man hadn't noticed me. I'd probably imagined things. He probably didn't live in the metroplex any longer, and if he did, he would never remember me. Why would he? Just because we played on the same tennis team in high school didn't mean anything to a person like that. If he could ignore me that entire time, as if I were nothing, why would he notice me now?

* ★ ★

After a deliciously buttery breakfast and a hot shower, I sprawled out on the floor in front of my couch. The fan was on low, and I watched the blades move. Lollipop curled up on my stomach and purred.

Peter Chen. He whitened his teeth. Did he feel pressure to do that because he worked in marketing? His LinkedIn account told me he was relatively new to my mom's company. Gently moving Lollipop off me, I got my laptop and scrolled through his profile.

Opening a blank document, I copied over his work history. Then I started scrolling through his Facebook profile. I had deleted all of my social media accounts when my mom started the divorce. I knew my dad had some accounts, and I didn't want to have a way for him to contact me. And so I'd started a new email account and started new profiles with a common enough name: Mai Nguyen.

Peter had two kids who were a little younger than me. I was surprised he was a father, though it really should have been stranger if he'd had no kids. The tone of his posts was a little puzzling until I figured out he was a third- or fourth-generation Asian American. He was more Americanized than me. What did he see in my mom? Would the things that caused friction between her and me be even worse between him and her? Or would it have some inverse effect? Would replacing Asian patriarchal customs with American patriarchal systems mean Peter would know a tiny bit about feminism? Would Peter's lack of trauma from war mean he could be loving?

In the pictures on his accounts, Peter was always smiling and always with groups of people. I followed him back through time to birthday parties, weddings, work lunches, campaign launches, and even memorials. I stopped when I put two and two together. It took me a while to find his children's mother. His first wife had died, and my hand stilled over my trackpad.

I tried to read the expression in the photos of her. How had she died? Had Peter caused her death? I switched over to his children. I couldn't think about his dead wife just yet. It rang too many alarm bells. My chest had already started to ache with heartburn.

His son was younger than me and named Felix. His daughter's name was Aurelia, and I laughed out loud. Was Peter that wealthy? Felix sounded like the kind of name someone from old money pulled out of a hat worn by their great-grandfather as he purchased enslaved people for his plantation. Felix had gone to a private high school, which explained how he looked so comfortable in his Ivy League college.

Had the money come from his wife's life insurance? I studied a photo Felix had posted over the holidays. I zoomed in and made out the cross streets. Google Street View gave me that address. The metroplex's city parcel database gave me her family name in the form of a revocable living trust. I had no idea what that was and learned. How responsible. Most plots in her neighborhood were listed as such, but I wasn't sure if that was a byproduct of age or wealth. Likely both. My parents probably didn't have a will or think about what would happen with all of their things when they died. I'd always believed I would be stuck wading through piles of bureaucracy, but I'd also thought that was normal. Felix and Aurelia wouldn't have to do that. Every penny would neatly fold into their bank accounts.

What did it mean for Peter to have so much money? What did that kind of comfort do to all of your thoughts? Why did he still take my mom to chain restaurants for dinner? Did he think she deserved no better? A hundred questions crossed my mind as I searched for ways to find out more about his dead wife. But unfortunately, there wasn't a way to get her death certificate. It hadn't been twenty-five years since her death. What could it tell me about Peter, anyway?

Orange rays of sunlight pulled my attention away from my computer. The entire day had elapsed, and the sun was setting. I stretched and then drank my whole bottle of water. Lollipop meowed, and I got up to feed her. At that moment, I couldn't remember what day it was or what day I usually gave Lollipop her soft-food treat. Shrugging, I gave her soft food anyway.

Tucking my phone and wallet into my jacket pocket, I locked my apartment door and set out with no destination in mind. It was Sunday, I remembered. And I'd spent this morning playing tennis with Peter, Nesbitt, and Karl. I squashed the thought of trying to cause Peter to twist an ankle during play. I'd just started to get to know him, after all.

Dog and Hound would be slammed with weekend partiers, and I didn't want to be there alone, but surrounded by strangers who were there with friends. There would probably be some sports game going on, and the place would be crawling with jerseys and men with beer breath shouting every few minutes. There would be bursts of laughter for jokes I wasn't part of.

I wanted to be alone but around other people. I wanted companionship but without the obligation of a relationship. I was lonely, and I hated it. Exhaling a breath quickly and loudly, I turned down a street filled with vine-covered brick houses. A bell jingled, and I looked, even though I didn't want to admit that it caught my attention. I hesitated, a half step in its direction, trying to pull myself away from that door that seemed to beckon to me.

The door had an arched top and a knocker in the shape of a hand. The building was more like a cottage and actually old. Not like Bourbon Cake with its fake rust. A tiny neon light blinked "Open" in a window. Under the vines, I could barely make out a painted sign: "The Green Ghost." The bell jingled as I pulled the door handle. I had to readjust my weight to move the heavy door and slip inside.

The scent of fire was so intense I was surprised that there wasn't one crackling in the fireplace. It looked used, but how long could or should the smell linger? The rooms were filled with wooden chairs and tables crammed into every available space so that I couldn't walk straight through the room. A wall that would have separated the main space from the kitchen had been taken down so a bartender could take orders from guests.

"First time?" asked a woman who popped up from behind the bar with a stack of glasses.

"Yes," I said, putting my elbows on the bar. The surface was sticky, and I immediately pulled away.

"Sorry about that. Closing shift gets lazy some nights. My name's Pam. We're just opening up. If you're not sure what you want, have a look around. The backyard is a quite nice place to watch the sun set."

"Sure, okay." I got the feeling I was rushing her, and she didn't want to move any faster.

"Oh, and tonight's meal is shepherd's pie. We only serve one meal option per night. And endless potato chips."

"Thanks," I said as I wandered to the back, where Pam had directed with a nod while she talked. One meal choice, the lack of options, was comforting to me. Like the meals my mom left me in the refrigerator every night throughout my childhood.

The backyard was five or six times the size of the cottage, and I wasn't sure how the single bar served the number of people that could fit out there. So, I sat down facing the door, but in the furthest seat away possible so I could see who entered the yard. The sunset was, indeed, spectacular. The clouds split rays and deepened the blues, purples, and pinks. Tree branches framed the sun as it fell below the horizon.

People drifted into the yard slowly. When the last bit of the sun disappeared, I went inside and ordered dinner. Taking a seat next to the fireplace, I had the impulse to message Hoa. This was the kind of place she yearned for, but would one bar convince her to stay in the metroplex? But then, I felt the urge to keep it secret. My own special place.

Pam dropped off my shepherd's pie and wine. The food was homey, comforting, and not trying to be anything it wasn't. As I ate, I was filled with nostalgia. For what? I wasn't sure. Several people around me were reading, and I wished I had brought a book. I noticed then that the Green Ghost was playing music over speakers, but quietly. Still, the music was not drowned out by customers' conversations. Everyone was sitting alone. Some read books, some wrote in notebooks with pen or pencil, and some sat looking at nothing and everything.

That was odd. Was this part of the bar's rules? I didn't see any signage or notes on the table. There wasn't a cell phone or computer in sight. I resisted the urge to pull out my phone to google the bar. I finished eating, then sat back with a second glass of wine and watched Pam work.

She wore dangling beaded earrings, had rings on every finger, and wore her dark brown hair loose. Tattoos were all over both her arms, and she used bright red lipstick. The kind of lipstick that never smudged and that I always suspected was poisonous. People kept arriving, but a line never built up at the bar. She seemed to know most people's drinks without asking. Were the patrons outside talking and carrying on like at a regular bar? Somehow, I knew that it would be quiet if I went back out. The cicadas would be singing, and I would just barely be able to hear people turn the pages of their books under the hum of the insects.

I stayed for a third glass of wine, trying to outlast the quiet calm. Finally, my eyes started to droop. I didn't want Pam to judge me for falling asleep my first night there, so I paid my bill. Next time, I would bring a book and stay until closing. Maybe then the clientele turned raucous. Pam had made it sound like it did at some point; otherwise, how could the closing shift get lazy?

The quiet of the bar made me miss a younger version of myself. Despite all the things I regretted from my past, there had been a time when I'd felt invincible. A time when I would go places alone, looking for danger and uncaring about making it to morning. A time when I surrounded myself with people so drunk you didn't know what would happen. Teetering on that edge made me feel like something remarkable could happen to me. It didn't matter what, so long as something did.

"HOW'S IT GOING WITH Peter?" I asked, helping my mom take out bowls of prepped dishes for our dinner. It was just the two of us, but she always made food as if I would be bringing three friends with me.

"Peter? I saw him weeks ago," Mom said, uncovering a bowl that held raw, marinated, thinly sliced beef. She would have sliced the meat while it was still half frozen, suffering through numb fingers to get it that thin. I smelled the aroma of marinated meat, and my mouth watered. A grill warmed in the middle of the table, and Mom cut off two tablespoons of butter and let them sizzle across the hot steel.

"Weeks ago, and you've forgotten him already? Because you're dating so many men?" I asked, teasing her as if I didn't know every time she went out. Her last date with Peter had been four weeks ago. She'd stayed home by herself for a couple of weeks after that. Some nights, I drove an hour to my mom's house to see if she was really home. As if she would hide her dating life from me. I'd read by street lamplight and watch her move around her house, turning lights on and off as she moved from room to room. She had made sure I had everything I needed growing up. Now it was my job to look after her, and I fully embraced it.

She began to spread the meat out on the grill, and I helped her untangle the slices. They had the perfect amount of fat that sizzled and started to crisp and brown with butter. She always went to extra lengths for meals, even when it was only me. Peanuts had been mixed into the mixture, and I let them char with the onions. Silently, we dipped rice paper into water and built spring rolls with vermicelli and the assortment of greens my mother had grown in her garden. I didn't know the Vietnamese or English names for many of the vegetables I'd grown up eating.

"Peter is nice," Mom said finally.

"But?"

"He's nice. There's nothing wrong with him."

"So, you're going to see him again?"

"Maybe." Mom pushed beef around on the grill, then turned it down. "Probably not."

"No?"

"It's too soon," she said. "I like being alone right now. I wasn't ever alone. In Vietnam, I had all my brothers and sisters. Then I came here, got married, and had you. Then work all the time. Now, it's quiet, and I only have one job and my garden."

"So, you're not going to get a cat."

"No cats. Cats are for you."

"You mean women who won't ever get married."

"You will, and you will have children. Even if you have a cat. But you cut off all your hair. How are you going to get dates now? When was the last time you went on a date?"

"It's been a little while."

"All you do is hang out with Hoa and play tennis. Don't you go anywhere to meet boys?"

"I've been on dates. They are generally not great." I shrugged.

It had been months since the last time, and I had deleted all of my profiles after that. My last date had been with a man who had a fetish. I was still angry at myself for not picking up on something that would screen him out.

"I don't know why you're bothering me about dates if you don't want me to ask you." My mom gave me a look I didn't think I'd ever seen from her. Defiance? A sense of humor?

"I just like to know when you're going out. So, I can be sure you get home."

"Okay, okay." Mom waved her hand in a way that said the topic was over. She turned the grill back on high and dumped another chopstick full of beef onto the sizzling surface.

Our conversation returned to safer topics, like some colleagues she'd started hanging out with and gardening. The people from work were several women who lived nearby. I was relieved, and at that moment, I saw how friends would help her. It didn't surprise me that she had invited people into her life. She was cheerful and happy. And now she could bring people home without worrying how drunk my father would be. I remembered how any mention of friends by my mom would send my father into a nonsensical, jealous fury. He'd expected my mother to be at work or at home. Nothing else and no one else. I turned my attention back to dinner and my mom. The light of the dining room made her glow with warmth. She was happier, I could see it. She'd left the specter of my father behind, so why couldn't I?

◆ 12 ◆

THE HOUSE IN FRONT of me was decorated with pink and blue streamers fixed to the patio railing. The railing and molding were painted white. The house itself was built with red brick. Brick that reached around the entire house and not only the front. There were hydrangeas planted in the landscaping around the house, and the sight of the flowers put me over the edge. My car share drove off before I could get back in. I regretted this decision already. Just because Hoa was leaving didn't mean I needed to spend an afternoon with Lauren and whatever she would drag me to.

Looking back at the house, I supposed the porch was technically a veranda. The building was, more accurately, a mansion. I double-checked the address on my phone and started writing a message to Lauren. There was no way in hell that I was going to knock on the door. I heard my name.

"You made it," Lauren said, pulling me into a two-kiss greeting.

"What is it?" I asked, stuffing my phone into my back pocket.

"You're going to love to hate this. It's a gender reveal. I couldn't stomach it on my own. And I knew you would provide the best commentary."

"Who is this even for? We have to stand far away from the reveal part. I don't want to die at a sex reveal party in this part of town. I don't want to die yet."

"Oh, I wish they did call it that. But don't you think people would get confused?"

"I'd much rather attend a sex-anything party than this."

"Noted. C'mon. We're already here. Just need to pop in, say hello, and drift away. Then we can go get dinner and drinks."

"I'm wearing all black. Aren't there themes to these things? And I don't have a gift or whatever."

"You're my guest, don't worry. I bought something. They make jewelry for kids to chew on now. Did you know that? Seems handy, though I wonder if they make something for the father. Chewable key ring? Chewable bottle opener?"

"This really is not my area of expertise."

"Sometimes you do things you don't like for people you care about."

"Whose party is this?"

"Some girl from high school."

"Does everyone here still hang out with people from high school?"

"You don't? Of course, you don't. You're too cool for the rest of us, Linh. You live in the metroplex yet manage to avoid everyone from your youth. That's impressive."

"It's simple. I don't go out. You should try it."

"I am so flattered right now. C'mon. After this you can say you've gone to one!"

"This is by no means on my bucket list," I said, following Lauren into the house.

Lauren's brown hair was down and curled at the ends. It was strange to see her with her hair free and in everyday clothes. She wore a pastel pink dress and cork wedges. She fit in with everyone around us, who were also wearing pastels and cork wedges. The shoes must be in right now. I stood out in my black collared shirt, skinny black jeans, and black leather Oxfords. My hair was down because it was now too short to pull into a ponytail, and I had put on the warrior-named lipstick. Even the men wore pastel polos with their khakis and boat shoes without socks. How stinky their big feet must get, or did wealthy people's feet never stink? I searched for a trace of a tattoo or some other marking of a secret punk or goth to no avail.

The interior of the house looked like something that could be on the cover of *Country and Guns*. Or was the magazine *Home and Country*? I usually averted my eyes when I was faced with those magazines at the grocery store.

It was only because I lived and stayed so close to the university that I managed to forget this part of the metroplex. With their rebellious, high-fashion styles, the students blotted out the khaki bleh of the rest of the city.

But here I was, in a suburban house with a white veranda; fertilized-until-glowing green lawn; and the perfect blonde, square-jawed, whitened teeth, and expecting couple. Children with absolutely no stains and ironed clothes played quietly, daintily. I wanted to barf and grabbed the glass of champagne decorated with raspberries that Lauren held out to me. She winked as I brought it to my lips. It was sparkling juice.

I followed Lauren around as she said hello to people and introduced me. When I caught a glimpse of the kitchen through a swinging door, I broke away. Kitchens usually led to back porches, and back porches were typically deserted. Squeezing through servers, I saw that I looked just like them. The help. This part of the metroplex was the rich-as-God part. Why didn't I stop the rideshare when I noticed? How could my social anxiety blind me so completely? We probably only passed Range

Rovers and Porsche SUVs after a certain point in the drive here. I hated Porsche SUVs. How dare they make such a car under that name, but it was probably saving the company from going under.

I took a deep breath and shut my eyes.

"Do you need a refill?" a voice asked from behind me.

"Yes, but only if you have real wine," I said, thinking I would find one of the servers behind me. Instead, I met the green eyes of Chandler Lindquist. Older but unmistakably his. I would know because I spent most of my middle through high school fantasizing about him and staring at him. It had been him on the tennis court. I had hoped I had imagined him. I had hoped I'd never see him again. And yet my stupid body was excited to see him again. I felt my heart rate increase, and my skin tingled when he reached toward me.

Chandler took my glass, poured it out over the banister, and refilled it with red wine before handing it back to me.

"You're Linh Ly, aren't you?" he asked.

"Yes, how do you know that?"

"We went to school together? For years? We played on the tennis team together." He assessed me again as if I'd been in some accident, and he ought to be able to tell if something wasn't right with me.

"I remember. I just didn't think you knew I existed."

Chandler had been more popular than popular. He'd only attended my sequence of schools because he had been kicked out of so many before. At least, that was what was rumored. Thinking about it now, I wasn't quite sure how a fifth-grader could get kicked out of all available schools.

"Of course, I did. You are memorable," he said, putting the bottle of wine on the banister between us. "Intense."

"You mean I was a nerd?"

"No. I mean intense. And I didn't mean it in a negative way. I wouldn't describe someone as a nerd."

"That's nice of you. I just mean it as common high school nomenclature. I suppose we're all adults now. Unclassifiable."

Chandler didn't reply, but leaned against the banister, which meant his arm was quite close to mine.

"How do you know the happy couple?" I asked.

"Rob's a childhood friend. The dad-to-be. We were neighbors and ended up going to college together."

"Shouldn't you be inside mingling with folks?"

"I wanted to see what you've been up to," Chandler said. "I haven't seen you around before. I would have bet you were the type to leave."

I met his eyes and tried to smile, buying myself a second of time. In that second, always a second, there were always so many things to consider. How much stronger a man was. How much he weighed in comparison to me. Was he dangerous? All men could be dangerous. Where was the nearest person? If I shouted, would anyone hear me? If I screamed, would another man hear and ignore it? I had accepted his wine too. Was I already drugged? And what if Chandler was utterly harmless? No. I frowned. Men were never harmless.

"Thank you," I said. I'd been drawn to Chandler on what seemed like a cellular level, and that had not changed. He still had his green eyes, long eyelashes, and his hands with well-defined veins. Had my haircut and makeup rendered me pretty enough for his notice? Did I wish for my long, unstyled hair back to hide me from his consciousness? I put my hand on the bottle like I was going to pour more. The thick glass reassured me. If you got hit on the side of the head with a wine bottle, it would hurt.

"Hey," said Lauren, shutting the back door behind her. "I've been looking for you."

"Me?" asked Chandler, smiling his blinding smile.

"Linh," Lauren said. They didn't need to introduce them-selves because they already knew each other. Everyone here likely had known one another since they were in diapers. Would he turn his attention to her now? She fit in his world. They went together without trying. I could envision Christmas cards and beautiful towheaded babies. Chandler leaned back against the banister. I almost wished it would break, so we could leave him and be on our way.

"Time to leave?" I asked.

"Yeah, I was looking for you so we could sneak out through the gate," Lauren said.

"Can I join you?" asked Chandler.

Lauren looked at me, and I shrugged.

"The more the merrier," Lauren said.

"Do you two want to come to Barrick's instead?" Chandler asked. "Rob's having a bit of an after-party there."

"Is it for men only? I don't want to crash that," I said, eyeing Chandler.

"It's simply not for Ashley's set. Are you part of Ashley's set?" Chandler asked.

"Not anymore," Lauren said, smiling. "See you there."

"Tell them you're part of Rob's party," Chandler said. "This should be over soon. After the fireworks or whatever they're doing."

I made eye contact with Chandler as a way of saying good-bye and followed Lauren around the house. It surprised me how quickly cork wedges made it through thick grass.

"Look at you," said Lauren when we were walking down the street past the endless line of SUVs. "Getting chummy with hot dudes on back porches. I didn't have to worry about you at all."

"We went to school together. That's all. I'm surprised he remembered me."

"Chandler's quite the fish. Did you get his number? Did I interrupt? Oh no, I interrupted."

I smirked. "No, you did not interrupt. You can have him."

"Nope, no. I will not. He wasn't into me even a little bit. He was definitely into you, though. I'm so happy to be hanging out and learning more about you. I can be the best wingwoman. Just wait. And, Linh, you got us an invitation to a Barrick's party! We should hang out more. Good things just happen to you like that." Lauren snapped her fingers.

"I thought it had something more to do with your energy."

"Not even my parents are wealthy enough to keep up a membership there. Well, let's be honest: they're way too into their television shows and the comfort of their couches."

"Why don't you have a membership yourself?"

"It's really much better if your parents or husband pays for things like that, Linh. So much better. I almost wish we had our tennis racquets. I bet they never use a ball twice there."

"So, we're going?"

"Of course, we're going—are you kidding me?" Lauren laughed. "Did you drive here? Let's call a fancy car."

"Don't you drive an Audi? I took a car share here."

"I like this about you. Always up for something exciting. Have you been to Barrick's before?"

"I'm not exactly Barrick material. Isn't it for the top .001 percent or whatever?"

"The only people too good for Barrick's are, like, royalty or some shit. This is Texas royalty at the highest level. I'm so excited to be with you for your first time. And you're going there to meet one of the most in-demand guys, no less!"

"I should be prepared for cow rugs? What else?"

"God, yes. Taxidermy birds, big cats, and probably some endangered animals. You know, killed before they were endangered. If I don't see at least five sets of spurs, I am going to ask for my money back. And they probably would pull out stacks of money to make up for my displeasure."

"I'm going to stand out."

"What? No. People will probably think we're fishing for rich husbands three times our age, and who says we're not? Honestly, the people there will be too plastered or high to notice. They don't care about us. We're not members, so we're nothing to them."

"You know, that's not as comforting as you think it sounds," I said. A black Range Rover pulled up to the curb in front of us.

"Off we go," Lauren said, opening the car door and sliding into the giant vehicle.

I cracked the window after a single breath of cologne-soaked air. The driver had rigged up a light system for the back seat. Reds, purples, and blues flashed over us, and he played dub music. It was only six. I wasn't ready to be in a club.

"Are you looking for a wealthy Barrick's kind of husband?" I asked quietly, as if the driver cared what we talked about. He leaned back in his chair, his hair was buzzed, and he wore a very tight shirt to accentuate this puffiness.

"I would absolutely consider it. You should too. Chandler is an excellent catch. He's one of Rob's set, then? Rob is god-awful loaded. Half the women at that party would murder Ashley if it meant they could slip into her place. Maybe all the women, even Ashley's best friend."

"She's pregnant. Maybe we shouldn't talk about things like that? And Rob's having an after-party following his child's sex reveal party?"

"Oh, stop. You know that kid is going to have a nanny and be shipped off to a private boarding school as soon as it's old enough. Ashley and Rob will hardly notice they have children. They just need them for Christmas pictures and to ensure their wealth stays in the family. More importantly, tell me more about Chandler."

"We were on the tennis team together."

"Oh, a second-chance love!"

"Hardly. He spoke two words to me the entire time we were in school together. Impressive, don't you think? I was a nerd. He was popular."

"Well, nerds get the last laugh, don't they?"

The driver had stopped at the entrance gate to Barrick's and rolled down Lauren's window.

"We're here for Rob's party," Lauren said to the security guard, flashing him a big smile. As we drove down the lane, I looked out my window. I hadn't ever driven past the club, as it was tucked far into the kind of neighborhood you didn't go joyriding through. Not unless you want to be tailed by an older woman, driving her Mercedes, with diamond rings bigger than the size of your eyeballs.

It was everything I'd expected. Leave it to Barrick's to fulfill all of your wishes. Ivy-covered stone walls, as if the club were in England and not the drought-ridden state of Texas. Sprawling, dark green lawns that probably drank more water than I would use in my lifetime. The main clubhouse was a picturesque Southern plantation construction. Altogether, the buildings were a uniquely grotesque Texan aesthetic of gaudy new money.

I had the urge to tear through the rooms, swinging a golf club and breaking every glass surface I could strike. The image made me feel less anxious.

"We're going to have fun," Lauren said, straightening her dress. "Follow me."

Lauren walked in like she belonged because, in all the important ways, she did. She was cut from the same cloth as everyone here. It was only through what sounded like the laziness of her parents that she was not a member. At the same time, I bet her parents could walk in at any moment and reclaim their place. Lauren followed a staff person to the dining room. I wanted to call them a servant, but they were not servants; it was the twenty-first century, for God's sake.

"I did entice you out with a promise of dinner, yes?" Lauren asked as waiters pulled our chairs out and pushed them back under as we sat.

The table was set with two more spoons and at least three more forks than I knew what to do with.

"The trick is to give no fucks," Lauren said, pushing all the utensils to one side. "Just like that." She put her phone down in the space she had cleared. "Do you think Tiffany and Jessica might be lurking around these parts?"

"If they're members, why couldn't we come here with them?" I asked. "Instead, we're crashing some stranger's party. Is this where I get murdered and put through a meat grinder because I'm Asian and wandered where I don't belong?"

"Do you watch a lot of horror movies? Is that it?"

Our waiter cleared his throat as he came up to our table. "Evening, ladies, my name is Derrick. What may I bring you to drink?"

"We're here with Rob's party, Derrick." Lauren said. "Would you start us with the best wine for our meals? I'll have the duck breast entree. Do you know what you want, Linh?"

"The steak. Rare, please," I said, not even looking at the menu.

"Perfect," Lauren flipped her menu shut. "Please send us an appetizer of your choice and whatever else you think we'll like." Another smile. Her glossy pink lips glistened even in the low light. The sommelier opened a bottle of wine, and I motioned for Lauren to taste and approve.

"You're a natural here," I said when the sommelier had left.

"Of course, I am. I'm white and from Texas money. This place was made for people like me. Pretend you're in a movie, Linh," Lauren said. "That's all it is. Not one of your horror movies, mind you. The movie of our lives. We probably won't see anyone here ever again. We can also go if you don't want to be here. I thought it might be amusing to you. See the strange animals in their environment and all that. Good for you for getting the steak. You know it'll be wagyu, right? And our dinner will be put on Rob's account."

"You might see all these people again when your husband's membership brings you back. What if Rob holds it against you?"

Derrick brought us a cheese plate and duck-fat fries.

"You're an angel," Lauren said as he arranged our tablescape. "We ought to spend more to help him meet his spending requirement for his membership. That's how it works. You pay for membership and then you're required to spend a certain amount. I don't really know who all that money goes toward. Barrick's shareholders who are also members? It's a circle jerk. It's not really important in the end. I'm boring you."

"Do you know who else might come?" I asked. "Of Rob's 'set'?"

"Oh, probably every square jawed, soft-handed guy at the party. And then some of the sour-faced women that I mentioned before, who would kill to be in Ashley's place."

"Not enough rich boys to go around?"

"Not that rich, young, and virile. Not around here. You'll have to watch out around them and Chandler. I'm sure he has to fight them off. But tell me how your training for the tennis fundraiser is going. What's Karl like? Does Nesbitt have a chance?"

"Karl is already in love with her," I said. "Their tennis is one long flirtation. Sometimes, I don't even have to hit the ball through a set unless I'm serving."

"And what do you think of Peter?"

"He's nice. Disgustingly nice. I can't find a single thing wrong with him. But my mom isn't going to see him again. So, I'm wasting my time with this fundraiser."

"Why did she decide that?"

"He's too nice? For now?"

"Oh, the kind you marry." Lauren gazed off into the distance.

"Oh," I said. I hadn't thought that my mom would actually consider marriage with anyone after her relationship with my father. I'd assumed she would never remarry. Simply date around the rest of her life. Meet some new lady friends and live happily ever after with them. Did this mean she would return to Peter when she was ready? Peter was a bigger threat than I'd originally thought.

★   ★   ★

After we finished our appetizers, entrees, desserts, and after-dinner drinks, Derrick showed us to the room for Rob's party. One side of the room had four French doors that opened to a shallow pool. White curtains blew in the wind. All the outdoor furniture was white rattan. No one was in the water, and four women sat at a table beside the pool.

The furnishings in the room were more modern than in the dining room, but there were still Texas stars and cow prints here and there to ground guests. Lauren asked for a gin martini at the bar, and I nodded for the same. I had noticed Chandler out by the pool as soon as we entered, and now he was making his way to us.

I was always surprised when someone recognized me from school. As if I had metamorphosed in college. In reality, I had become even more ingrained in my unbrushed hair and black wardrobe. Only recently had I changed. And then Chandler had sought me out. He had been the golden boy in school. I'd dreamed of him like every single kid who was into boys did. The only thing that made me different was that I could stare at him more because we were both on the tennis team. I did a lot of staring in my youth. As if I thought I were invisible because I felt invisible. But it doesn't quite work like that in reality, does it?

"I'm glad you came," Chandler said. He put his hand on the back of the chair I was sitting in. "I thought you might disappear on me."

"Ghost Barrick's? Unlikely," Lauren said. "Tell us about the people here and who we should watch out for."

"Everyone," said Chandler.

"Just like movies," I said, raising my glass. Lauren and Chandler raised their drinks, and we toasted.

"Tell me how you know my dear friend Linh," Lauren said. "We play on a tennis team together."

"Yes, well, we played on a tennis team as well," said Chandler. "I was your typical jackass, and Linh had this Daria thing going on. Too cool for the rest of us. Maybe I still am considered a jackass?"

"We'll have to get back to you regarding your current jackass status," Lauren said, her eyes catching on a guy entering the room. "Speaking of jackasses, excuse me. I see someone I must annoy. Linh, don't leave without telling me."

"Daria thing?" I asked Chandler. He sat down in Lauren's empty chair.

"You had a green coat? I always thought it was a Daria reference."

"No goth skirt or boots, though. I'm surprised you know who Daria is, that's all."

"We had a TV."

"I mean—oh, never mind," I said. I wanted Chandler to go away, and I wanted him to stay. I didn't understand why he was here talking to me. "Those women by the pool look like they want to kill me after they do away with Ashley."

"Vipers. I've always tried to keep away from them."

"Even as a kid? So you got in trouble purposefully so you could attend a school in a poorer town?"

"Made life more interesting."

"And you could still get your legacy admission to your family's Ivy of choice, thus not ruining your future?"

"Exactly," Chandler said, drinking from his glass. His facial hair glittered in the candlelight. I wanted to feel that against my neck. I leaned closer to him to try to catch his scent. Could I smell a dangerous man? Would my pheromones fail to respond to a man who could cause me harm, and would they lead me astray?

"I'm surprised your parents didn't ship you off to boarding school."

"My mom wanted me around. She does love me."

"So, you watched Daria," I said, not wanting to talk about moms. "What else do I not know about you that would interest me?"

"I wanted to be Trent?"

"Do you still live at your parents' house? Are you going to bring back the soul patch?"

"No, I live in a condo downtown. And facial hair isn't really smiled upon in my line of work."

"What's your line of work?"

"I'm an eye surgeon."

"What kind of eye surgery?"

"The kind that requires that I do a lot of travel."

"You give the gift of eyesight to the blind that can afford it?"

"Just about."

"I suppose that's more interesting than living off your family money and playing golf all day."

"It would be tennis, at least."

"Do you still play?" I asked.

"Yes. Would you like to see the courts here? They're quite nice."

"Another time." My mind was swimming in alcohol, which was the only reason I'd been able to talk so light-heartedly with Chandler. Even in my fog, I was aware enough to know that I didn't want to die on a tennis court.

"Right. I didn't mean to try to—"

I waved my hand. "We should stick around here and show support for Rob, shouldn't we? These are your 'set' as you say?"

"Yes, we've all known one another practically all our lives."

"So, we have," a man said, coming up and slapping Chandler on the back. "Can we talk about that . . ." He didn't even bother meeting my eyes as he pulled Chandler away like I didn't matter.

Emboldened by the gin and half bottle of wine I'd had with dinner, I got up and joined the vipers, who'd been staring at me while I talked to Chandler.

"Hello," I said. "I'm Linh."

Dee, Monica, Valerie, and Cor introduced themselves. Monica and Cor waved their empty glasses and moved off to the bar.

"They've been drinking since ten AM," Dee said. "It's better that you don't have to talk to them."

"Tell us about yourself," Valerie said. "I haven't seen you at Barrick's before."

I hated the breadth of that question from women like Valerie. Her hair was dyed blonde, and her lips were ballooned with Botox.

"I'm a friend of Chandler's," I said simply. Let them make what they would of it.

"You're his current exotic thing," Valerie said.

"Is that what he likes?" I said, cutting her racism with bluntness. As if I could win somehow.

"Valerie is jealous," Dee said. "And we've been drinking since eleven."

I leaned back in my chair. *"Pretend you're in a movie."* "Tell me about Chandler."

"He's perfect. He's the one who always gets away," Valerie said, looking wistfully at Chandler.

"He's the type who might not cheat on his wife all the time," Dee said. "But then again, what do we know? He travels all the time. But he's never been quite like our other boys."

"What does that mean?"

"Like Rob," Dee said, waving her hand. "Getting married. They'll probably have a baby or two in the next three years. All that. At some point he'll get tired of Ashley, but they'll stay together. He'll get what he wants on the side, and so will she."

"Which one is Rob? Isn't this party for him?" I surveyed the room, though I realized I didn't remember what Rob looked like. Blond? Brunet? Square-jawed? Polo shirt and khakis? There were twenty men around that could be Rob. "What's he look like again?"

"He's disappeared," Dee said.

"Probably showing someone the tennis courts," Valerie added, smirking.

If I'd had a racquet, I would have liked to bash her head with it. Lauren stepped out onto the patio with two fresh martinis and dropped into the seat next to me.

"Dee, Val, how are you two? Long time," Lauren said. "Still viciously drinking?"

"Right into our graves," Valerie said. "It's Valerie now."

"Sure. Giving Linh a hard time?" Lauren asked.

I sipped from the new martini before stating, "You all know each other."

"We go far back with Lauren. We all go far back. We're just telling your friend all about Chandler." Dee raised her glass up toward the bar and moved it so the ice cubes clinked. "How sweet he is and how everyone still pines for him just like we were children. Can you believe he's pushing thirty and not even one marriage under his belt?"

"Oh dear, at this rate he won't be able to toss his children up in the air," I said.

"He will if he gets his wife pregnant tonight." Valerie stared at Chandler, much like I had spent my school days doing.

"You know you'll end up marrying Sid, Val. Why are you dragging your feet?" Lauren said. "I still see you two on Instagram. Don't you have eight versions of an engagement announcement by now?"

Valerie waved her hand in the air before downing her drink. "Sid is safe. He'll always be there. I've only turned twenty-eight. Plenty of people have babies at thirty now. I still have time."

"To what? Fall head over heels in love? With Chandler?" Dee asked. "You two have known each other for years. It would have happened by now."

Valerie stood up just as the bartender with Dee's drink came up. Her elbow hit the edge of his tray, but he caught the glass and set it down in front of Dee. The tray rolled off into the pool.

"I'll get that later," he said. "Heading to the bar?" He held his arm out for Valerie.

"How are these bartenders trained?" I asked Lauren. "That was like magic."

"Movie magic, remember?" Lauren said.

"They can make extra money however they want, if you're interested," Dee said from across the table. "I'm afraid I've offended Valerie. She's sore because Sid hasn't actually proposed, but who can blame him for hesitating? She'd rather have Chandler, as if that's an option. And the rest of us are settling down. Closing in on those thirties, you know?"

"Clearly," I said, but Dee had already started getting up to leave. "You want this?"

Lauren smiled. "I have it whenever I want it. It's not a question of wanting. I came over here to tell you I'm leaving with the friend I needed to annoy. Will you be all right? Are you waiting on Chandler?"

"I'll walk out with you and call a car," I said, getting up.

Lauren hugged me goodnight before climbing into a blacked-out Hummer. As I pulled my phone from my pocket, I felt calloused fingers on my elbow.

"You're leaving?" Chandler asked. "Let me drive you home."

"What? Yes. No."

"They might not let a rideshare through the gate."

"Oh." It was getting chilly and late. I unlocked my phone. "Fine, but I'm messaging a friend now to let her know."

I messaged Lauren, even though I knew that she might not see it. She might be too engrossed with her Hummer man to check her phone before the morning. The alcohol had pushed me to that special place of uncaring. I wondered if my mom felt like this on her dates. Reckless. Free.

Chandler nodded at the valet.

I didn't bother trying to talk as we waited for his car. A two-door blue sports car was pulled up. Maybe I wasn't giving Chandler enough credit. I'd thought he would drive a ubiquitous luxury SUV. I was surrounded by his smell in the car. The fact that I noticed was annoying. I wanted to hate Chandler. I was embarrassed about how infatuated I had been with him as a teenager. I wasn't sure how it came to be that I was leaving Barrick's in his car.

"Your vipers are going to kill me when they find out you've taken me home," I said after telling Chandler which direction to drive. "They talk about you like you're a cut of steak. Do the men talk about the women like that too?"

"Yes." Chandler accelerated as we hit the highway. "Would you like to drive around or go straight home?"

"Show me how fast you can go," I said.

"Are you sure?"

"How fast can this car go?"

"Faster than what I can do on a city road."

"Do you go out to the tracks?"

"Yes. There are a lot of places where you can drive fast when you have enough money."

"That's the answer to many things."

The car revved deeply as he changed gears.

"Why do you come back here?" I asked. "Couldn't you live anywhere?"

"I like to see my mom, and she likes it here. Have you lived anywhere else besides Texas?"

"No."

Chandler merged onto a toll road. The overhead cameras flickered to capture his license plate number to bill. Lights flashed in the center console, and a small screen lit up with the letter *K*.

"Is that your batman light?" I asked.

"Cop radar detector." Chandler slowed down to the speed limit.

"And it flashes *K* like that over and over?"

"Yes, *K* over and over. When a cop is around the *K*'s speed up. Funny, isn't it?"

I gave Chandler a little more credit. There was a flicker of hope for me, for him. For him and me? I exhaled and dismissed the thought. We passed lot after lot of fluorescent-lit car dealerships. The sky was as dark as it could get, with the pollution of streetlamps casting an unnatural glow. It was almost two in the morning, and I didn't know when or where the hours had slipped by me.

At night, I could pretend the city was another city and that the metroplex that sprawled out was someplace else. I had forgotten that feeling. The feeling of driving fast, quietly, with no destination in mind. I felt his hand on my knee, and I moved my leg closer to the center console. I kept my head turned away as if I were captivated by the cityscape. Instead, I looked at the reflection of his hand on my leg in the window.

★ ★ ★

I had planned to have Chandler drop me off at the front of my apartment complex. But by the time he asked where I lived, it was just past three, so I directed him to my building. Instead of saying goodbye, I kissed him. He brought his hand to the back of my head and turned my head so we could fit our mouths together.

"I have a flight in a few hours," Chandler said. His lips were wet and shone with our saliva.

"Were you planning to sleep?" I asked, opening my door. I paused on the curb and looked back at him. The alcohol had run through my system, but I was still acting like this was a movie. I was letting my short hair and my lipstick empower me. I didn't care why Chandler was here. I wanted him, and he was there for the taking. If we did have sex and then he left my life forever, that would be it. A period at the end of something I hadn't realized I had left hanging. It would be a neat and tidy ending.

Chandler followed me inside, and I poured us glasses of water. We drank quietly, hydrating as if we knew we needed strength. White light from the parking lot cut through the blinds and gave Chandler's shirt stripes. He watched me as I moved around the kitchen, and I watched him set his empty glass on the counter, as if we had done this all the time. As if we knew each other enough to be familiar.

I was still excited about speeding on the highways. Or maybe it was Chandler's kiss. Or maybe it was Chandler. Or maybe it was that I hadn't ever let someone inside my apartment. It was easier to leave if you weren't in your own place. We made our way backward, forward, and sideways toward my bedroom, discarding shoes and clothes on the way.

I imagined my desire uncoiling, growing, and wrapping itself around my body. It was invisible but the fiercest thing I'd felt in a long time. We lingered in the doorway to my bedroom, his fingers exploring me, warming me. I pushed Chandler toward the bed. I pulled off his underwear slowly. He watched me as I admired his body. And as he watched, I felt myself become luminous. Before he slipped on a condom, I ran my hand along his smoothness.

Chandler tried to push me onto my back, but I resisted. When he felt how wet I was, I felt his cock jerk with desire. As I lowered myself slowly onto him, he put his hand on my shoulder. His thumb pressed against my collarbone. If he pressed hard enough, could he break my clavicle? I made eye contact and moved slowly but firmly against him.

I surprised myself by coming twice before I let him roll us over. Everything about Chandler was sharp and defined. He had one of those *V*'s that brought your eye to his groin. He had learned to last and learned to pleasure. His hands were calloused, and the texture tickled my skin where he caressed me. I went twice more, and on the fourth time, he let himself go with me. When he rested his head next to mine to catch his breath, I felt the scrape of his facial hair against the tender skin of my neck.

Chandler went to the bathroom, and I listened to the water run. I'd never had sex like that before. No one ever told you it could be so different. Could my body have known all this time? I went to the bathroom after him and was surprised when he was back in bed when I opened the door. I thought he might leave while I was getting ready for bed. I moved by touch, my eyes momentarily blinded because of the change from the light of the bathroom to the pitch black of my bedroom.

He reached his arms around me, and I wanted to say he didn't have to do all of that. He didn't have to comfort me before he left my life forever. But I couldn't get the words out before his warmth and breath on my shoulder lulled me to sleep.

I didn't hear him leave in the morning, but I imagined him still smelling of sex on the airplane. Would the flight attendant get so close to him that she could smell us on him? Would it disgust her, or would she excuse it because he was Chandler?

Slowly, I got up and started coffee. I looked around at the countertops and tabletops for a trace of him. Even if he had wanted to leave a note, he would have had to rummage through my things to find a sheet of paper and a loose pen. There was nothing like that out in the open. I hadn't asked for his phone number or offered mine. I would probably never see him again. The only way I knew I hadn't dreamed of him was a soreness in my legs.

APRIL WAS WHEN THE last muggy thunderstorm washed the concrete before the ground was baked in unrelenting heat. My mom had taken a break from dating. My days fell into a rhythm between feeding Lollipop, working, feeding Lollipop again, and playing tennis. We had to move practice later in the evenings or in the mornings, to protect ourselves from the intensifying heat.

I took to driving past my father's apartment on my way to tennis practice. It ate up time and kept me from arriving so early that I needed to make small talk with people. At least, that's what I told myself. A little voice in my mind reminded me that my father was full of anger. I didn't know how he released it now that I wasn't living at home with him. I remembered the control he'd exerted over my mom and me when I lived at home and had to speak to him. What if he still felted entitled to controlling my mom? What if he was following her?

"You're getting better fast," Lauren said. She put her bag down next to mine as practice ended.

"That's what happens when you play with two coaches and a higher-ranked dude every other week." I poured iced water from my bottle onto a towel, then wiped my face. The surprise of the cold made goose bumps spread over my arms.

"Come get dinner with us after practice," Lauren said. "It's been a minute. We miss you?"

"Is that a question?"

"I didn't know if it would sell it or make it less palatable. Which is it for future reference? It'll just be the four of us. Jessica, Tiffany, me, and you."

"It hasn't been that long." But as I said it, I thought back to the days and nights that had drifted together and blurred. My entire life was like that. A routine that I'd settled into. A repetition of work, Lollipop, tennis, and following my mom. I liked it that way. It made life simple.

"I knew it. Small groups. All eight of us together isn't fun anyway. Two or three conversations and all that. We've become barflies at this place called Bourbon Cake. I'll message the address."

"All right," I said. What would we look like all together? After practice they looked like they'd played a fun set abbreviated with champagne and strawberries. I looked like I had run a few miles and lifted too many weights. My face would stay red for at least an hour.

At the bar restaurant, the hostess showed me to a corner booth that had been reserved for the group. The three had drinks in front of them, and I had the feeling I had agreed to a trap.

"How have you been, Linh? It's been a minute," Tiffany said.

"Order a drink," Jessica said. "We want to know about your Chandler."

"He's not mine," I said after asking our server for wine and a burger.

"You didn't tell her." Tiffany looked at Lauren.

"I was waiting until we settled in." Lauren rolled her eyes. "Never any nesting time with these two."

"Life's too short," Jessica said. "I'm going to be married and popping out children soon."

"It's not like you're dying," Tiffany said.

Jessica patted Tiffany's hand. "Anyway, spill, Chandler? The Chandler no one could catch?"

"How did you even know?" I looked at Lauren.

"Nope, they knew before I could even think about saying anything," Lauren said. "The beauty of an incestuous community like ours."

"What did you have to tell me?" I asked.

"Chandler wants to see you again. Somehow, he didn't manage to get your number?" Lauren asked. "What did you two get up to?"

"We went for a drive," I said.

"Is that still an in-use euphemism?" asked Tiffany.

"Literally," I said. "Then we had sex. I don't know why he wants to see me again. I figured it would be just that night. A box he wanted to check off checked off."

"Oh, was he bad? The reports on him have always been better than good." Tiffany sipped from her drink.

I was saved from answering right away with the delivery of our dinner. Cobb salads for the twins and greasy burgers for Lauren and me.

"He was fine in bed," I said, not wanting to tell them just how good it had been. "I just don't get why he wants to see me again. He can have anyone."

"Does he know you're playing hard to get?" Tiffany asked. "That's risky. He might think you're not interested."

"Well, I'm sending you his number. I didn't give him yours yet. I thought it might be fun to keep him hanging." Lauren typed on her phone, and I felt mine vibrate. "He's so desperate he's talking about it at Barrick's. You'd better watch out if you see Val on the street. She'll probably run you over now. And you know she could get away with it."

"I didn't see her!" Tiffany said, pitching her voice higher and bringing tears to her eyes.

"Wow, you can do that, just like that?" I was truly impressed.

"The things you learn in finishing school," Jessica said.

"A gal must be prepared to manipulate her husband," Tiffany said in a deep Texan drawl.

"Well?" Lauren asked. "Are you going to see him again?"

"He does have a nice car," I said, letting a small smile curl one side of my mouth.

★   ★   ★

But I didn't reach out to Chandler right away. Mom was going on a date with a new man. His name was Matt, and I didn't trust what I saw online. He'd moved to Texas recently, which made it harder for me to track down traces of him and verify it. I was lucky he had some social media accounts, but he was obviously careful. I couldn't find exes or children, which made me wonder if there were too many to count or none at all. Did both mean equally bad things about this new man?

Mom was still letting men pick her up from home, and I tapped my fingers on my steering wheel to calm myself down. Matt drove a faded blue beat-up truck, and I wondered if he was financially secure. Mom didn't deserve anything less. She had a right to be taken care of after years of taking care of me. I wouldn't let him have her if Matt couldn't do that.

As they ate dinner at Chili's, I ate a cold sandwich I had packed with a bag of potato chips. While I watched the restaurant, I ordered flowers for Mother's Day. The flower store had a special where they would handwrite poems on the cards. I scrolled through the options and stopped at a poem by Lola Ridge.

Your love was like moonlight
Turning harsh things to beauty.

The moon was full and bright tonight, so I took it all as a sign of alignment. I selected the poem and took a screenshot to read it with more attention later.

I was almost done with the entire bag of potato chips before they left. How many drinks did Matt have? Was he a drinker? Would my mom want another heavy drinker? I was annoyed that he took my mom to a Chili's for dinner. I wanted her to have dinners at restaurants that required reservations so that it showed an ounce of effort on the man's part.

Matt held the restaurant door open for my mom. That was a small plus, I supposed. He drove out of the parking lot but did not go toward my mom's home. I turned down the music in my car and followed them at a distance. A drive? Maybe they were going for a drive. I got closer to them to ensure I could still see my mom in the car.

She was there in the passenger seat and laughing at something. Everything was normal. She was fine and alive and having a good time. I let another car get between us but continued to follow them. The streetlamps didn't reflect off the faded paint of Matt's truck. I almost missed it when he exited.

We were a ways out of the city, in a quiet neighborhood. I let Matt drive half a block in front of me. When he pulled into a park's parking lot, I drove past the entrance and down the street. When they didn't pull out of the parking lot, I pulled over and took out my phone. It was a big park. Would they walk around it after dark? It was technically closed, but I watched other cars enter the lot. So, I followed.

It was infuriating that a man would take my mom to a park to make out, at her graceful age. She deserved more than that. She was worth more than a thirty-five-dollar dinner at Chili's. I drove right past Matt's truck and flashed my high beams. I saw their two heads move apart. Were they making out? Why would my mother stand for this?

She couldn't possibly be attracted to Matt's shirt tucked into his jeans, his tennis shoes, or his beat-up truck, could she? I circled the parking lot and flashed my lights at Matt's truck again. The longer they sat there, the more aggravated I got. Matt wasn't good enough for her. How dare he bring my mom to a park after dark to mess around as if they were sixteen?

I was about to turn past the entrance on my third loop when a police car turned into the parking lot. I drove out and parked along the street. The cop made two loops around the parking lot with his lights flashing in silence. That was the single positive experience I have ever had involving a cop.

When Matt drove back to the highway, I followed. What would I do if he went inside with my mom? I pulled over as Matt turned onto her street, and sent Mom a message. Maybe a message from your daughter could kill the mood.

Me: *How was your date?*

The three little dots didn't appear immediately, so I pulled onto her street and parked. Matt's truck lights were on, so presumably Mom was still in the car. Were they making out again? Would she invite him inside?

I ducked when the passenger door opened, even though it was too dark for my mom to see me. She walked up to her door, and no matter how much I squinted, she looked perfectly fine. There was no limp, no sign of being hurt. Matt drove off, and

I watched the lights of Mom's home turn on in the living room and then the kitchen. I waited for her to message back and to make sure Matt didn't come back. If Uber drivers hung around, why not someone you dated? I hoped my mom locked the door behind her. The street was quiet, and the seconds stretched to minutes and then half an hour before my phone vibrated.

Mom: *Fine, nice guy.*

Me: *Think you'll see him again?*

Mom: *I don't know. No. Sleepy, going to bed.*

All the lights in Mom's house were off, and I was alone, heart still beating fast from adrenaline. I drove slowly down the street. Opera was playing on the classical radio station, and I turned it up loud as I merged onto the highway. There were always so many cars on the highway. No matter what time of day, the lanes were filled with semitrucks speeding to their next stop.

I always thought people looked caged in cars, and their cage was forever moving with them. There was an accident that brought traffic to a standstill. I didn't have to pee, and I had no other plans, so it didn't bother me. I didn't have to look at my phone to know that the accident was bad.

There was a distinct smell in the air that I knew from spending my entire life driving on highways and toll roads. At the first whiff of it, I shut my windows and pressed the button to recirculate the air inside the car. Even if I had wanted to drive by the wreck fast, the onlooker pattern had already been established. There were ambulances and burnt shells of vehicles. An overturned semi. What looked like a minivan. I held my breath as I drove past and was grateful for the darkness of night, which kept the shapes on the ground blurred with shadows.

◆ 14 ◆

BUDGET CUTS AT WORK meant that I had to pick up extra projects to prove my worth. Because the staff who were responsible for raising money for the university did not like to do paperwork, I had to input reports into the university's database. My supervisor had joked about proofing the information as I did the work, and it turned out it was necessary. The fundraisers did not care about grammar, clarity, or spelling. Some wrote like children. Some wrote like professors trying to make one idea last pages, with overwrought language. The more insecure the fundraiser, the worse the writing. They misused big words and connected sentences as if length made statements more intellectual.

But getting access to the database meant I had another way to look people up. All kinds of tiny pellets of information are kept in databases like that. I found out that Peter's late wife was an alumna of the university. It was a gold mine of information if I wanted it. I shut her file as soon as I found it, though. Peter was in my mom's past. I had only wanted to see what might be possible. I explored the database between submitted reports. Found connections and divorces, saw how much people might be worth, and traveled backward through their family lines. I told myself I was familiarizing myself with the database. I was practicing just like I would practice my forehand.

Summer always lulled me into a heat-induced stupor. Working from home intensified the fogginess of my days. I finished my work more quickly now that I did not have to make small talk or keep tabs on where people were to avoid those I didn't like. I could attend department meetings virtually, which meant I could toss up a headshot of me smiling while I sat and frowned. The headshot I used was old. I had not yet cut my hair and had never bothered to wear makeup at work. Maybe my colleagues wouldn't even recognize me in real life. Perhaps they would pay attention to me now. Even as I thought it, I knew it wasn't true.

Eventually, I put Peter's dead wife's name into the search bar again. There was an endowment built after she passed, with a long list of donors to it. I went through each name and printed every screen. I bought banker's boxes for the print-outs. Of course, I had to buy labels for the folders and create a color-coded system. Paper files made it feel more like real research. If someone saw the files, I could say it was just work. Who would go through boxes of paper files anyway? That was laborious in the age of command plus *f*.

When I grew tired of researching Peter's dead wife's wealth lineage, I was on the couch, petting Lollipop as we both watched the clouds float by through my window. Besides tennis, I didn't leave my apartment often. Grocery delivery was the best thing in the world. My days were still and simple when my mom wasn't out on dates.

There wasn't an exact schedule I followed. If I didn't have work, my days would have blurred together and become nameless. There was simply daylight and darkness. There were my costumes and cars. The metroplex is a place built for driving.

A group of cities that sprawled into one. There were mornings when I woke up at six so I could start my day with people like my parents. People whose financials put them on the edges of the metroplex, and there was no way to get around an hour and a half commute. Always, I left with a full tank of gas, as if I might keep driving until it was empty and only stop when I ran out. I watched people put makeup on at stop lights. Others ate breakfast sandwiches with one hand while steering with the other. I saw a man typing on a laptop propped on his steering wheel. I drove as far as I could before I turned around, went back through morning traffic, and returned home to log into work.

Afternoon rush hour was harder for me to get through. There was something about the harsh glare of the sunlight off the car in front of me that made me sleepy. I considered whether I should ask to work in the office again to keep the days from slipping endlessly into one another, but, no, I didn't want to be around people who looked through me. What kind of life was that? It was easier to work remotely. I could bear it that way. My colleagues were only rectangles of pixels. It was about as much thought as they'd ever given me.

The traffic was a comfort to me. My mother was settling into new rhythms. Her replies to my messages took longer. If I called her on a whim to see if she wanted to watch a movie, she more and more often already had plans. When I was not checking Mom's windows or watching her parties from down the street, I watched my father.

I ordered sunglasses and jackets online and had them delivered to my apartment. Delivery boxes accumulated. I threw them into a corner, not bothering to break them down or take them out to recycling. The pile had fallen against the wall and then kept growing. It was as tall as me now.

As if it could help me understand my father, I watched him get home from work and then head to the strip club. He and his friends had a handful of regular spots. One needed to vary the places where you drank your Coors Light, I supposed. I usually didn't follow them into the clubs. Once, when I sat for too long near one of them, someone knocked on my window with their penis in their other hand. I drove away as fast as I could.

My father's appearance became more and more unsettling as the weeks passed. He had always looked the same in my memory. His age showed by five or six more white hairs on his head for every decade. But all at once, he seemed to look every minute of his sixty-one years. He had never called me all this time, so I didn't dare call him. What would I say? "Hi, it's been a year, but have you gone to your doctor?"

I had a favorite bridge that I used to merge onto one of the loops around the metroplex. It was exceptionally high, and in rush hour traffic, you crawled along with it. On windy days, the car would move with force. There was something exhilarating about sitting so high. At the apex of the bridge, it looked like I was going to drive out into the open sky. I wanted that. I wanted to know what it felt like to travel through space fast, free, and weightless. How fast would I have to go to slam a car over the side of a bridge? Would the car fly, or would it crumble, with me inside, against the cement?

◆ 15 ◆

BECAUSE I DID FEEL strange after the fourth or fifth day without seeing another person, the Green Ghost was where I
stopped for a nightcap. Pam was always the bartender. I never
worked up the nerve to ask her how, but everyone who came
knew they could not bring friends and could not talk. It was
a bar for individual contemplation. Almost a larger version of
the clubs that met to read together in public. Except people
could do anything here, including staring vacantly into space.
The chairs were facing paintings that often were changed. That
small detail was so thoughtful. Did Pam do that for us despite
the brusque attitude she put on?

It was that kind of night, and I was admiring a painting of
Gertrude Stein when I noticed a familiar figure out of the corner of my eye. Chandler.

As he went up to the bar, I pressed myself into my wingback
armchair. Pam chatted with Chandler, which meant he was a
regular. To new men, she was often taciturn. Or maybe he was
new, but Pam was struck silly by his looks and charm. I could
see her being attracted to a man like Chandler. Anyone would.

My back started to sweat against the chair's leather. When
Chandler finally walked away from the bar, I turned my head

away as he passed behind my chair. If he saw me, I don't know what he would do. He couldn't talk to me here, could he? What was he even doing here? I had been going to the Green Ghost for weeks now and had not once seen anyone remotely familiar. Was Chandler following me?

I looked at his phone number. My finger hovered over the "Message" icon. How long had it been since we saw each other last? And what if he'd found someone else at that time? Surely, he had. It would take less than a minute at Barrick's for Chandler to be surrounded by options.

It was only Thursday night, so I had one more day of work to get through, and my glass of wine was empty. Paying my tab, I stood exactly where Chandler had stood, as if I would be able to touch his essence. When I was back on the street, I walked in the opposite direction of home. It struck me then that I had brought Chandler to my apartment. He could have remembered it and driven out here to try to find me. But no, it was pure coincidence that Chandler had come to the Green Ghost. So, if Pam knew him well enough to chat with him, how had I never run into him before now?

I'd completed a circuit of the block and was in front of the Green Ghost again. There was Chandler's car. I remembered it. I admired it under the orange glow of the streetlamp. It was a nice car. The logo was the shape of a crown. I pulled my phone out again. The bright white light made my eyes water, and I turned down the brightness.

"Linh," Chandler said from behind me.

I jumped and dropped my phone. "Chandler."

Chandler bent to pick up my phone, which was unlocked, and smiled when he saw what was on the screen. "Were you about to call me?"

"No," I said, snatching my phone from his hand. "I was not. Message maybe. Maybe not. I was still thinking about it."

"Should I leave then?" His car keys jingled in his hand.

"Probably so," I said. I shrugged and began to walk away.

"Linh," Chandler said, reaching for my elbow, then pulling back after a second of contact.

"Come over," I said.

Chandler motioned to his car, and I got inside.

"Were you going to message me?" Chandler asked as he pulled into a space in front of my apartment.

"We'll never know."

"I'm not talking about tonight. I mean in general."

"Come in. If you want," I said, getting out of the car. It still smelled new. Did it only smell like that because Chandler was always traveling? I sat down on the couch when we were inside and watched him look around. "Do you want water?"

"I'm okay," he said. He pulled the blinds back so we could see out the window. The plastic rattled for a second as he sat next to me. "Have you lived here long?"

"Four or five years." I wasn't sure why I didn't tell him my usual lie that I'd just moved in. That I simply had not had the time to get around to decorating. Instead, I let him know I preferred this: empty walls and sparse furnishings.

I picked up his scent after a moment. He didn't wear cologne, and it wasn't body odor. His pheromones made me want to jump into his lap, which made me frown.

"How have you been?" Chandler asked.

"Fine." I moved closer to him. I willed myself away but seemed to be inextricably pulled toward him as if he had his own gravity. "How was your trip?"

"I've been on three since the last time we saw each other."

"And let me guess, you have another tomorrow?" I picked at a white fuzzball that was stuck to my jeans.

"I do."

"Where are you off to?"

I turned toward him but did not meet his eyes. Not yet. I studied his hair, the same hair I used to stare at in high school. The same neck I would watch get more tan throughout the tennis season. But it was thicker now with age. Where he had been slim before, he was now muscular and solid. The boyishness had left his body and movements.

"I'm leaving for Monaco tomorrow," Chandler said, reaching out and running his fingertips from my knuckles to my wrist.

"Is this why you haven't married any of the vipers? You travel too much?"

"Not at all. They would love an absent husband."

"Why aren't you sitting at Barrick's with one of them?" I resisted the urge to flip my hand over and weave my fingers through his.

"Because they only want my money."

"And I'm exotic." I pulled my hand away, but that meant his hand fell onto my knee. I hated that I wanted him to run his hand up my leg.

"No, Linh. I'm not like that. You're you," Chandler said. His voice was soft and kind. He took his hand away. "I think you're interesting. I want to know more about you."

"We knew each other for years, and you never talked to me then."

"In high school? And middle school? I was an asshole. And you were intense."

"I'm still intense," I said, meeting his eyes now.

"But I'm not an asshole." Chandler pulled me against him, so my shoulders were resting under his arm. I didn't dislike the spot. It was warm and cozy. I leaned my head back, so it rested on the meat of his shoulder.

"What do you want to know?" I asked.

"You have a pet? Cat? Ferret? Badger? There are bowls on the floor in your kitchen."

"Lollipop."

"Was I right? A badger."

"She's my cat. She's hiding from you." I didn't want to talk about myself. I hated that, the slow revelations. The childhood storytelling. I turned into Chandler's neck and took a deep breath. His scent alone caused my body to warm and relax. I bit his neck lightly. It was salty. When he turned toward me, I kissed him.

★ ★ ★

He was gone again in the morning, and I still had not given him my phone number. Perhaps we were destined to run into each other on nights before he left town. He had left the keys to his car on my kitchen table with a note.

Enjoy my car while I'm away. I think you'll like it.

The paper had the logo of a hotel at the top. He must have gone to his car to get paper and a pen. Then he'd had to come back in to leave the note on my table. I liked the idea of him coming and going from my apartment.

The car, though. Was this the kind of thing rich men did for their current flings? I shrugged and opened my work laptop. I'd mindlessly read a few emails before realizing what the car could do for me. I didn't have to be as cautious if I wasn't driving my car. I could be unrecognizable.

16

"How is the job search going?" I asked Hoa. We had met for lunch and were now walking around a mall together. This particular mall drew residents from across the metroplex and tourists alike. There were rides, multiple food courts, a skate park, and glass ceilings along the main concourse. We walked through clouds of pizza, cookies, and popcorn odors. Hoa led me into one of her regular stores, and we went straight back to the petite section.

"It's good. I've got a trip coming up soon for an interview in New York," Hoa said. She held a gray, knee-length dress up to her body. "Do you think this looks professional?"

"I'd go for the oxblood." I pulled out a dress in her size.

"Did you abandon all the clothes we bought before?" Hoa asked.

I'd worn my typical outfit of all black. I considered telling her how I only wore those clothes when I followed my mom around so that she wouldn't recognize me. "No, I guess I defaulted to my usual today."

We made our way to the dressing rooms, and I sat by her door as she changed.

"How have you been? You seem distracted or something? Different?" Hoa said from the other side of the door.

"Fine. Everything in my life is fine."

"How is it working from home? I don't think I could do that."

"I like it. Wouldn't you like to not use bathroom stalls?"

"Sure, I guess. But you don't miss seeing people?"

Miss people from work? I thought of the men and their cologne and loud voices. I remembered how they leaned over me and my desk as they explained the email they had just sent to me, as if I could not read. Then there were the men who looked you up and down when you entered the room, as though you were not able to see them doing it. I thought of the women who actually thought they were equal to the men, and if they were white, they almost were. Almost, and that almost made them unpredictable. I thought of the bias and diversity training. I thought of the smell of someone else's excrement. I thought about how I could hear the men not wash their hands as they left the bathroom, the toilet still flushing as the bathroom door opened and shut. How then, those poop-handed men touched the doorknobs, copier machine, and water dispenser.

"I don't miss those people," I said as Hoa stepped into the three-way mirror, wearing the dress in question.

"Oxblood definitely looks better." Hoa turned to look at her backside. "I won't miss the people from my work either. Do you ever think of leaving?"

"It's fine now. I doubt I interview well."

"There are how-tos for that. I'll send you the ones I'm using. How is your mom doing?"

"She seems okay. Goes to work and comes home and gardens."

"But, like, how does she feel?"

"I don't know."

"Don't you ask?"

"Why would I ask her that?"

"Well, how are you feeling these days?"

"Why are you trying to talk about feelings?" I crossed my arms as Hoa closed the door to the dressing room to try on another color of the same dress.

"We're friends, aren't we? Not enough people talk about their feelings. As if we're supposed to be robots or something. And I think robots probably feel, don't they?"

Hoa opened the door and put her hands on her hips. The fabric complimented her complexion. In that dress, in that color, Hoa's beauty was unmistakable. She had always been the pretty one.

"You'll need to get both colors, Hoa," I said. "This is for a date. The oxblood is for the interview."

"How can two colors change so much?" Hoa pulled her hair up off her shoulders.

We both looked at her reflection in the mirror.

"I'd say you should wear that to our next night at Dog and Hound, but that seems cruel to Daylon."

Hoa rolled her eyes and went to change back into her clothes.

"Are you going to tell him?" I asked.

"There's nothing to say. I'm only interviewing. We aren't anything. I wouldn't even call us friends."

I waited for Hoa to check out, and then we continued. I'd never let her drag me out shopping before now, and she was taking delight in it. The first store we visited was for petite clothing. She had a different favorite place for accessories, but the staff there always looked at you oddly, Hoa said. Like you didn't belong there. Hoa had a different store for casual clothes and another for shoes and makeup. Then she planned to take me to an Asian shopping center for fun.

"You brought your protégée back," Max said, holding my face and studying it. "Technique on the eyeliner is progressing. Go smoky when you're not sure. Beautiful lip stain job. And the hair. What a well-done cut."

"Your recommendation," I said, pulling my chin out of Max's hands.

"I just bought these." Hoa pulled out the dresses. "What would you suggest?"

Max motioned for Hoa to sit and started pulling boxes out of drawers. As Max and Hoa chatted, I wandered away. The last time I'd seen Chandler, I had been makeup-free and wore black jeans and a T-shirt. He must only be interested in the sex because I'd never been dressed to impress when I ran into him. I thought about how he left his car with me and wondered how long he would be away. What if his trip was six months long? I hoped there wasn't a dead body in the trunk, and made a note to check when I got back home. The car had sat in my extra parking spot for the last week without me touching it. Since I still hadn't given him my number, would it simply disappear one day, much like Chandler tended to disappear in the mornings?

Hoa took me to a popular Asian shopping mall because she couldn't believe I had never been. So much so that she kept asking me to confirm the fact every few minutes. I had brought it up because I thought the shopping center would have what I wanted. Wigs. If I was to take advantage of Chandler's car, I wanted to take full advantage. And for that, I needed a wig to be ready for my mom's next date.

The main store was packed with handbags and jewelry. It was chaos, and I almost left immediately after entering.

"Ah, yes, I see why you wouldn't come here by yourself," Hoa said, tucking my arm over her elbow. "Stick close."

"How do you even find what you're looking for?" I asked.

"How do you know what you're looking for until you see it? Take it slowly. Peruse. It's not about going into a store and leaving it in record time. We'll go aisle by aisle and then store by store."

"Every store? Every aisle?"

"Yes, Linh. You really haven't been here before?"

"The parking lot is always crowded. The shops are always crowded. And I don't use a lot of bags."

"But now you will? As part of your transformation? You know, I like that you're doing this now. It's better to squish through all your options then have it all figured out by the time we turn thirty. Now we won't be like everyone else having a meltdown on their birthday."

"Is that why you're looking for a new job and trying to move?" I picked up a purse made of the same material as a wicker basket and tried to imagine the occasion for it, unsuccessfully.

"I suppose so. I don't want to live here my entire life. There's nothing wrong with that, of course, but I don't want to. And I can feel myself slipping into that kind of life."

"Even if it's with Daylon and you have a happily ever after?"

"I don't believe in that. I don't really know Daylon anyway. It could just be pheromones, and that might make for a few good nights in bed, but what about all the rest? I do like Daylon, but like I've said before: we're on two divergent paths. Why do you keep bringing him up? You're hardly a happily-ever-after type."

"I'm not, but that doesn't mean I can't want one for you."

Hoa dropped the purse she was looking at and grabbed my arm. "That is the sweetest thing you have ever said to me. No. That you've ever said, period. Are you okay? Are you dying?"

"We're all dying, Hoa," I said, shaking her hand off me.

"You've met someone?"

"I had sex. That's probably released some dopamine into my system. That's all."

"Who is he?"

"Just a guy," I said. I didn't want to admit it to Hoa.

"Oh boy," Hoa said. "I'm going to let you off the hook right now, but we're going to go all day long, and I'll get this out of you. I'm seeing fish and chips for dinner."

"And the long lashes of Daylon?"

"You betcha. I have to feast my eyes on him as much as possible. Maybe he'll be lucky for this interview."

"Well, maybe you ought to get extra close. Maybe rub him for luck."

"Shush." Hoa's eyes were bright. "Let's do something fun."

"Like what? Wigs?" It came out of my mouth before I could hesitate. I was on a mission, after all.

"Wigs? Absolutely not what I would have ever guessed you would say. But absolutely yes. There's a wig shop here."

Hoa convinced me to get three purses and more scarves. I probably had enough scarves to cover both my arms at this point. We purchased large and loud dangling necklaces in bright colors. We got bubble tea and mani-pedis. At the wig shop, I selected a red, shoulder-length wig. Then I added a blonde, curly one that went past my shoulders. And last, one with straight, bright blue hair that went halfway down my back.

"What are you going to do with all of these?" Hoa asked. She decided she'd rather buy more purses than wigs.

"Use them for Halloween? Wear them while watching movies at home? I don't know. But they're fun, aren't they?"

"You're going to dress up for Halloween now? Are you doing all of this to try to make me stay?" Hoa squinted at me.

"Maybe. Maybe not. Maybe I'm trying to have some fun before I die."

"You'd tell me if you were?" Hoa asked. "I mean if you are dying sooner than we all are already dying?"

"Yeah, of course, but I still wouldn't keep you from moving and all that." I shrugged. "You know, we should buy you a knife. Or pepper spray. Or both. Maybe bear spray?"

"Aren't those sprays the same?"

"No, and a percentage of people don't react to pepper spray. Which you don't know, until you know. Hence the knife." I dumped my pile of wigs on the cashier's counter.

"Is that how it works? How do you know all of this? Do you carry both in your pockets?"

"Don't you? You carry nothing to protect yourself?" I held up my car keys, which included pepper spray and a whistle. "I don't carry bear spray, but I'm not moving to New York. You'll have plenty of room in your purses for it."

"And now you will too. The metroplex is a big, dangerous place too, you know. You don't have to worry about me."

"We drive around by ourselves in our cars here. Not subways. Have you even read about what happens on subways?"

"No," Hoa said, clapping her hands over her ears as we walked into the parking lot. "Do not tell me anything you've read before I go. Let's get dinner!"

Hoa jogged away from me laughing, her hair blowing in the wind, and her bags blew every which way as she dodged between cars. Watching her open joy, I felt myself wanting to cry. I was going to miss Hoa.

★   ★   ★

"No way. Chandler fucking Lindquist?" Hoa put her glass down. Wine splashed and ran down the side and onto the table.

"It's not a big deal."

"I mean, not really. Except that you were obsessed with him in high school. I mean, everyone was. But you were also obsessed. And even through the last two years of our high school, when he had already gone to college. The staying power of that dude is absurd. So, what's he like? Is he an asshole? Most guys like that are probably assholes for their lives."

"He's nice. Travels a lot."

"Where? Wait—I don't actually care."

"Why don't you care about that? He travels all over."

"Linh, don't get hurt."

"Why am I the one getting hurt?"

Daylon arrived with our baskets of crispy fries and golden battered fish filets.

"Have you met Linh's new boyfriend?" Hoa asked Daylon.

"No, should I have?" Daylon asked me.

"He's not my boyfriend. So, I haven't brought him here." I squirted ketchup into a corner of my basket to show them the conversation was over.

"You've been around less these days, actually," Daylon said. "Have you found another bar?"

"Shouldn't you two be flirting and not interrogating me?" I asked.

"Feisty," Hoa said. "How are you, Daylon?"

"Good. Busy." Daylon smiled at Hoa before leaving our table.

"Did he wink at you?" I asked.

"Doesn't he wink at everyone?" Hoa squirted ketchup into her cup of tartar sauce.

"I don't understand winking. Is it supposed to be cute? Or is it an insult? Like, I don't view you as an equal, so I'll wink at you. You and children. Or does it convey some information about the winker? Like, more than the fact that they can carry off a wink without it looking like they've flinched?"

"I think it's supposed to be, like, amusing? Cute probably?"

"The winker is cute for winking? Aren't they even communicating anything to you? Just a factoid about their cuteness? So, winkers are egotistical. Did Daylon really wink at you?"

"He did. Does Chandler wink at you?"

"I can't remember. No, probably not. I think if he winked at me, I would be cured of him. I feel like everyone has been winking. Is that trending?"

Hoa laughed. "I don't have to ask you more about Chandler if it means we stop talking about winking. But really. Where did you run into him? How? Are you two dating?"

"It's nothing. I ran into him at this baby-sex-thing my tennis teammate tricked me into going to. Then we ran into each other in the neighborhood."

"Are you dating now?"

"We haven't really had a conversation about whatever we're doing."

"I see."

"See, what?"

"You're still not ready for commitment."

"Still? Why do I have to be? He might not be either. We haven't talked about it, so I can only assume neither one of us wants to talk about it."

Hoa laughed and changed the subject. We finished dinner and had another round of drinks before calling it a night. When I got home, I dropped all my shopping bags next to my door and found the one with the wigs. Straightening each one carefully, I set them on my coffee table. I put the blue one on and looked at myself in the mirror. I put on pink lipstick, then darkened it with purple. If I added a pair of sunglasses, I could be anyone.

I could commit to this. I would commit to the protection of my mother. I thought about what Hoa had said about commitment. It was the loveless marriage, the arguments, and the growing apart but staying together that I didn't want to commit to. Chandler was beside the point. Right now, he was a good fuck. Who cared about our future? I wouldn't hope for it. I'd spent all of middle and high school hoping for him to notice me. It was still embarrassing.

I was already committed to my mom and Lollipop. I was committed to my job because I needed income. I was committed to Hoa and tennis. I wiped the lipstick from my mouth and set the blue wig down with the others. I turned on my bedside lamp and surveyed my empty walls. Did my apartment make Hoa worry about me? We never stayed here long. She was allergic to cats, so when she picked me up, she poked her head into the doorway while I put on my shoes, but never entered. If I had known she would judge me for my blank walls, I wouldn't have let her see. I would have hidden this about myself from her. But no, Hoa had known this about me since we were children. Of course, as a child I had been afraid of my father coming into my room and tearing everything off the walls.

What I needed was to stop thinking. I opened my laptop. I still checked Peter's social media posts and those of his children. Peter posted about lunches with colleagues. Boring corporate stuff. His daughter was getting married soon and posting engagement photographs every two days. I was sick of seeing photos of her kissing her future husband, and wondered why she didn't simply kiss him instead of posting the images. His son only posted pictures of himself with his fraternity brothers in suits, smiling their blindingly white smiles. It felt good to remind myself that my mom wouldn't force us into a family like that. I wouldn't have to be the dark cloud that constantly rained on their picture-perfect lives.

17

EVEN AS EARLY AS eight, the hot mornings made me sweat after a few minutes on the tennis court. I covered a yawn as we warmed up, playing mini tennis near the net. As expected, I'd improved through the weeks I'd spent playing with people who were better than me.

Tennis was an extremely social sport, even though you spent most of your time across the court from the other player. I thrived on how nonverbally social tennis was. Even while playing singles across the net, the two players influenced each other. Senses heightened as you tried to read your opponent. You learned their body language better than their families did.

Peter and I had finally found a rhythm. He knew I would go for every ball that lurched in my direction and even those he was better positioned to hit. I was eager. I was accustomed to playing singles. I knew he could be accurate within centimeters if he had the time. I also knew that he never aimed at someone's body, even if he could, even if it was the best shot. He probably knew that I always went for the body shot or straight for my opponent's feet. I could be aggressive in tennis in ways I couldn't be in real life, and so I was merciless.

The coaches usually beat us every time, and this morning was no different. But we were getting closer, and today we only lost by three points in the first set and two points in the second. After two whole sets, I was out of breath and tired. My clothes were soaked with sweat. The sun was high enough that there was no shade.

"Let's get breakfast, shall we?" Karl asked. "It'll be good to really focus before the big day."

I could see Nesbitt's excitement at the prospect and wondered why they didn't go off on their own. I started to decline the invitation when Peter spoke over me.

"That sounds like a good plan. We should talk about our strategy more, Linh," Peter said.

"Fine," I said, bristling at the decision to join being made for me. Was this the kind of person Peter was?

The restaurant Karl chose was overrun with their Saturday brunch rush, and it was faster to get two tables for two. I watched Peter flip through the menu and hoped my mom hadn't started going out to brunch without me knowing. What if she saw us? What would she think? I zipped up my jacket. My damp clothes had begun to chill in the air conditioning.

I sorted the people around us into two groups: one nursed their hangovers with mimosas, and the other juggled the sticky, busy hands of children. Between the loud music playing and the shouts of kids, I felt like I was at a bar at two AM instead of breakfast at ten AM.

"What problems do you have with my game?" I asked after our coffee was delivered.

"None. I just figured Nesbitt might not go to breakfast if we didn't all go," Peter said.

"Did Karl split our tables on purpose?" I tried, unsuccessfully, to see where Nesbitt and Karl were sitting. "This is an awful way to start the day. We can just eat and go. Or we can get our breakfasts to go?"

"If you have to go somewhere, you can," said Peter. "I didn't mean to force you to breakfast. I was trying to help out those two."

"Did you only agree to this to be Karl's wingman? I don't have to be anywhere. I didn't mean to be rude. It's just loud," I said, drinking more coffee as it might soothe me.

I supposed it would be unkind to leave him to eat alone. And if Nesbitt saw me going, she might too. She was so skittish around Karl. But I knew too much about Peter to keep the small talk going. I never liked small talk anyway, so I sat quietly. Something I was quite good at.

"What do you do outside of tennis?" Peter asked.

Our server refilled my coffee cup, and I poured cream into it before answering.

"I'm a copywriter at the university," I said. I didn't want to ask him what he did.

"That's interesting. I work in marketing."

"Yeah, I work with our marketing team a lot. They're very energetic," I said, leaning back as our server set down our food. "How long have you played tennis?"

"More years than I can count. I'd stopped playing for a long time, though. But I liked the classes and how Karl teaches."

"It's all muscle memory, or so they say."

"I went to a lot of clinics too. Even went out to Arizona for a couple of weeks. A vacation, sort of. If you find exhaustion from tennis relaxing."

"I haven't been to Arizona."

"If you ever do, you'll learn that the elevation is higher than the metroplex. The first time I played tennis, I didn't last for more than thirty minutes. My lungs were on fire. A clinic in

Florida was easier. It's humid like it is here. And you get the beaches and all of that."

"And hurricanes and unstable infrastructure," I said.

Peter gave me a funny look, then started talking about his kids. I focused on breakfast and keeping my mouth full, so Peter would have to keep talking. He'd lived all his life in the United States. I knew this, but at the same time, I couldn't assume anything about him. I wasn't sure how deferential he expected me to be to elders. I wasn't sure if he expected silence and submission from women like my father did. He seemed to talk to me like an equal, but that could be my wishful thinking. It was easy to get carried away by what you wished. Then a simple sharp word would put you back where you belonged.

And so, I balanced my responses. Participating but saying nothing. Admitting nothing. Showing no opinion. Reflecting a diluted version of the man I was talking to so as not to offend in any way.

Peter continued to talk about tennis, and I nudged him into talking about his favorite players. Like most sports fans, he could keep going without much encouragement. I tried not to think about his children or accidentally say their names, so I thought about Chandler and his car. I had finally checked to make sure he hadn't left me with a car full of drugs or a dead body. The length of time he had been gone stretched into weeks, so I reasoned that I needed to drive the car to keep the battery charged.

Karl paid for our breakfast, and we parted ways. I had parked far away from the entrance on purpose because I had driven Chandler's car and did not want anyone to start associating it with me.

Chandler had left a credit card in the cup holder, presumably for gas, which was strangely thorough. What kind of person leaves a car and credit card with an acquaintance? Did he assume

I wouldn't do anything bad because I was a model minority? Was he watching the transactions wherever he was? I struggled to puzzle out what Chandler meant by it all. The car was fancy, so I pumped the most expensive gas into it and was grateful for the credit card as the miles accumulated. Was this what a sugar daddy was? But weren't those typically at least twice your age?

I could have messaged Chandler and asked him my questions. But that would have led to long message threads and a never-ending conversation. I wanted to see if the car would disappear one day or if Chandler would show up on my doorstep. Or worse, would cops show up? Would I be arrested for something and disappear?

The car no longer smelled new. It probably stank of tennis balls and my sweat. The seat was probably imprinted with the shape of my ass, which might make it forever uncomfortable for Chandler. The knowledge that I had changed something of his permanently made something spark inside of me, but I squished it every time I felt it.

Like every Saturday after practice, I went home and took a shower to relax my muscles. Dressed only in my underwear, I flopped onto my bed with my air-conditioning running and the ceiling fan going on high. I could stay like that for hours without moving. Sometimes I went back to sleep. Most times, I watched the fan's arms go around and around, marking the passage of time. It was soothing. It was nothing. It was everything to me: the quiet, the peace, the uninterrupted aloneness.

18

I SIPPED A COFFEE, chocolate, and banana smoothie, hoping it had enough caffeine to wake me up, but not cause me to pee every ten minutes, and that it had enough sustenance to get me through the fundraising match. I resolved to muddle through our first—and probably only—game. Families were milling about, and errant children were shouting. They always seemed to yell at the top of their lungs with their high-pitched voices. It was like a carnival, and clearly these people had not rolled out of bed twenty minutes ago.

Nesbitt and Karl were helping set up chairs and tables for the barbecue lunch that was supposed to happen after the matches. A group of people were unloading beer kegs and carting out ice from the shop's machine. I put on my sunglasses and shut my eyes. If I propped my head up just so, I could sleep for a few minutes. Would that make it better or worse?

Worse. I woke up to Nesbitt nudging my shoulder.

"Didn't get a good sleep?" she asked. "Are you hung over? What is happening to our team this year? Half of you are always hung over."

"I couldn't sleep last night," I said, rubbing feeling back into my arm, which had gone numb. "What time is it? Are we starting soon?"

"Almost nine. We've had some issues. Peter hasn't shown up, along with a number of other players. Might have to reshuffle. I came over to ask if you would be okay playing singles."

"Sure. What's happened to Peter?"

Nesbitt frowned. "Not sure—he's not answering his phone. The other players are sick. Probably hung over. They shouldn't have done this on a holiday weekend. Karl's a bit worried about Peter. But the sooner we play, the sooner we can finish."

I followed Nesbitt to see the bracket. There were about half as planned, but everyone was in good spirits. They had already reached their fundraising goal, and these matches were for fun. There was nothing like watching a tennis game early Saturday morning for pleasure.

Karl was flirting with Nesbitt, like usual, and I watched them, struck by the strangeness of my being there at all. It had been almost two years now of taking classes with Nesbitt and then joining her team. I had agreed to participate in this tournament, to help her love life, without thinking. As if we were friends. She was my coach. She spent an hour each week criticizing me. We'd never had a conversation longer than five minutes.

And now I had to play one of the other coaches in my first match. A coach named Steve walked around the place like it was his private country club. This was a court run by the metroplex, and no one was turning pro around here. Maybe I could get points for the shortest match ever played. Maybe I would faint during the first game. Maybe I could throw up. No, my stomach was calm. The nap had taken off some of the edge from lack of sleep, after all.

I jogged out to the court to wait for Steve. The sun was bright and beginning to gain strength in its rays. I hadn't put sunblock on and felt rejuvenated by the rays on my skin. I already had become noticeably darker. My father would have sneered at my skin. *"Too dark,"* he would have said. Some might argue he was trying to protect me. But I knew better. He was just as racist as anyone else in this country. I'd never know if it was something he'd learned after he immigrated or something he'd learned in Vietnam. It didn't really matter where he'd learned it. It mattered that he taught me at a young age to notice. And every summer, I let the sun darken my skin, which it did even when I applied sunblock.

Steve jogged out onto the court and bounced on the balls of his feet as he took out his racquet. I stood flat-footed and stretched my arms. This was for fun. This was not serious. The faster it went, the quicker I could return to bed.

I served the first game, and Steve gave it to me. I honestly tried during the second game and then let it all go during the third. We were on court five and far away from the bleachers. I could tell Steve was hitting it back at me directly and without any added force. Most of my balls moon-balled, their arcs high, slow, and predictable, back to him. I let his balls return to his side of the court, only fueled by what was left from his strike. The game was pointless. I was supposed to be playing with Peter. Maybe if Peter were here, he would be playing Steve, and I would already be home and in bed. The following games went by in a blur. I didn't bother noting the score. The crowd was watching court one, where Nesbitt and Karl were playing another team of coaches.

After I finished losing my match, I asked the teenager at the front desk about Peter. They looked at me for a few seconds. I reminded them who Peter was, and they gave me the name and address of a hospital. I shrugged off my annoyance and took the slip of paper. Did this mean Peter was hurt?

It felt natural to drive to the hospital and ask for Peter at the front desk. It felt natural to let them assume I was a family member and show me to a waiting room. Only when I saw his daughter in a chair did I consider whether I had gone too far. Luckily, she was the only one in the room.

"Are you Peter's daughter?" I said slowly. I had spent so much time looking at her social media that I didn't really need to ask. I knew she took after her mother and appeared to be white if you weren't used to the certain shape of her cheekbones. I held my breath as she drew herself back from whatever thoughts she'd been thinking. Was I jealous of her ability to pass? Her closer proximity to whiteness? No, we were all fucked just the same.

"I'm here for my dad," Aurelia said. "You are . . .?"

"We were supposed to play a tennis game," I said, looking down at my outfit. "We've been practicing for months. I was worried."

But Aurelia was already leaning back in her chair wordlessly.

"Do you want to be alone? I can leave." Suddenly, I was embarrassed that I had rushed to the hospital. I should have waited for Karl and Nesbitt to finish their matches. Maybe people outside of the family weren't allowed to be here. I'd slipped through but didn't even have flowers. Did you always take flowers with you to hospitals?

"It's okay. My name is Aurelia. I'm his daughter. It was road rage. They ran him off the road in broad daylight," Aurelia said. "Dad said they were shouting things at him and making racist slant-eye gestures. You know? A woman who saw the accident drove here and waited so she could send me the video she recorded. I couldn't finish watching it."

I sat down next to her. I knew too much about her. Where was her fiancée? Why wasn't he here with her? Why was she alone?

"He should be fine," Aurelia continued. "His leg was broken, and they had to do surgery. I guess he won't be able to play tennis with you for a while."

"Today was the tournament. It's all right." I remembered the obituary about her mother. It hadn't said how she'd died. I suppose obituaries weren't the place for that. I wondered if Aurelia had called her brother immediately or was waiting until after the surgery so he didn't have to worry. An older sister might do that to protect her siblings. If she could, she might never tell her brother.

My phone vibrated with a message from Nesbitt asking if I had gone to the hospital to check on Peter. I messaged her that he was in surgery and had broken his leg. Then I messaged her that I would stay, and she should celebrate her match with Karl.

"You don't have to stay with me. You can go if you need to," Aurelia said, glancing at my phone.

"The rest of the team were wondering if Peter was okay. I'll go if you want. Or I can stay if you don't want to be alone."

"Okay," Aurelia said, settling back in her seat.

Okay to which I wasn't really sure, but I pulled a magazine from the side table next to me. Aurelia sat silent and unmoving. I could smell her perfume faintly. It was the same one that Lauren, Jessica, and Tiffany wore. It smelled expensive, although I didn't know its name. I knew enough to know that usually, a certain kind of woman wore it. That was most of what it needed to communicate, wasn't it?

After four magazines, a doctor came through the swinging doors.

"Family of Peter? I'm Dr. Iqbal," she said. "Peter's doing fine. We're getting him settled, and then a nurse will show you to his room. We were able to set the bone without any trouble. It will take some time to heal, and the nurses will go through therapy options. Do you have questions about the surgery that I can answer?"

"He'll be fine? He's awake?" Aurelia asked. I'd felt her body release tension, and watched her from my periphery in case she might faint.

"He will be fine. He's got a medium road to recovery, but there's no reason to worry. I'm here if you think of any questions, as are the nurses," Dr. Iqbal said, squeezing Aurelia's arm and then mine before she disappeared back through the swinging doors.

When a nurse came to show Aurelia to Peter's room, the nurse approached me first because, by his name, I looked like I matched Peter more than Aurelia did. The misstep made me feel sorry for Aurelia, so I said something about having an appointment and left quickly.

I had driven my own car. The cars had become part of my costumes. Like lipstick or the shoes I decided to wear, they were physical indicators to my body and mind of what I might undertake. I wondered what it could mean that I'd gotten into it this morning, when Peter would get hurt by a hate crime that no one would call a hate crime. My car still required using a key to start the engine. I turned on the air-conditioning and sat with my seat belt on. What would I do if I were confronted with what Peter had been? I ran through scenarios. I'd read some interview where a trained military man talked about knowing what to do in situations before the situations happened. Maybe we were still fighting a war.

Aurelia hadn't been prepared for something like this. When life felt unjust, I felt that my parents had raised me to survive. In a world like this, maybe it was better not to be coddled and not to know what love was. Sitting in the waiting room, I felt how much Aurelia cared for her father. I knew her depth of feeling was vastly different from mine, whatever mine was.

19

I'D FINALLY CONVINCED MOM to stop having men pick her up from home. Peter's accident was another log on the fire of my purpose. Mom drove slowly to the restaurant, to avoid being early, and I followed her three cars back. I wore the red wig because it was the shortest, and we were in the hottest months of the summer. This restaurant had a separate entrance for its bar section, so I took a seat where I could peek into the dining room, and ordered a drink.

It was another box chain restaurant. It was more family friendly than Bourbon Cake. There weren't two menu pages full of beer and cocktail options. But they could easily be the same chain. Everything in the metroplex was similar. It was no wonder Hoa wanted to get out.

Mom had said the man's name was Eric Ryan and hadn't given me any more information. I wasn't sure where she'd met him, and there were too many on the internet to narrow it down. I needed to see him clearly enough to see if I could identify him as someone in an old photograph I'd found online. I wanted to watch his movements and mannerisms. I needed to see what kind of man he was. I needed to write down his license plate. I needed to protect my mom.

He must have already been at the restaurant because they were both seated and looking at menus by the time I was situated. Eric was balding and had a bit of a potbelly. He was cleanly shaven, and his shirt was free of stains. I couldn't see what kind of shoes he was wearing—as if that would hold the key to how his soul measured up. I pretended to take a selfie as I took a picture of him.

I sat at the bar and ate dinner while I watched Eric talk. He talked a lot. He allowed my mom to respond with a few words, but, from my vantage point at the bar, it looked like the Eric show all the way. I hoped my mom wasn't okay with that. But she had been brought up so differently from me. Did she think there was anything different from what she'd learned as a girl? Could she even imagine having a relationship different from the one she'd had for so long?

I spent the next hour watching them talk. Eric paid for dinner, and they parted ways outside. There was no look back from my mom. Eric watched her walk away, and I scrambled from my seat to keep an eye on him. He drove a large, red truck. Either it was very new, or he never used it like a truck to actually carry things. I hated that kind of person, but the height of the vehicle allowed me to track him as he backed out of his parking spot.

Adrenaline pumped into my blood as I followed Eric while he followed my mom. He kept his distance, just like I had in the past. I called my mom and put her on speakerphone, knowing she would pick up, even though we were supposed to drive hands-free.

"Hi, what do you want?" asked Mom.

"Are you home? I am in your neighborhood and wanted to see if you wanted to hang out."

"Almost home. Are you okay?"

"Fine. Just thought we could watch a movie," I said. "Did you go on a date tonight? Am I interrupting?"

"No, I'm done."

"See you soon," I said, letting her hang up.

A red light stopped Eric and me, and I took a picture of his license plate. What was his plan? I wanted to run him off the road to keep him from knowing where my mom lived. I was driving Chandler's car, though. I pulled over next to Eric's giant truck, put the car in neutral, and hit the gas. I'd never tried to rev my engine at someone, so when it responded loudly, I exhaled a deep breath. If I could get Eric to race, to drive straight through the next intersection, we would lose sight of my mom's car. His truck was so high. I couldn't make out if he noticed me. I put the car back in drive and waited. I could see my mom ahead of us, turning right.

The light turned green, and I hit the gas. Eric followed me. I merged onto the highway and swept into the left lane and sped up. Chandler's car purred with the fast acceleration, and I felt euphoric with speed. Eric caught up with me in his truck and maneuvered in front of me. I stayed close behind, as if I wanted to keep speeding, then swerved through a tight opening across three lanes and exited. I lost sight of his taillights in the endless line of cars traveling on the highway.

Even though it would be impossible for Eric to backtrack to my mother's house, I still sat in my car for fifteen minutes to see if his truck came down the street. I had to park a couple of houses down to hide Chandler's car, and I slowly walked to her front door. I held a flashlight in one hand and pepper spray in the other, but no one drove up the street. I dropped both items in my purse before knocking on my mom's door.

"Come in—it's unlocked," she said, holding the door wide for me to enter.

"You really should keep your doors locked," I said, slipping my shoes off.

"I usually do. You said you were coming over, so I unlocked it for you."

"I have a key."

"So why did you knock?"

"It's your house. It's polite to knock." I took the glass of water Mom held out to me. "How was your date?"

"Boring. He talked a lot. I won't see him again."

"Did you say that to him?"

"I said thank you and good night. What else do I have to say? He may not call me again. If he does, I won't pick up."

I nodded and drank water as adrenaline ate at my insides. What had that man planned to do? Message my mom while sitting outside of her house? Jack off in his car as he talked to her? Force his way into her home?

"Do you think you should get an alarm?" I asked.

"I talk to the neighbors all the time. They're always home. This isn't a big city like where you live."

"But you're alone."

"It's fine out here. Don't worry so much. It'll make you wrinkle." My mom poured a glass of iced tea for herself. "Movie?"

We settled on the couch, and I let her pick something out. The movie she chose was a quiet family drama with the kind of acting that never really makes you believe it's real. I slept through most of it. Following my mom was quite exhausting. The rushes of adrenaline were what would give me wrinkles.

It was past midnight by the time the film ended. My mom had fallen asleep but woke up when I turned off the TV. I waited until I heard her lock the door before I walked back to Chandler's car. The moon was so bright that it felt like I wasn't out at night. It was like I was on a black-and-white movie set. If I wondered far enough into the set, could my real life slip away forever? And then, what? I'd go on following my mother for the rest of eternity?

I was tired, but I still looked up and down the street, expecting to see the dark cab of a truck somewhere. The hairs on my neck prickled as if I were being watched, and I locked the car doors immediately after I got in.

At home, there was a piece of folded paper wedged into my doorjamb. I saw the clean lines of a hotel logo on the top of the page and knew who it was.

Missing you. I hope you're enjoying the car.

"Missing you" echoed through my mind as I took my shoes off and set down my things. As if he was still missing me at this very second. I set the note on my dresser and stared at it while I brushed my teeth. Chandler had been here, but he had gone again.

It wasn't an encounter I would miss. It was more important that I had been with my mom tonight. What would have happened to her if I had not been following her? Had I not distracted Eric from following her home? What would he have done to my mom? Chandler didn't have to worry about what could hurt his mom. Chandler probably didn't have very many things to worry about that he couldn't fix with money. He had simply stopped by for his preflight fuck.

◆ 20 ◆

WHEN I ENTERED MY father's favorite club, I found an empty booth and sat down quickly. I hadn't really had a plan. I had only known that I needed to see my father more closely. Someone had turned on the haze machine, and the view below was like looking through to another universe. The strobe lights made people's movements glitch. It looked like they were a simulation. There was a dancer on stage, and every time the light flashed back on, she was in a different position. It made her look like a puppet.

My father looked unharmed and all in one piece. He had his row of empties in front of him, and he was jostling the man who was sitting next to him. He was with three others, all men in their sixties or seventies with empty beers and glasses in front of them. They could drink more than me, and I was still in my twenties. I wondered what they would feel like the next day. Wouldn't they be hungover? Would it give them diarrhea, or were their bodies inured to the alcohol?

"They are getting worse," a woman said as she stood next to me. "Come with me. You shouldn't sit here alone."

I thought she was kicking me out, so I shrugged and followed. Maybe women weren't actually allowed in the club? But instead of going out the front doors, she led me to a hallway that a man was standing in front of with his arms crossed.

"That's Sebastian. He'll know to let you through now."

"Will he let me leave too?"

"He's here to protect us. Every woman in the building, including you. It's better if you're upstairs than out here with the drunk men."

She had a point. I met Sebastian's gaze and hoped I was right in seeing kindness written into the laugh lines around his eyes. I followed her up a dark stairwell. At the mezzanine level, she waved to a sofa.

"I'm Jane, and you look like a wine woman." She held out a small bottle.

"Thank you," I said. The top twisted off, and I drank from it like a beer.

"Who are you following?"

"I thought this would be a no-questions-asked kind of place." I twisted the cap back onto the wine bottle.

"We aren't in a movie." Jane reapplied her lipstick without a mirror.

"My father."

"Worried about him?"

"No. I'm worried about my mom."

"I see." Jane leaned forward, looking down. "I'm more protected here than you are out in the world with men. Isn't that strange?"

I watched my father stand up. He wobbled and laughed it off. The other men got up too, and they stumbled outside. I leaned back on the couch and stared at the ceiling.

"Do you like it here?" I asked, but Jane was already gone. I stayed and finished the bottle of wine alone.

Even though I had given my father a head start, I caught up with him when he was nearing his apartment. His car wove in the lane, and I hoped a cop wasn't nearby. I kept a distance from him but tried to keep other cars from being directly behind him. I didn't want someone to call the police. I didn't want to watch him get arrested. I could feel the heat of shame creep into my face at the thought. I didn't want to watch him get into an accident either, but I didn't know what else to do but follow him.

My father did not get out of his car immediately. He sat there with the lights on, and I almost got out to check on him. The door swung open and bounced back, probably leaving a dent in the door of the unlucky car next to his. The scene wasn't new to me. How many times had I watched it as a child before I, like my mother, stayed away from home? As a teenager, with my mother working two jobs and my father out every night drinking, I didn't even have to sneak out of the house. I didn't have to hide when I came home because my father was usually passed out in his bed.

He was so drunk that he wasn't able to shut his car door completely behind him. He used cars to lean on as he made his way through the lot. It was a long way, because he'd had enough experience to know that he needed to park at the end of the lot, where there were fewer cars he could hit.

The air was cold on my skin. It was early enough that birds were starting to chirp. Lonely, light sounds, almost as if they were still sleeping, and these songs were their snores. I had always loved this time of the night, between those who stayed up late and those who got up early.

My father vomiting brought me back to the moment. I bumped my hip against his car door, to shut it all the way, and walked over to him. My wrists were covered in jangly bracelets, and I did not speak. I merely leaned down and helped my father up. He groaned and mumbled something in Vietnamese. I took his keys from him, and we staggered toward his door.

I didn't bother turning on the lights. I didn't want him to know it was me. Was it possible to be so near your child and not recognize her? My father had spent so little time around me, so maybe for him, it was possible. Besides, he was drunk, it was dark, and I was wearing a wig and sunglasses.

The apartment was messy, which I knew would be the case. Women cleaned. Men like my father did not, even when there wasn't a woman around to take care of him. There was the odor of stale beer that I expected at any place my father lived. Empty bottles and full ashtrays covered every tabletop. Aside from those things, the apartment was bare.

"Whore," my father said.

I ignored him. I wanted to believe he couldn't recognize me.

"You and your mother are both whores. Worthless. She took all my money. She owes me. I'll get her back."

I dropped my arms, and my father stumbled against the wall. He used it to hold himself up and went into the bedroom.

I heard him throw up again and flush the toilet. When I went in to check on him, he was face down on the bed, one shoe on, the other who knew where. I was glad the lights were off. I was glad I couldn't see him. I could imagine his face, the mole on his check, how he looked when he was unshaven. But I also knew his entire life consisted of war and strife and uncertainty. His life hadn't been anything like my life, so how could I judge him? What haunted his dreams? I could never imagine. I didn't want to know, and he never talked to me about his past.

It was hard to look at him, even in the darkness, because the mixture of emotions wasn't something I could describe in

English. Maybe I could have if I knew enough Vietnamese. Maybe there was no way. When I read about parental love, I never found the words to describe how I felt, how I felt like nothing and everything simultaneously. I lived in a culture that taught you one way of loving when the way my parents showed love was so different. Did that make it something else?

I set a glass of water on the side table and shut the bedroom door behind me. Taking deep breaths, I pushed my feelings into a pile. I imagined sweeping them up, holding them in my hands, and then flinging them into the wind. I put my mind into being peaceful, tranquil, calm, stoic, and strong. My chin quivered, and I clenched my teeth.

Scanning the mess of my father's apartment again, I resisted the urge to clean. My attention caught on a long dark box under the coffee table. It was made of heavy plastic with latches to open it. The shape was unmistakable. The gun case. Could I take it? What would I do with it? What happened to people who stole guns from other people? Adrenaline flooded my body. Was this how he intended to get my mother back? I was about to reach down for the gun when I heard someone come down the metal apartment stairs. I couldn't walk out with a gun case in my hands.

I left my father's apartment and shut the door behind me. I leaned against the door. My heart was beating like I had gone for a run. Would I be responsible for ensuring my father died with decency? Was I already a shame to all of my ancestors for letting him live like this? But most of all, I wanted to know why he had that gun.

♦ 21 ♦

I COULDN'T USE MY usual tactic for parties with Hoa's goodbye party. Usually, I arrived late. Usually, that meant everyone would be on their second or third drink, the time at parties when things got fuzzy. No one remembered when I came or left after that. I could stay for five minutes or an hour, and it didn't make a difference.

But Hoa had enlisted my help in getting things ready, so I was there to set up and would be there at the very end to help her clean up. She had wanted to host it at her apartment, to make it more comfortable, but she was also packing, so her apartment was about as bare as mine. The day before the party, she had sent me a schedule of when to leave and the things I would pick up on the way over. She'd preordered everything, down to bags of ice. My errands, even though I ran into hiccups and long lines, ran on her schedule. It was like she could see the future and had accounted for the delays. Hoa had always been organized like that.

When I looked out over the world, I saw the chaos that made me retreat into my home, onto my couch or bed, where I could comfortably watch the clouds float by. When Hoa looked out at the world's chaos, she dove into it to help get it in order and move it along. Along to what, I wasn't even sure.

I generally was not a party person. Or a gathering type of person. I didn't look forward to hanging out with Hoa's friends. They all were shackling themselves to each other and in the process of reproducing. It was becoming more and more difficult to muster the high-pitched squeals upon hearing about engagements and pregnancies. When I saw gemstones, I thought only of how many people had died to acquire those diamonds and emeralds. When I thought about babies, I couldn't stop myself from thinking about the rising sea waters, floods, droughts, and pollution. What kind of person brings a new life into certain disaster? How delusional did you have to be? How self-assured did you have to be to think you could protect your children from the harms of the world?

I clenched and unclenched my body to shake off my thoughts. The party was starting. Even though Hoa had sold most of her furniture, her apartment exuded warmth and comfort through her decorations. People had come with flowers that dotted the table and kitchen counters. The wine bottles they'd brought began to crowd the table space. I shouldn't have been surprised at the number of people who had showed up for Hoa. She had always been there for me, and so she probably had always been there for everyone in the room. Helping them. Giving them her time and her insight and herself. Was she leaving because of that too? Because if she stayed here, we might take from her until she had nothing left? And still, she probably wouldn't stop giving.

I had expected there to be an hour of awkward small talk, but within ten minutes of the party's start time, people filled the kitchen. Then they filled the living room and balcony. Children ran underfoot, and I found myself dodging their sticky hands and sharp elbows. Most everyone here had children, were pregnant, or were actively trying. I could see the unbridled desire in the eyes of those trying for their tiny version of themselves. The not-yet-fathers doubled down on their beer.

The unbelievably high-pitched squeals, the conversations around day care, and the stories about the fantastic things their mini-mes had done recently drove me out. I used the excuse of taking a box of empty wine bottles to the recycling bin. In that box, I had included a not-quite-empty bottle for myself. I didn't have anything in common with anyone there. What was I going to do? Talk about how I was so worried about my mom that I had taken to following her around town? Talk about my father's alcoholism and his gun? Rain my sad family stories onto their conversations about how best to keep their white sheets white?

Loneliness in a crowd wasn't new to me. It was harder for me to think of a time when I hadn't felt that way. I tossed the box of bottles into the recycling, accidentally throwing the bottle I'd brought for myself in with it. Typical. I laughed. My stomach was already souring from the alcohol I had consumed, so maybe it was better this way. How had my father numbed his body to alcohol? Maybe mine was becoming sensitive to it because it was trying to keep me from turning into him. I let myself into the apartment pool area.

The pool had a row of lounge chairs. The plastic squeaked against my weight. Music and laughter from the party drifted to me, carried by a breeze, and I took a deep breath of chlorinated air. The light pollution from the metroplex drowned out most of the stars. There was a sliver of moon and Orion's belt. In college, I used to do laundry while I slept off the night before, next to the pool, on Sunday mornings. It was the best, most religious-type experience I had done for myself. I was alone those mornings too. Was I happy then? Would I have been happier if I had been with someone? Had I not changed since those years, and was that the problem?

Had Hoa noticed that I had been gone longer than it takes to walk to the garbage and back? Probably not. There was an apartment full of people celebrating her, as it should be. I was such a small part of her life, and yet she was such a big part of mine. Were relationships always so unbalanced?

I took deep breaths, counting like I'd heard that people do to calm themselves. It was time to go back to the party. To smile through the pity I'd see in people's eyes because I was single, and that must mean something was wrong with me. To smile through the fact that Hoa was leaving, and probably leaving for good.

✦ 22 ✦

FALL WAS MARKED BY the teasing scent of winter on the occa-sional breeze. It would take another month for the leaves to change colors and drop. I ignored the frenzy over artificial coffee flavorings and added another ad blocker to my internet browsers. But the cooler weather meant that I could buy more jackets. The season's trend turned out to be oversized sweaters, and for the first time in my adult life, I moved with the trend.

I couldn't leave my car running in the winter like I could in the summer. The exhaust would rise up as white smoke and make my presence obvious. The sweaters came down to my mid-thigh. I purchased knit ones made with thick cotton yarn. I bought ones with cinched sleeves. They were dress-like, and I resisted the urge to add a belt. It was fashionable to strike a blob-like shape, and I took advantage of it. When I was parked and watching one of my parents, I could draw my knees up into the sweaters. I wore thick wool socks so I could keep warm as the temperature dropped.

The pile of discarded shipping boxes in my apartment touched the ceiling. I considered buying Christmas lights and repurposing the boxes as a tree. It was the right shape. Christmas decorations were already on store shelves. At this rate, I wouldn't be surprised to see them out next year as soon as the independence holiday passed. Holiday decoration shopping seemed like a very normal thing to do. Maybe I would do it to show that my life was fine.

★   ★   ★

Mom had put out some sort of autumn decoration on her dining room table: a wreath centerpiece. The fake leaves had painted orange edges. She had placed a vase of fresh flowers in the middle of that. Pine branches with white roses. The vinyl tablecloth disrupted the tableau.

I'd gone to Mom's house while she was at work, because her friends had stayed so late the night before. They were usually respectful of weeknights. Several bottles of wine were in the recycling bin, but that was not unusual after one of their visits. There were two boxes in Mom's living room that I'd seen her friends carrying, and I lifted the flaps with my pinky.

Both boxes were filled with worn paperback books. I picked one out. The cover depicted a man kissing a woman's exposed shoulder. Her old English dress was barely clinging to her breasts. The book edges were soft, and the spine was wrinkled. All the books were in similar states of use. I dropped the one I had picked up into my bag.

In all of my life, I had never seen my mom read a book. We hadn't had books at home except for my textbooks, now that I thought about it. I went into Mom's bedroom and looked around. She hadn't made the bed this morning, and there was a box on her nightstand with discarded wrapping paper. As I approached, the unmistakable shape of a vibrator came into focus. My mind emptied. I froze for seconds or minutes. I turned away from it as if it were something shameful. It wasn't, but it also wasn't something I should see.

My mom's bedroom windows looked out on the street, and I watched the clouds move across the sky. I could see Chandler's car where I'd parked it. A cardinal landed on the neighbor's bird feeder. As I watched it maneuver for seeds, a red truck drove down the street. The truck's windows were tinted, but it was familiar. I took out my phone to take a photo of the license plate. Cars on the street blocked my view. Still, I knew the numbers would only confirm that the truck belonged to one of the men my mom had dated, the one who had tried to follow her home. He'd done what I had done with so many men. He'd looked up my mom's name in the county's property database. He'd found her address. He knew where she lived.

The truck did not drive down the street again. I waited for an hour, until the sunlight started to change. Mom would be home soon, and I didn't want her to find me there.

Back at home, I dug through boxes until I found where I'd put my notes on Eric Ryan. That box had since had empty delivery boxes piled on top of it. I kicked away plastic sleeves of air used for packing as I looked for the file. It felt like years had passed since I'd first researched him, instead of months. I had printed out every hateful blog post Eric had written and screen-shots of every racist post on social media.

Google Street View showed that his house was on a small street on the outskirts of the metroplex—a part of town where Chandler's car would stand out; a part of town where I wouldn't be able to camp out in my car. I switched to satellite view. The parcels of property were large, with either a shack out on the land or a mansion with annexes and pools, not much in between. Eric's home was one of the former. A mobile home that had seen much better days. He must have put all his money into his truck.

I'd let myself be distracted by Hoa's move. I had let my guard down. I needed to have a good schedule and system to watch over my mom. I needed to refocus.

EVERY NIGHT THAT I did not have plans, which was almost every night, I sat at my post in front of my mom's house. Just to check. Just to be sure. I had been forced to cut this night shorter than usual because I'd forgotten to pack a protein bar. Then I realized I had eaten a protein bar for dinner for the past five days and decided to treat myself to the Green Ghost. Pam never asked me what I did or what I had been up to. I liked that the bar did not ask anything of me. Thus it did not own any part of me.

Bolognese with a house salad was this evening's dinner. I settled into a seat by the fireplace so that I could enjoy the scent of ashes. Someone sat in the chair next to mine, and I turned the page of my book without looking. I didn't think the bar had gotten busy enough that people were forced to sit next to one another. Usually, everyone quite diligently sat far away from each other. But maybe this person also found the smell of a fireplace comforting.

The words on the page blurred as I thought about Eric Ryan again. I had hoped he would forget my mom. Should I pursue him to stop him from harming anyone? But what would I do if he did follow someone else home and break into their house?

Call the police and describe how I had been following Eric? His social media posts were filled with rants and links to questionable news sites. I made sure to click only on links he posted on my work computer. I'd be happy if that machine got infected with a virus.

Why had he gone out with my mom in the first place? He was openly racist. I shuddered to think of him buying her dinner and then using that as a reason to hurt her. To prove that she had taken from him, so he could take from her. Night after night, I watched the cars that drove past my mom's house. And so far, I had not seen his oversized truck again. So far.

Pam set down plates of salad and pasta on my table and my neighbor's. I looked over and met Chandler's gaze. He smiled and held his glass up. I did not reciprocate and glanced around to make sure no one had noticed. What if we were caught talking to each other? I wouldn't be surprised if Pam had to throw us out. No one at the Green Ghost talked to anyone besides Pam. I did not want to break a rule and be banned.

Chandler had already started eating, so I did the same. We were both facing the empty fireplace, but he had angled his chair so that I was in his line of sight. I kept my chair facing the fireplace. There wasn't anything else to do but eat. What would Hoa say if I told her our first meal together was at a silent bar, next to each other but not with each other?

The time it took for her to respond to my messages had grown longer and longer. Even in this digital age, distance pulls relationships thin. I ate slowly so I might outlast Chandler. As if it were some competition. When Pam came to take away our empty dishes, I signaled for a second drink and opened my book again. After a few minutes, I heard Chandler get up. I thought he was leaving, but instead he dropped a piece of paper on my table.

You're not really reading.

The paper had a hotel logo on the top.

Do you always keep hotel stationery on hand?

I wrote this and pushed the paper to the edge of my table, so he was forced to get up and retrieve it.

Let's go somewhere else.

Chandler dropped the paper off and then went up to the bar. I watched him leave and considered my options. Leave now or wait and chance that Chandler might leave without me? How had he found this bar? I was driving his car, I remembered. He could have his spare key and leave me here. But I was close to home and perfectly able to walk. I drummed my fingers on my book's cover for a second before getting up.

"You didn't have to pay for my dinner," I said once I was outside. Chandler was leaning on the hood of his car, and I tossed him his keys.

"I was trying to be a gentleman," Chandler said. "How do you know this bar?"

"It's in my neighborhood. We've seen each other here before."

"I thought you had walked by and seen my car. Not a lot of people know about this bar."

"I haven't told anyone about it. It's not just *your* bar. Unless you actually own it or something like that?" I asked. Chandler could own it. Maybe he was from one of those families that owned entire city blocks. If he was, why did he even bother working?

"I don't own it, but that would be a nice thought. To preserve it."

"Aren't you rather far from Barrick's?"

"Exactly."

"Should I bother asking how your trip was? Or should we skip it? You don't have to lie about maybe having a family in another city." I'd stopped a few feet from Chandler. I wasn't quite sure what I wanted. To walk home? For him to take me home? For him to take me someplace else?

"No secret families."

"Let me guess: You're leaving to go somewhere else tomorrow?"

Chandler tossed me the car key. I caught it, my tennis reactions saving me from getting hit. Was he embarrassed that he was leaving again? Was I upset to be only his preflight fuck?

"I just got back into town this morning," Chandler said.

"You don't need to tell me that," I said, making up my mind. I wanted to be reckless. I wanted a divergence from the sameness of all my nights. If I was going nowhere at all, at least let it have some scenic outlooks. I walked to the passenger door and opened the door. "You drive."

He got onto the highway and drove east to merge with one of the loops that would take us around the entire metroplex.

"What do you think about when you drive?" Chandler asked. "It looks like you drive a lot."

"The point is not to think."

"I get that."

The lights blurred past you if you focused straight ahead. The repetition of the strip malls wasn't so disappointing when they created a rhythmic beat to the night. The cars alongside you meant you weren't alone. But I didn't tell him this.

"Have you ever wanted to leave the metroplex?" Chandler asked.

"Did you drive another car to the bar tonight?" I asked.

"I got a rideshare. Have you thought about it? Leaving?"

"My mom lives here. Why do you keep coming back here, of all places, if you don't have to?"

"My mom lives here too." Chandler pulled into the HOV lane and accelerated.

"Do you do track days?"

"Yes. I spent last winter learning to drive on the ice and in the snow. There's a track in Russia."

"I'm sure there are plenty of things in Russia if you have enough money."

"I was a little nervous the entire time. If I crashed and died on the track, I would be so far away from my mom. She's all I have. For some reason, that bothered me. I felt isolated. Like no one might care. Do you know what I mean?"

"Your mom would care."

"Yes, she would, actually. I'm lucky to have that."

"There are hordes of women at Barrick's that would care."

"Maybe for as long as it was take them to say *'Damn.'*"

We were going past downtown now, and the skyscrapers lit the night. A red Corvette pulled up alongside us, and Chandler lifted the corner of his mouth. He didn't ask me, and I almost said *"Go"* when he hit the gas. The Corvette accelerated with us, and our cars sped down the lanes. Both of us had to leapfrog around slower cars, and we crossed from lane to lane. Chandler had turned on his police radar, and it beeped. The driver of the Corvette braked a second after us.

I had grasped the door handle to keep myself from sliding around as we moved. Chandler took the exit that would take us back around to my apartment, and we drove up a curving bridge. If we had still been doing the same speed as moments before, would the bridge have made it feel like we were flying?

Chandler followed me into my apartment. I didn't turn on any lights. My apartment was full of empty boxes and dirty laundry on the floor. Would Chandler run away at the sight of it?

"When is your flight?" I asked. I led him back to my bedroom, and we sat on the bed.

"Early." He was so close his breath blew my hair.

Chandler turned me to him, ran his hands up my arms, and then kissed me slowly. He got on his knees on the floor as he unfastened my jeans and pulled them off. I leaned back, resting my weight on my hands. I relaxed into his movements until I was so warm, I couldn't feel the difference between our bodies.

Afterward, I listened to Chandler's steady breath. He'd fallen asleep in the time it took me to use the bathroom. There was a balled-up tissue on my nightstand, presumably holding the used condom. The air was humid, and I could smell latex and the bleach-like scent of semen. I resisted the urge to throw the tissue away, to immediately start erasing Chandler's presence.

I turned away from Chandler, to sleep, and froze when I felt him snuggle into my back. He buried his face, covered with my scent, into my hair. Chandler wrapped his arm around me and pulled me close. I hesitated for a second before resting against his hot skin. The fan was off, and we had a sheet pulled over us. I concentrated on my breathing to forget about the heat of another body in bed with me. I felt Lollipop jump onto the bed and thought I felt her curl up on the other side of Chandler. He was stuck against me now, and I was trapped in his embrace.

It felt like I'd just fallen asleep when I heard his alarm go off. Chandler slid out of bed. I listened to him turn the water on and off in the bathroom. Cold air trickled against my back where he had been. I didn't move at all and kept my eyes shut as he fumbled around in the dark for his clothes. I felt him stand near the bed, then he leaned down and kissed me on the forehead. Then he left. I was about to get up when I heard my door open again. I hoped with every cell that it was Chandler. The door shut again, and then I listened to the sound of a car door closing.

I fell asleep before I could muster the energy to lock my door. When I woke up again, bright sunlight filled my apartment. I got up and pulled on underwear as I went out to the kitchen. He had left a note on the table.

I won't be back until Christmas. Call me? Message me?

Under that, he'd written his phone number, which I already had. Then his email, various social media handles, and messaging apps I'd never download. What did he want from me? What did I want from Chandler? I yawned, locked my door, and got into the shower.

★　★　★

"Late! Too soon! Pull back! Why aren't you ready!" Nesbitt yelled at us from across the court as we ran a drill.

"Why is she being so hard on us today?" Lauren asked as we jogged off the court.

I shrugged. We were paired together and got into the back of the line. Jessica and Tiffany hit their balls perfectly, as usual, and then jogged into line behind us.

"Karl proposed," Tiffany said.

"Bless her," Jessica said. "Shouldn't that make her nicer? She hit me a ball a few inches out of my range. On purpose."

"Aren't that what coaches are supposed to do? Challenge us?" I asked before jogging up to the baseline.

"We've missed you, Linh. Come to dinner after with us," Tiffany said when she had hit her ball and run to the back of the line.

"Please, I can't hold up the sarcasm on my own," Jessica said. "Mother says I need to stop too. Before I show my fiancé that I'm not actually good wife material. Mother says I only need to get through the wedding, and then I can show my true colors."

"Is he the type to be gone all the time on business trips?" Lauren asked as she ran back in line.

"She loves him," Tiffany said. "But don't make her say it. You should see them together. Lovesick puppies."

"Speaking of it, I want you to come to the wedding. I have an invitation in my bag. I wanted to hand it to you, so you couldn't say it got lost." Jessica adjusted the sweatband she always wore on her right wrist.

Nesbitt blew her whistle. "Time's up. Pick up balls!"

After shoveling tennis balls into Nesbitt's hamper, I picked yellow fuzz off my skirt. I was bloated. My body was forewarning me about the nearness of my period. I pretended to stretch, so I could look up my skirt and make sure I hadn't started my period already. No stains. I should have put in my menstrual cup, but I almost wanted to free-bleed. To let my body be unrestrained.

But no, that wouldn't be possible. I couldn't free-bleed if I wanted to go to restaurants after tennis. I couldn't free-bleed if I wanted to hang out with women like these. It had been a little while since I had joined them. I had been fixated on watching Mom's house. Watching for Eric's ominous truck. Watching for danger. But seeing Chandler had knocked me out of my routine. Maybe spending time with these women was what I needed to knock me back.

Everything at Bourbon Cake was the same. I don't know why I was surprised. We were seated at the same booth, and the server had memorized Lauren, Tiffany, and Jessica's orders.

"Here is the invitation." Jessica handed me a heavy cream envelope. "You will come? I marked you down as a 'yes.'"

"What will you do if I don't show up?" I asked.

"I'll use your seat to escape our mother," Tiffany said.

"More importantly, who will you go with? Chandler, I hope?" Lauren asked. "He's on the invitation list, you know.

Give us details. Are you still seeing him? I hear from people that
Chandler hasn't been seen around Barrick's much these days."

"Are you friends with those people? Should I be careful?"
I nodded thanks to the server who delivered my glass of wine.

"Keep your enemies closer, Linh," Jessica said.

"Right," I said.

"Tell us about Chandler. Tell us what you've been up to."
Lauren put her head on her hands and waited. Jessica and Tiffany put down their utensils and looked at me as well.

"I don't know if Chandler will be in town." I looked at the
wedding invitation. January first. "You're really doing it on the
first day of the year? Isn't everyone hung over that day?"

"Everyone is always already hung over by the wedding day,"
Jessica said. "What kind of weddings do you go to? Besides, I
wanted to keep the 'yes' RSVPs low. Just two or three hundred
guests, you know."

"Well, are you going to ask him?" Lauren asked.

"Chandler? You just said he was invited." There was no
way I was going to ask him. Going to weddings with someone
meant something, didn't it?

"But you two could, like, go together," Lauren said.

"He might be out of town. I don't know what he has
planned." I shrugged.

"So message him and find out," Lauren said, a fry halfway
to her mouth.

"I don't talk to him when he's away." I said.

"Like . . ." Jessica leaned forward. "At all?"

"Right, he doesn't have my number, so we don't talk," I
said.

"So, you write letters? That's goddamn beautiful," Tiffany
said.

"No." I swallowed a bite of my burger. "We don't talk."

"Oh," all three of them said. They leaned back in their seats, then spoke at once.

"Does he have a woman in every city he visits?" Tiffany said.

"Does he get off on that?" Jessica asked.

"Is this a kink?" Lauren said.

I took a long drink of water before responding. "I don't know. I don't know what he wants from me. Do you? He left his car with me. Who does that? What is that?"

I hadn't told anyone about the car, but I needed someone else's explanation. Maybe it was some rich person's code. They were from the same world as Chandler.

"His car," Lauren asked, mouth agape. "Look at you, Linh."

"We need another round," Tiffany said to our server, who had only taken half a step in our direction.

"I drive it sometimes. It's a nice car," I said, watching their reactions.

"I bet," Lauren said. "And still you don't talk to him? Why?"

"There's no point," I said. "I don't get what he wants from me."

"Well, obviously, *you*," Jessica said.

"Oh." I wasn't sure what to make of that. "Well, then can we talk about something else now? Your wedding, Jessica? Anything."

"Of course," Jessica said. "The wedding theme will be a spring wonderland in the middle of winter. Mother wants to have snow and tulips."

"Real snow? Or Like potato flakes as snow?" I asked.

"Oh, that's a fun idea." Tiffany smiled down at me. "But we've already ordered snow machines."

Lauren, Jessica, and Tiffany drifted into a conversation about flowers and fabrics. I listened and nodded when appropriate. I doubted they wanted to hear my treatise on the ecological harm of the flower industry. I doubted they wanted to know the issues that came along with fabric dyes. I doubted they wanted to know my hot takes on the wedding industry.

The three of them had become closer over the last few months. I could tell by how much of the conversation was conveyed through body language. It was easy enough to spend time with them. They had enough self-assurance for multitudes. If I was giving off any nervous energy, it was probably quickly diluted by their ease. Loneliness brought me to the table, and did loneliness always drive people into friendships? And yet, there was something missing. Something off. Could I ever escape that feeling of not belonging? Of being different and some unnamable sort of unease?

♦ 24 ♦

I HAD TO TURN my car on every fifteen minutes to stay warm enough while I watched Mom. A cold front had swept into the metroplex early in the day, and the temperature had dropped instead of increasing. I ran my car heater on high until it was warm enough, then shut it off. The heat of my body fogged up the windows as the warm air leaked from the car. I had turned my car on for the sixth time, when I saw Mom leaving the restaurant.

I gave her a long lead because I was driving my own car. It wasn't until I'd caught up to her on the highway that I recognized the truck that was right behind her. It was the large red truck that Eric Ryan drove. I tightened my grip on the steering wheel. Could it be a coincidence? Of course not. It wasn't a coincidence that either one of us was following my mom at that moment.

He was getting close to the back of her car and then dropping back and then creeping up to her again. It was dark, so my mom must have noticed. How could you not notice the glare of headlights filling your mirrors? The next time Eric dropped back, I swerved behind Mom's car. Her exit was coming up, and I didn't think twice. I had to get him away from her. The truck was accelerating behind me as we all turned onto the exit ramp. As soon as we were off the ramp, I hit my brakes. Mom's car kept moving forward, and I shut my eyes as the truck behind me hit my bumper. I pulled to the side of the road and put my car in park.

Cars illuminated the interior of the truck as they passed, and I thought I could see his mouth opening and closing. I could imagine a train of obscenities flowing from him just like it would from my father. I was raised by a man like him, who could do no wrong, who was wronged by the world, and who reacted in indignant anger.

I heard his car door shut behind me. I closed my eyes for a moment to collect myself. I had learned in childhood how to take the drunken, angry shouting of my father. I could take it from anyone. My face hardened into a mask. My mind slipped away. My body shook as if I were cold, and I flinched when someone knocked at my window.

"Are you okay?"

A woman stood on the other side of the glass. Did she stop to check on me? I rolled the window down.

"Do I need to call an ambulance?" she asked.

"I'm okay. I just needed a minute." I unclipped my seatbelt and got out.

"It looks like your bumper has a dent, but my truck doesn't even have a scratch. These new cars, you know? They brake for you in incidents like this. Was there a dog on the road or something? Was that dent there before? We should exchange insurance and all of that."

"Yes, okay," I said. She was not Eric at all. Had I imagined him?

"I'm sorry I hit you at all. This exit is too short. It's always causing fender benders."

I took a photo of her insurance info and pocketed the slip of paper she handed me with her name and number. The woman cocked her head again when she was saying goodbye, to ask me silently if I was okay. I gave her a smile and probably a half grimace. All this time I had thought every red truck was Eric Ryan's. I scoffed at myself. There were hundreds of big red pickup trucks in the metroplex. How could I be so stupid?

25

I took a deep breath as my rideshare pulled into the parking lot of a restaurant I would normally never be able to afford. I needed an escape from feeling foolish. I resolved to try to be cheerful. I didn't want to ruin Jessica's bachelorette celebrations.

"You look so elegant," Lauren said as she forced me into a hug. She had been standing at the restaurant entrance, waiting for me. Her heels were so tall and thin, I didn't quite understand the physics of them.

"Hi." I let her hug me, even though I hated hugs. Her perfume would stick to my clothing for the rest of the evening, but I told myself again I would be cheerful. I would try to be what they wanted. I didn't have the energy to resist a hug anyway.

"Give your coat and suitcase to this gentleman here, and come, come—we're down the hall." Lauren took my arm and led me back into a private dining room. The restaurant walls were covered in cloth, which must have provided soundproofing, because our footsteps sounded muted. The light bulbs were all warm oranges. Every hallway and room was separated by curtains and doors. I didn't even catch a glimpse of another group of diners.

As instructed in my bachelorette weekend prep email, I took a carshare to the restaurant and packed for two nights. I'd had to wear one of the long coats I usually wore to watch my mom, on account of the cold. The low was predicted to be in the thirties. Whoever had taken my coat and bag disappeared through a sliding door. As the email called it, "The Adventure" kicked off with dinner at the kind of restaurant that didn't list prices on its website. A server poured wine and sparkling water as I got settled in my chair, and disappeared before I could even say thank you.

"Linh, these are my longtime friends Cor and Sandra. You met Cor at Rob's thing. That's Liz and Amanda over there— they're cousins of Tiffany and Jessica." Lauren glanced at her phone. "Speaking of, they're pulling up now. Get ready."

"Ready?" I asked.

Tiffany opened and came through the door first, then opened it wide for Jessica, who threw her hands up as she entered.

"Raptor!" everyone shouted. They repeated it until they were chanting.

The door swung shut behind Jessica, and everyone seemed to shout louder until some invisible conductor motioned for them to stop.

"Ladies, thank you," Jessica said, taking her seat.

Tiffany sat down next to her, and the door opened again as servers in a single-file line came in. Each one had a plate, and they set them down in front of us in unison. I shifted in my seat. Salads were on the plates, thank God. Ordinary salad made up of frisée and the thinnest slices of tomato, tossed with a lemony dressing. I expected some sacrifice to happen at any moment, and I hoped the weekend didn't end with my death. My mom wouldn't be able to find me. I had the most melanin in the group. It was a rule that we got singled out and killed, wasn't it?

"I know you," Cor said. "I met you at Barrick's one night, didn't I? You've taken Chandler from Valerie."

"Yes. We did meet. I haven't taken Chandler from anyone." I drank wine and then water. Perhaps I should stay clear-headed. The mixture of the two liquids was sharp on my tongue.

"Sure, you have—own it. She knows it. She's even set a wedding date for her and Sid. It's about time. It's better for her to get married."

"Or she'll never get married?" I asked. "What's so bad about that?"

"She would be lonely and feel disappointed," Cor said. "I worry about her. What do you and Chandler do? We barely see him around Barrick's anymore, and that was a rarity to begin with. How long have you two been together now?"

I put my fork down on the plate, and it tumbled onto the table.

"A toast," Tiffany said from across the table. "To my wonderful sister, who is so lucky to be becoming an official raptor."

"Thank you," Jessica said. "But we have a special guest with us. Linh! It's so good to see you. Someone, tell her about all of this raptor nonsense."

"Our family, like a sorority—I guess that would be the easiest for you to understand," Amanda said, looking down her nose at me. "We become raptors when we marry."

"Right," I replied when it was clear she wasn't going to say more.

"Raptors can kill prey larger than themselves, which are metaphorically their husbands," Lauren elaborated as several separate conversations broke out over the table.

"This is rich-people shit?" I asked. "Or magic? Will Jessica turn into a sea eagle at the altar?"

"Now that would be rich-people shit," Lauren said, patting my arm. "Remember? Pretend it's some sort of movie."

A single-file line of servers entered and removed our salad plates, followed by another group that set down a plate with one bite's worth of food. Nonetheless, the women picked up their knives to cut the morsels into even smaller pieces to delicately bring to their mouths.

I took tiny sips of wine, but I didn't have to do much to hide how little I drank through dinner. Our glasses of wine were changed with every other new plate. It had been long enough between now and the last time I had hung out with Lauren, Tiffany, and Jessica that they felt almost like strangers again. Had I ever felt really comfortable around them?

Dinner finished without any more chanting. I had lost count of the plates, and yet I was still left hungry. Tiffany directed us into a large black SUV that pulled up to the restaurant entrance. I climbed to the back row and could see our bags piled up behind the seat. Everyone was chatty and giggly now. Cor slid into the seat next to me and did not put on her seat belt. I could smell her perfume and wondered how much money it took to make you feel like you could handle whatever happened to you if the car crashed and you were not wearing a seat belt.

Tiffany got into the passenger seat next to a driver. At least we wouldn't die in an alcohol-induced accident. Jessica shouted song requests, and Liz and Sandra started to sing. Sandra could actually sing. Liz was the opposite. Sitting in the back of the car, the sameness of all of their highlighted hair, manicured nails, and tailored clothing was accentuated. I sighed. Maybe I had miscalculated. I had felt so stupid for thinking that man was following Mom that I'd made another stupid mistake in going out with these women I hardly knew.

★ ★ ★

I dozed as we made our way to the lake house. What they called a house I would describe as an estate with a lake in its backyard. The temperature had dropped more, and we hurried through the door with our bags.

"I told you we should have flown to Hawaii or somewhere warm," said Tiffany.

"We can go to Hawaii anytime," Jessica said, tossing herself onto a couch in the living room. "This is my favorite lake."

"Anyone want a nibble?" Liz said, opening the fridge in the open-plan kitchen. It was stuffed with limes, boxes of strawberries, and packages I couldn't make out from my distance.

"What's the schedule?" Liz asked.

"You didn't read your email!" Tiffany popped a bottle of champagne. "There's a schedule printed in all the gift bags."

"But you can do whatever you want." Jessica spread her arms wide over her head. "Just try not to drown in the lake or anything like that."

"Sure, I'll keep myself from drowning," Amanda said. She turned toward the steps. "Any room?"

"Any room," Tiffany said. "Except for the one with Jessica's name on the door."

"How many rooms does this house have?" I asked.

"Twenty?" Jessica said. "And a library. But most importantly, the lake."

"You're going to force us to go fishing, aren't you?" Liz sighed and took her bag upstairs.

"Charming cousins you've got," Lauren said. She'd opened a bottle of wine and brought it and a handful of glasses to the living room.

"We had to invite them. Family and all that." Tiffany said.

"More like inheritances at stake," said Jessica, kicking off her shoes.

"Cor? Sandra? Linh? Still drinking?" Tiffany held up the bottle.

I sat in an armchair and accepted the glass Tiffany held out to me.

"Was this the only way to escape your mother, Jessica?" Sandra asked.

"She's obsessed." Jessica leaned her head back on the couch. "Tell me now if you've hired men or any of that." She lightly kicked Tiffany's foot.

"Oh, wait and see," Tiffany said.

"I could use a man," Sandra said. She had taken off her shoes and pulled her feet up under her on the sofa. She massaged her foot with her free hand. I wondered what she had spent all day doing.

"There's a gift bag at the top of the stairs for everyone." Tiffany fussed with a lever until a flame leaped up in the fireplace. "There should be at least three things, maybe four, that ought to get you through the night."

I watched the fire—one of those gas fireplaces with fake logs made out of ceramic in the grate—leap and flicker. Tiffany had let the gas run before the flame caught, and I could smell the sickly sweet scent of it. The women lounged casually in their dresses that cost more than my monthly pay. They were more comfortable than I could ever feel. I sipped wine and could taste its expense in the complexity of the grape.

"What's your betrothed doing for his bachelor weekend?" Cor asked. "Strip clubs in Vegas or something like that?"

"I have no idea," Jessica said.

"Want to swim in the lake?" Lauren asked me.

"Now? Absolutely not," I said. "Who knows what's out there in the dark. And it's freezing out."

"No fun," Lauren said.

"I'm with her," Cor said. "I don't want to die by snake bite or alligator attack."

"Are there alligators here?" I asked.

"No, no," Tiffany said, waving her hand. "Please, this place is too posh for wild things like that. But you know—don't push your luck. It's been a while since our family has used this property with frequency. Though mother thinks Jessica might set up out here and get started on breeding."

"That might be the only thing my mom and I agree on," Jessica said, returning with two bottles of wine. "Minus the children. She'll never forgive me for that."

"No children!" Tiffany screamed. "That's our mom. Almost every day. She was so disappointed that you weren't pregnant and trying to rush a wedding. We learned not to let her around our birth control. She'd figure out a way to slip us a packet full of sugar pills."

"Don't worry, ladies, I assure you we're both using IUDs for this very reason," Jessica said.

"But if your cousins have children, will your mom spitefully write you out of her will?" Sandra asked, setting a tray of dips, chips, fruit, and cheese onto the coffee table.

"Marry richer and you don't have to worry about being cut off," Jessica said, admiring her engagement ring. The diamonds sparkled in the light. "And, Linh, the lake will be warm. No matter how cold it gets, it always stays warm."

★   ★   ★

I walked down the long hallway and chose a room at random. It was only for a couple of nights, so I didn't really care. Nevertheless, the room was nicer than any hotel room I'd ever stayed in. The furnishings were Western themed because of course. There was a cowskin rug on the floor, longhorn statues on the side tables, and a painting of cowboys riding across a plain over the bed. The bathroom rugs were even cow patterned. I dumped the contents of the swag bag onto the ground. There were two different vibrators: a leather bag that probably had another something battery-powered and bottles of lubricants. Leaving everything where it fell, I put my hands on my hips and shrugged. I could simply stay in the room and masturbate all weekend.

The window looked out over the lake, which I could only see because it reflected the moon. I touched the glass and was reminded of the temperature. A lake swim tonight probably would have been deathly cold. Had Jessica been joking? Or had she been serious? Was the lake warmed by some method so all these wealthy people could swim whenever they wanted? Whether it was here, at Barrick's, or at after-tennis dinner, being with these women always felt like an out-of-body experience. I didn't put my clothes into the wardrobe or dresser drawers. I took off the dress I was wearing and draped it on the back of an armchair. It looked wrong on the leather ranch-style chair. Too somber for its surroundings. The cool air on my skin caused me to shiver, and I climbed into the four-post bed. The mattress felt like high-density foam. I went to sleep thinking about how the indentation of my body would disappear from the bed the moment I got up.

★   ★   ★

I woke up to someone banging on my door.

"Breakfast is ready!" Tiffany shouted.

I could smell bacon, coffee, and syrup. Mom had not messaged me. I had told her I would be away all weekend, almost as a warning. *Don't do anything dangerous* is what I'd wanted to say to her. I made sure my phone would vibrate with anything new and put it in my back pocket.

Downstairs, there were plates of pancakes, waffles, and bis-cuits on the island in the kitchen. There was a platter of bacon and sausages, bowls of fruit and yogurt, and jars of jams and syrup.

Tiffany held out a cup of coffee, which I gratefully took.

"Oh, and this," she said, holding out a bottle of Pedialyte.

"Isn't that for children?" I asked, adding cream to my coffee.

"Best hangover cure," Tiffany said. "Try it. Load up your breakfast plate and join us. We're out back."

"Is it cold out?"

"We have heaters. We're not out here to camp, you know."

"Did someone make all of this?"

"Ha ha. No, silly. Well, I suppose someone as a human made it. But not one of us. A chef drops by to make our meals." Tif-fany covered a yawn. "You're here to relax. Everything's taken care of."

"Okay." I covered an open biscuit with gravy. I had forgot-ten to look at the schedule and didn't know what was next.

"C'mon. Everyone's up but the cousins. We're placing bets on whether or not they've already left." Tiffany had piled her plate with bacon and scrambled eggs.

"Would they?" I asked as I followed Tiffany out. I'd put more than I could dream of eating on my plate, and wondered if everyone on the patio was eating yogurt and fruit.

They proved me wrong. There was another platter of only bacon in the middle of the table. Jessica dipped a charred strip straight into the gravy boat.

"It should warm up today," Jessica said. "Highs are supposed to be in the seventies."

"God bless climate change," Tiffany said, sitting down.

There were bottles of Pedialyte scattered over the table, as well as pitchers of mimosas.

"Isn't changing weather normal for Texas?" asked Sandra.

"Don't you think that's why we've been fed that line since we were children?" Jessica asked. "So, we wouldn't be concerned as the climate disaster unfolded?"

"Climate aside, here's to the almost-raptor," Tiffany said, raising a champagne glass.

I toasted with my coffee and then focused on my food, which tasted like a home-cooked meal. Everyone must have thought so because the table fell into silence only interrupted by requests to pass the gravy boat or bacon plate. I wasn't hungover, but drank the Pedialyte anyway. Maybe it helped to drink it in advance. If the speed at which the pitchers of mimosas were disappearing was any indication, I had better prepare.

★ ★ ★

When I went back inside, the house was busy with strangers carrying suitcases and lights. I zigzagged through people to get back to my room to use the restroom. I glanced at the schedule and tried to commit it to memory.

Our day started with haircuts and makeup sessions. There were two stylists per person. Mine complained about how my hair type always stuck into her skin like splinters and didn't even wash off easily. I gripped the armchairs tightly under the plastic cape. When she was done, she briskly walked away to begin the process of washing me off her. I hoped my invasive hair had buried itself into every crevice in her body. The makeup artist used so much eyeliner and lashes that I looked like an anime character. I hoped the eyelashes were easy to remove. I had never been tempted to change my lashes.

My transformation was done first. I stepped out onto the back patio to escape the fumes of hair products and some strange thing they sprayed on our faces to keep the makeup in place. I was fast on my way to developing cancer from something in those bottles—I knew it.

"Come on, Linh," Lauren said from behind me. "That's next."

She pointed to a tent that had been erected next to the house. Had it been there last night? I didn't think so.

Inside, yards and yards of soft white curtains disguised the fact that you were in a tent at all. Two chandeliers diffused warm light throughout the room. Along an entire wall were full clothing racks. Two mirrors were placed by pedestals. Three changing areas were curtained off. A white sofa set and low table full of macaroons and fruit surrounded chilled champagne bottles.

"This stylist is one of the most in demand stylists. Flew out from New York just for this session with us. Aren't you excited?" Lauren poured champagne.

I guessed I was supposed to have recognized the name from the schedule I had smushed into my back pocket. I wasn't sure what you did with famed stylists. Did you ask for their autograph?

"Are they here to help us pick out dresses for the wedding?" I asked.

"Oh no. They're going to transform how we use clothes to express ourselves for the rest of our lives."

"Like *Queer Eye*?"

"Like what?"

"Never mind." I took a bite of a macaroon, and it promptly got stuck to the roof of my mouth.

The other women arrived in a cloud of fragrances, and I coughed as my nose and throat closed up and my eyes watered.

"Let me see the bride-to-be," a deep voice said, from I wasn't sure where.

The stylist was dressed in all black. He was at least six feet tall, and his head was bare and so smooth it shined. His voice was Barry White deep, and I braced myself for the particular vulgarity of white women preening for a Black man, as if it made up for everything else when it only reinforced the status quo.

As the woman tried on dresses, their comments and the ways they touched the stylist got more and more sexual. When it was my turn, the stylist handed me a dress, and I dutifully and quickly put it on. Because I was short and small, the stylist chose a dress that made me look like a doll. He had probably never dressed a person with such short limbs before. He could probably tell by my clothing that I wasn't someone who would increase his earnings for this gig. I left the frilly dress in a heap when I changed out of it.

"I'm famished already," Lauren said. She was now wearing a soft fur top made of—I don't know; bunnies you can only find on Mount Everest?—over light beige leggings that showed a shadow of everything.

"It's noon—lunch should be set up," Tiffany said, glancing at the new watch she'd picked up from the accessory table. I could see the crown logo of Rolex among the diamonds.

I wondered if I could resell the things I acquired from the table, but thought that was a particularly poor person's way of thinking, wasn't it? And weren't showers only a different way of selling things? I walked past the table without looking at any of the glittery items. I didn't want a bill in the mail that would send me spiraling into debt.

As Lauren and I walked out of the tent, I couldn't help but notice that she didn't even have cellulite sprinkled along her backside. Her body had no imperfections. My throat and eyes cleared up at the first touch of fresh air.

Lunch consisted of a long table of eight different salads and a chef to make and press a panini. I stuck with Caesar salad and then combined all the prosciuttos and salamis that I could with mozzarella into a panini. Dainty rattan tables and chairs had been set up facing the lake.

"Isn't this fun?" Lauren asked.

"Oh yes." Salami grease from my sandwich was dripping down my hand and onto my salad.

"You don't get seasick, do you? The afternoon will be on the lake. Look, the boat is pulling up now."

Boat is a word that implies a lot of sizes until you get into the range of things called yachts just before you go to ship. I didn't know a boat that big could be on a lake, but apparently there was a lot for me to learn.

"No, I don't think I get seasick." I put down the sandwich anyway.

"There will be snacks on there too—don't worry." Lauren took a small bite of her non-leaky sandwich.

"Oh, Linh, you're still in your own clothes," Jessica said as she sat down with us.

"I didn't realize we were supposed to keep things on. Then get on a yacht?"

"That's the fun!" Jessica clapped. "But you do you."

Jessica was wearing a Roaring Twenties–type dress that had tasseled fringe coming off from everywhere. I was wearing my own black jeans with a black button-up blouse. The blouse had flowers on it and was made of silk. Washable silk and very small flowers. I had tried.

"How deep is this lake?" I asked.

"As deep as any artificial lake can go." Jessica shrugged. "Of course, it's a bit lower due to the droughts. They bring in water, though, so you don't see those horrid lines along the edges."

"How nice," I said.

"Time to move!" Tiffany rang a small bell at the entrance of the tent.

I got into the boat first and sat back by the engine. There wasn't a life jacket in sight. It took fifteen more minutes to get everyone else out of the tent. They made their way across the lawn in heels effortlessly.

"I could have just eaten him up," Sandra was saying as she sat down next to me.

The engine started and I looked out at the lake to hide my grimace. I counted to ten, then repeated that two more times to quell my blood pressure. The driver took us out into the middle of the lake, so far that I could not distinguish our dock along the shore. There was no escape. If I jumped out of the boat, I'd probably get a cramp from swimming and drown before even making it halfway to shore.

When we stopped, we were allowed to wander around. Tiffany guided us all to the upper deck. Another food spread was laid out on a table. All single mouthfuls of assorted things with fish, shrimp, and caviar, providing protein. I thought about all the food left over back at the house. Would all of that get thrown away after serving its purpose, which wasn't nourishment but rather the appearance of plenty?

Pop-country-rap music started playing, and I decided it was time to start drinking. Strange men appeared from nowhere and started dancing. I moved to the edge of the deck and did not smile. I did not want to be touched by the entertainment. The idea of a man paid to entertain me made my skin creep. It was too much like my father's preferred entertainment. The other women had no hesitation.

"No pictures of this part," Tiffany said, wagging her finger at me.

"Just checking email," I said, but I was only looking at the home screen of my phone. There were no new messages from my mom.

I edged around the mass of people grinding on one another and went to the lower deck. I wished I had a book. I wished I had an eBook even, but I'd never liked reading on a screen. There was another boat on the lake, speeding across the water, then back again, as if the lake were not big enough for its desire. I kept my phone in my hand so I could feel if I got new messages, and watched the birds in the sky. The temperature was mild, like we had been taken away from winter. Birds swooped in the sky, and I imagined I was on some coastline far away from the metroplex.

The sound of an engine coming close brought me back to reality. The speedboat was nearing us, and I could hear the cheering of men. They turned out to be teenagers as they got closer. I could tell by how they still had not yet fully grown into their limbs. Teenage boys to me were the most dangerous kind. There was too much energy and too little understanding of the consequences.

They sped toward us, then swooped away, waiting until the very last moment to turn away from us. Their arc kicked up a wave that jostled our yacht. I threw out my hands as I lost my balance. Forgetting my phone was in my hand, I let go to grab the side of the boat. Between the noise of the other boat's engine and the sound of the water, the phone seemed to slip silently into the lake.

"Idiot boys," Jessica said, sitting down next to me.

"You're missing out on your party." I looked into the opaque water.

"I needed a break and wondered where you went. Did something go overboard?"

"My phone."

"I'll send you a new one when we get back. The latest model just came out too—you're lucky."

"Thanks, that is really nice of you." I didn't want the latest model. I had actually planned on getting the dumbest candy bar phone available next. But I couldn't say no to Jessica. Most times, when people offered to give you something, they took offense when you told them what you actually wanted, especially if it didn't cost as much as what they had in mind.

"You didn't want to dance with the men? They're quite nice."

I shrugged.

"It's not like you're cheating on Chandler. You won't even say you two are dating."

I shrugged again. "I don't really like physical contact."

"Oh, I see!" Jessica smiled her bright smile, then patted my knee as she went back upstairs.

I wondered exactly what she thought she saw. Did she assume I had some condition that made me special? Was I an even more prized friend now because I brought more to the table then my melanin? I pulled my legs onto the seat and rested my head. I'd slept through plenty of parties in my childhood and drank through the parties in my adulthood. Maybe it was time to make the switch back to sleeping.

★   ★   ★

When we pulled back onto the dock, I stayed back and watched the others make their way barefoot back to the house. A couple of the hired men helped everyone back to their rooms. I didn't see them come back downstairs as I made my way up, so I assumed they were not quite done with their jobs.

We were given a few hours of open time before dinner. I showered and scrubbed the makeup off my face. Whatever the stylist used had stained my lips and took three washes to get off. It looked like the woman who cut my hair had basically trimmed my ends. Thankfully, though, their rush meant that they hadn't glued the lash extensions very well. I suppose it wouldn't have helped me since my eyelashes would have made them point down. I laughed at the thought of extensions that fell like my hair. It might make my eyes look like they were permanently weeping.

I stayed in the room to let my hair air-dry. Without my phone, there was nothing to do but stare out the window at the cloudless sky. My view looked out over the back lawn. The tent erected for the stylist session was already gone. If I hadn't been inside it, I wouldn't have known that anything at all had happened there.

Growing up without this kind of money made being around it feel like a mirage. A secret society that I'd been invited into, but one in which I would always be a guest. I'd spent so much time alone, driving, watching my parents from a distance. I'd made my own life into something surreal. The year was going to end soon, and what did I have to show for myself? I took a deep breath, then another.

Downstairs, Liz and Amanda were explaining the rules of pickleball to everyone else while hitting a plastic ball that looked like a dog toy, back and forth, with wooden paddles that were slightly bigger than table tennis paddles.

"Want to try, Linh?" Liz asked.

"No, thank you," I said. "I don't want to confuse my tennis muscle memory."

"I'll give it a go," Jessica said.

She got up and hit the ball back to Amanda like she'd been playing forever. I watched the ball if you could call it that. A sport with a plastic ball felt less serious, even though I did have respect for professional table tennis. This, though? A young sport made up by a few bored white men in Seattle, one of the capitals of tech bro culture? No, thank you. I saw how the people who played pickleball took over the tennis courts when they arrived. They put their things everywhere, brought chairs, tied their dogs to the tennis net post, and walked around like they owned the courts in a way only white people could do.

"Are you all hungry? Snacks and wine. Wine and snacks." Tiffany rang her bell. She seemed to really enjoy having that bell.

Two caterers dressed in all black rolled a table into the room, then passed out pre-poured glasses of wine. The table had an ice sculpture of a bird in flight, surrounded by flowers, as a centerpiece. I finished the glass of wine before getting up to fill a plate. The ice bird's beak had melted in the warmth of the room, and it now looked like a ghost coming in for an attack.

I'd eaten two cubes of cheese before distant chimes sounded.

"Dinner's ready," Tiffany said. She put down the paddle, and the ball Cor had been hitting back to her sailed by and bounced on the floor. Its bounce sounded hollow and cheap. Its plastic represented what I hated in the world. A seemingly harmless material that would last longer on the planet than I would. People buying more and more of a thing in a trendy craze only to feed the landfills. I'd have to look up how many years a single tennis ball would live. I wanted to stop thinking completely.

As dinner was served, I felt more at ease. At first, I thought it was because of the wine, but then I realized it was because of the addition of the service staff. I wasn't the only person of the global majority.

Dish after dish was served, and yet I was still hungry. I was hungry for relaxed meals where people had discard piles of cilantro stems and shrimp shells. A meal where people weren't afraid to use their hands. I was hungry for meals made with abundant love. I was hungry for hot pots and grills in the middle of tables with extension cords running between chairs. I was hungry for things none of these women could give me.

When the timing was right, meaning when everyone was drunk, I put on my jacket and walked out onto the dock. The yacht was gone, and the lake was quiet. The water hit the pier, and occasionally I heard an owl. I wished the owl would fly past, but knew I'd never catch a glimpse. They were so incredibly silent in flight.

★　★　★

The next morning, Lauren convinced me to go on a hike with her in the time we had before we would be driven home. We walked along the lake until she saw a trail that led into the woods.

"Why didn't you come back to tennis?" Lauren asked. "The temperature didn't stop you last winter."

"I've been busy with my mom."

"Oh, fuck," Lauren said. She pulled me to a stop with her hand on my shoulder.

I followed where her other hand was pointing and saw a movement in the leaves.

"Is that a bear?" I asked.

"It appears to be a bear."

I could feel cold sweat spill from my armpits.

"This is exactly why I prefer not to go wandering out in the wild," I said.

"It's not the wild! This is a gated lake community for Christ's sake." Lauren had come to stand close to me, and it occurred to me that she could push me if the bear charged us.

"What are we supposed to do? Do you think it's someone's pet?" I asked.

"Maybe it's someone's pet. But it's still a bear."

"What kind? I think there are two different kinds and you're supposed to do different things for different bears, but the things are opposite one another."

"Are you for real?"

"Yeah, I read about it one night on the national parks' website. I was trying to be prepared."

"Shh, it's moving," Lauren said.

"What kind of bear is it? Do you have your phone?"

Lauren put her hand over my mouth, and we started to walk backward down the trail. When the bear was out of sight, she pulled my shoulder to turn me around. We ran all the way back to the house.

"Hi," Jessica said from the porch. She held a glass of champagne and had a magazine open on her lap.

"Bear," I said.

Lauren grabbed the champagne bottle from its ice bucket and took a long drink.

"I'm sorry, what?" Jessica said, holding her finger on the page where she'd stopped reading.

"We saw a real-life bear," Lauren said. She wiped her mouth and held the bottle out to me.

I took the bottle and drank.

"Well, shout if you see it coming up the lawn." Jessica looked back at her magazine like bears were as harmless as deer.

When my heart rate calmed, I went up to my room to be alone. I stood by the window, looking out over the lawn and lake. Lunch was being served, and I could hear the clang of plates and the women laughing on the patio below. I shut my eyes and then reopened them. The lake glimmered with sunlight. Cor was walking barefoot across the lawn, and I looked for the bear in the tree line. Would it race out and eat her like the yeti at the end of that old computer game?

Eventually, I mustered the energy to go back downstairs and join the others for lunch. We packed and folded ourselves into the SUV to be driven back home. I watched the scenery change from wooded gated estates to shacks in the middle of farmland and then to the city. I had them drop me off at the entrance to my apartment, and I walked down the driveway. I expected Chandler's car to be gone, but it was still there. I'd almost expected my car to be covered in dirt, as if I had entered another world and had disappeared for years instead of days, like in that movie. I looked for a note from Chandler jammed into the doorway, but there was nothing.

When I opened the door, Lollipop meowed. I changed her food and water dishes. She sat on the coffee table with her back to me, as if retaliating against me for leaving her alone. I opened the blinds and sat on the couch. My bag could be unpacked later, or maybe it would stay packed and be absorbed into the general mess of my apartment. I shut my eyes and breathed deeply. Everything about the weekend had felt wrong. Like I had put on a shirt that was too tight and itched. I felt used but by whom and for what, I wasn't sure. I breathed until I forgot. I breathed until I remembered my purpose.

Ignoring Lollipop's meow, I locked my apartment door and got into Chandler's car. I needed to check on my mom.

26

MOM DIDN'T ANSWER HER front door, but I found her working in her backyard garden.

"Will you bring me that shovel?" she asked when she saw me come through the gate.

I was surprised to see that things were growing in the garden at all. It was cold and gray, and I was wearing a green knee-length puffy coat. The backyard looked different. Mom had added another raised bed and strung up lights above the patio.

"Did you do all this work by yourself?" I asked.

"Friends helped me."

"A particular friend?"

"Friends from work." Mom used the shovel to spread dirt evenly over the surface of the new planter. "We'll have dinner together on Thanksgiving and Christmas like usual?"

"Sure. I don't have other plans."

"Sit down. There's a chair over there."

I pulled a chair up and sat down. "How are you?"

"Okay." My mom kept shoveling dirt, the shovel making a shh sound as it cut through the soil.

There was something wrong. I cataloged every detail of my mother. She wasn't moving like she had been hurt. Silently she shoveled more dirt. But what if she had been diagnosed with something?

And then, like a child used to being lectured, corrected, and made to feel shame, I realized my mom must have found out about me. Maybe she'd seen how I'd gotten hit by that truck behind her. How could I explain everything to her? I started to feel hot.

"Your father," Mom said.

I let out all the air I had been holding.

"He died." My mom stopped what she was doing and looked out at the sky. Her face was turned away from me, so I couldn't guess what she was feeling. Some of her hair had escaped from her headband, and strands blew with the wind.

"How?" The question, the word seemed appropriate, although I never considered how appropriate I was in my conversations with my mom. It didn't matter so much that she thought I was normal as it did for me to keep as much as I could from her. But at that moment, I felt too much to figure out what was the best thing to say.

"I don't know. Probably the alcohol. I left what the police gave me on the table inside. His apartment needs to be cleaned out. Can you do that?"

I flinched at the thought of my mom being in the mess of my father's apartment. "Yes, of course."

"Thank you," said my mom before she started shoveling dirt again.

I watched her move the soil around. My father was dead. We would bury him, and my mother was working in her garden. I didn't know anything about gardening, so I wasn't sure what she was doing. My father was dead, and my mom had asked me to clean up after him one last time. My father was dead, and it seemed like I should feel sad. I should cry. I should mourn. My eyes watered but it was due to the cold wind.

★   ★   ★

The apartment staff gave me a key and didn't offer to help me. I supposed it wasn't a fun experience for them to have to deal with someone who had passed away in the buildings, though I had to doubt it was the first time that had happened here.

I hadn't read the police report I had taken from my mother's house because I hadn't wanted to know the details. When I entered, bleach was the first scent I noticed. Then I smelled the stench of beer that I always associated with my father. Underneath that, there was the sickly sweet smell of vomit.

It looked like someone had tried to clean up. I guessed that someone from the apartment had to, to keep the odor from spreading. The apartment management had insisted I come to gather his things as soon as possible. Anything I left would be disposed of the next day. They had made it seem like it was a favor to me. Leave anything behind and it would be gone; or not come at all, and everything he owned would disappear.

I hadn't thought to bring anything with me. I left the door open behind me to help disperse the smells. I tried to open a window to let more air circulate, but it had been painted shut. The roar of the highway came and went with the wind. I'd always imagined it sounded like the ocean might if we weren't hundreds of miles away from the nearest coast.

I made a pile of any paper bills I found. There wasn't much. Had I hoped to find a trace of me in his life? A family photo, as few as those were? Some mention in some form? The only personal objects in the apartment were his clothes, wallet, and phone. The phone was plugged in and fully charged. I tilted the screen toward the sunlight coming in through the doorway and could see where his fingers hit the screen most. It was an Android phone, which I was thankful for only because I did not have to guess the order of the numbers. The line he traced was clear, and I unlocked the phone.

One scroll through the images within his messages was enough. My face flushed with shame at the nudity. I unplugged the phone with its charger and added it to my pile of things to take. Rummaging in the pantry, I found a plastic bag to hold everything I planned to leave with. Was this all I had to remember my father by? Empty beer bottles, dirty laundry, and sexts? I backed up until I was flat against a wall. I didn't want to sit anywhere. I hoped he hadn't hidden anything in the bathroom because I could not bear to go in there. To see the filth in which he had spent the last days of his life. I didn't want to see the dirty shower grout, grimy ring around the toilet bowl, or used towels. I did not want to see the stains left behind.

Tears dripped down my face, but I did not make a sound. I had spent hours watching my father, and yet I had not been there the night he died. I'd been out at a lake house, eating things and drinking things he dreamed of being able to afford once he got to the United States. He'd been led to believe that if he worked hard enough, all that wealth could have been his. Except everything was made to keep that from happening. I had been out on a yacht, and his drinking buddies had had the wherewithal to wonder where he was. They'd found him relatively quickly, but not in time to save him.

How had I not seen how bad his drinking had gotten? How had I not realized I should not let him out of my sight? Had I been too used to it? Was I complicit in his drinking and his death? There was a large piece of me that felt like his death was my fault. After all, I was the only family member here for him.

I took a deep breath and held it to stop crying, but it only made it worse.

The rectangle of light that came through the door traveled across the carpet. It felt like so little time that he had lived in the apartment, and yet the carpet showed his most crossed paths from the couch to the kitchen, for beer most likely, and then in and out of the bedroom. I looked toward the sofa. I had not wanted to deal with the gun under the coffee table, but there was nothing left for me to do.

I was familiar with guns. Most everyone who grew up in Texas saw one and went out to the country to practice shooting. I did not understand why my father had purchased a shotgun. I pushed the case out from under the coffee table with my foot and then opened it. Why does anyone choose a shotgun? The black metal gleamed when light struck it. I looked at it. I didn't want to take it out of the case. I didn't want to touch it. Shotguns were heavy. The kick of firing had always bruised my shoulder in the past. What did my father want with a shotgun? A handgun, I could understand. A thing that could fit in a bedside drawer. A shotgun was an unwieldy, unapologetic, enormous threat. You could believe you might dodge a bullet. A spray of bullets was different. But that was the point. So you didn't miss.

There was something tucked underneath the gun handle, and I pulled the corner of a photograph free and unfolded it. In the picture, my father and mother sat next to each other at a wedding. Their wedding. I knew this because my mother wore a red áo dài. I felt like throwing up, but I hadn't eaten yet, so there was nothing to throw up. Anger at my father for being a threat to my mother made my heart harden. I stopped crying, but I felt closer to breaking.

I put the gun in the trunk of Chandler's car, which I had driven, as if it could be my mutual support friend, for lack of one. I wouldn't have dragged anyone I knew with me on this task. Who in my life did I want to expose to this depth of me? Who did I trust enough to show them the darkness in my family? I wanted to ask Hoa what to do with it, but she was hundreds of miles away. My mother didn't want to look at my father's mess anymore. She'd done it for her entire life. I hoped this was my last time.

When I got home, I put the heavy gun case on the coffee table. Then I put it on the floor. Then I pushed it with my foot until it was next to the pile of boxes that had grown and grown. I lifted the edge of a box at the bottom until I could wedge some of the hard plastic case under it. Once I had the leverage, the rest of the case slid under and out of sight easily. A couple of boxes fell down from the top like rocks that occasionally fell down mountains. I kicked them in front of the gun—out of sight, out of mind.

Only after going through all that trouble did I think about whether the gun was loaded. Surely not? In college, I'd heard about a kid I knew from high school who bought a gun for himself on his eighteenth birthday. Apparently, he took it out during his party to show people. How drunk do you have to be to look down a barrel of a gun? Or did it go off and hit him somewhere where they couldn't stop the blood? I felt most sorry for the others at the party, for the weight that they would carry for the rest of their lives. I didn't want to end up the same way. I didn't know how to unload a gun safely and really did not want to put that into a search bar. It would have to wait for another time.

★   ★   ★

We didn't have a family plot. My father had no family in the states. He hardly had any family left in Vietnam. In a culture of large, extended families, how exactly had that happened? But his family lived in Saigon. I couldn't imagine living in a capital city through war, but I also knew nothing about war. Here in the metroplex, wars were thousands of miles away and not right outside your front door.

Mom hadn't cared where my father was buried. I selected a plot in a cemetery near my childhood home. A cemetery I grew up driving past multiple times a day, if not every day. There wasn't a grand entrance to it, and railroad tracks ran along one side. There was a tree or two and a street that ran through the center and led to some corporate warehouses. It was one of those cemeteries that simply appeared adjacent to a neighborhood. An old cemetery that the city grew around.

The headstone was carved with his name and dates. No epitaph. What would I say that wasn't a lie? He wasn't a good husband. He wasn't a good father. His life was destroyed by imperialism and war.

The funeral home who helped me with arrangements had asked if I wanted to share the details of the funeral with anyone. I hadn't known who to invite, but my father's employer had found the information. Word had gotten around regardless. That didn't mean a lot of people showed up. It only meant that for the first time I saw my father's strip club friends in the daylight. They looked like anyone's uncles and fathers. A bit scruffy due to the cold. Their jackets hid their clothes, so if they were unwashed, I would never know.

I wore a white shirt and black pants. My green coat and high boots hid my clothes. I had no idea what my mom wore under her even longer and puffier purple coat. She had pulled the hood up, and the faux fur trim blew in the wind.

A cold front was in the midst of dropping temperatures on the metroplex. We had not planned for any remarks or anything at all. Two cemetery workers stood a distance off, trying to hide their shivers and impatience. There wasn't a ceremony planned at a temple. The nearest temple was forty-five minutes away, and neither my mom nor I had wanted to make this longer than necessary.

My mom and I stood at the foot of the casket. There was a small arrangement on top of it. I didn't think of making the floral arrangements larger. My father hadn't liked flowers or girly things, so why make him suffer through it in death?

We all stood quietly as the wind whipped around us. I hadn't tied back my hair, and it flicked across my face. I couldn't distinguish between the sting of hair and the sting of wind. My mom was the first to take a step back and turn away. Slowly, my father's friends did as well. I wondered what the funeral staff thought of us. Did they think we were barbaric for facing death with silence and our own thoughts? But they probably didn't think anything of us. It was too cold. It was another death in the endless deaths they dealt with.

As I stood there, I thought of Lucy Ramirez, the staff who was wounded at the university shooting. She had eventually succumbed to her injuries. It had been a single sentence in a long email to staff from the university president. It wasn't anything like the emails they sent when deans left or arrived. People like Lucy, people like my father, people like me would live and die without lengthy remark from people who became presidents of universities.

The sky was darkening, and I turned. I was the last one. I didn't want to keep those that would actually do the burying out in this weather for too long. They were still alive. They needed to stay warm. I got into my car and turned on the heat and watched the two men push the button that lowered the casket into the ground.

It wasn't like the movies. Life is not at all like the movies. As one of the men packed up whatever was used to lower the casket, the other drove a small bulldozer down the dirt road. He had to drive right over another grave in order to push the dirt into my father's open grave. It took them fifteen minutes to complete the task and leave. I hadn't even noticed the pile of dirt; I had been so focused on the casket.

Would my father have liked the casket? He abdicated his choices when he left no plan for his death. I'd had to calculate the cost as the funeral staff walked me through choices. All of my savings disappeared so quickly. Would my father have imagined a long service at the temple? It hadn't occurred to me to go light incense for him. Had my mother? Had his friends? Would my father think more than a handful of people would go to his funeral? Would he have imagined a party afterward? A raucous or subdued one? But, of course, my father was dead. He didn't think anything. Funerals were for those who were still living.

27

IT FELT STRANGE TO be in my mother's house when she was home. So often, I let myself in when she was out or watched from the street when she was inside. I set the pumpkin pie I had promised to bring on the counter and watched her fuss with the turkey legs in the oven. She'd spent all day cooking. That was clear. Egg rolls, fried rice, stuffing, and mashed potatoes were already on the dining table. She had set out two empty glasses next to an open bottle of wine.

"Do you need me to help with anything?" I asked, pouring wine. I wondered if we would talk about my father. The funeral had been a little more than a week ago, but I wasn't going to bring it up. I didn't know what to say, and it was my mother who knew my father's history. It was her place to bring him up or not.

"Relax, drink wine. I'm almost finished." Mom took the temperature of the turkey legs and closed the oven again. "This is better than cooking an entire turkey. Rachel and Nara were right."

"Those are your work friends?" I glanced around the kitchen.

There were dirty bowls piled in the sink, vegetable peelings on the counter, and a paperback book tucked under a towel, as if Mom were trying to hide it, but I knew what it was. The gifts from her friends. I had borrowed several romance books by now and found myself drawn to the historical ones with ladies and dukes, where women could be ruined and then saved by marriage, which was what happened over and over. And yet I still couldn't see how happiness could be achieved in today's world through romance, and certainly not through marriage. Marriage didn't solve problems.

"They're my friends. Do you separate your friends from work? How is work?" asked my mom. She was setting the pie I brought onto a plate.

"Work is fine. This wine is nice."

"Nara gave the wine to me. She wanted to give us something nice for the holiday," Mom said. "Do you have to work on Friday?"

"No, I have it off. I don't go back until Monday." I relaxed a little. Maybe we wouldn't talk about him at all.

"Food is ready."

As usual, there was entirely too much for two people. There was too much food for three people, even. We filled our plates with a mixture of American and Vietnamese food. Our Thanksgiving spread was like our lives. Two cultures were eaten together and swallowed with no consideration of how the flavors would or would not mix.

Looking over the expanse of food Mom had cooked for me, I paused, as if deciding where to start. This is what I had missed during the bachelorette weekend. All the food that had been made, while not bad, had a particular taste to it. Too much salt and too much butter. I had missed the sweet sour of pickled vegetables that had been sitting for two days. I missed fish sauce. I missed the particular combination of spice, sweetness, and freshness of Vietnamese food. Even the turkey and stuffing were different. Mom had made the stuffing from scratch. There was no taste of preservatives or artificial flavorings. She had made everything with love in her heart.

"Peter finally came back to work after his accident," Mom said.

"Your Peter at work was in an accident?" I pitched my question mark a note too high. "That's odd. I played tennis with a man named Peter who was in an accident. I think he hurt his leg."

"Broke his leg," my mom said at the same time.

"You said your Peter plays tennis, didn't you?" I asked quickly. That could be it. It could be easy to admit to meeting Peter through tennis. Mom didn't have to know about anything else, as if admitting to this condoned all of my behavior.

"It's a small world. That would be nice if you already knew him. Maybe you two already have something in common. That's good."

"And why would it be good?"

"He's really nice. Maybe we can all have dinner sometime." Mom blushed.

"Sure." I could feel the happiness I'd gotten from the food leaking away.

I focused on building up a perfect bite in my bowl. I found myself judging my mom for thinking of Peter instead of my father. Father was her ex-husband. Did I expect her to feel guilty, to feel remorse, even though I knew all the pain he had put her through? I didn't want to think about Peter at all. I had wanted to spend time with my mom. We lapsed into my usual silence, punctuated with forks scraping plates.

After dinner, we packed the food into the fridge, and she filled several containers for me to take home. Then we watched a romantic holiday comedy. It was probably the only thing Mom watched these days, along with reading her paperback books. I fell asleep somewhere in the middle and woke up as she took our glasses into the kitchen. Our goodbyes were always awkward. I knew I was supposed to say "I love you" or something like that, but the words still felt strange on my tongue. I didn't doubt the feeling was there, but the phrase would never flow off my tongue easily. I said goodnight and listened for the sound of her turning the deadlock as I walked away.

My hair was still short enough that the wind blew it out from under my coat collar. I pulled the zipper up higher and tucked my chin into the warmth that came up from my chest. As I walked to my car, I looked up at the sky. It was a cloudless night, and I could see some stars twinkle. It was like they were beckoning me, but to what I wasn't quite sure.

28

THE WORLD WAS SHOPPING on Black Friday, so I went out driving early in the morning. I was amazed at the lines of people who still went out and sat in front of big box stores to score deals like it was some game. I purposely got stuck in crowded parking lots, people honking at pedestrians like they didn't have the right of way. I drove Chandler's car because it made me feel good to drive an expensive vehicle through mall lots. The windows were tinted, and I wore a wig of light brown hair. I felt like I could be anybody.

I drove past a valet station and watched the boys jump up when they heard my car's engine. I still marveled at the fact that malls had valets now. There were probably valets for grocery stores if I looked hard enough.

I parked at the far end of the parking lot of a mall that was so wealthy it was a tourist stop. A place where I would be anonymous. As an afterthought, I slipped Chandler's credit card into my wallet. The rectangle of plastic gave me courage. I pulled on a beanie to keep my wig from blowing off. Everything inside the mall sparkled, readied for Christmas a month ago. All the walls seemed to be made of glass. The floor was injected with crystals, so it blinked in the light. What would happen if someone fired a gun in a place like this? Could the bullet travel the length of the mall if no obstacles, say, like a human body, got in its way? I shook the thought from my head. Did everyone think about the possibility before they left their house? I tamped down the fluttery fear inside my chest.

I went to the restaurant inside a pricey department store, to distract myself. I wanted alcohol to dull my sharp edges. It was the kind of store where the salespeople could tell you didn't have enough money for their time in a fraction of a second. The kind of store where I was always afraid I would break something and have to pay for it.

Since I was alone and without any shopping bags, I was seated in a crowded corner. I ordered a sandwich and a glass of wine. One wall was all glass and overlooked the atrium. Everyone who walked beneath me looked the same. There were the women who wore yoga pants everywhere, even when it was freezing outside, and had the kind of arms that should be soft and plump but had been strained into fitness. The men all had square jaws, bleached teeth, and predatory eyes. There were entirely too many cable-knit vests over collared shirts. Even the children sported sweater vests. That particular shade of golf-club green made me think of Chandler. Chandler, who I had not seen in months. Who I still had not contacted. Whose car I still drove. It probably needed some annual service that I was neglecting. I frowned at how easily I slipped into caretaking and worrying.

I had resisted the urge to look Chandler up on social media. With my luck, he would be the one man who kept his accounts private. Or maybe he wasn't on social media. Sometimes I thought he wasn't what he said at all. Maybe he worked for the government. Spies were real, weren't they? Was he patriotic like that? What if he knew everything about me and the things I spent my time doing?

My food and wine arrived, and I ordered a second glass of wine from my server. I didn't want to be bothered by servers, and that always made them keep their distance. I imagined that it was a line in their new employee handbook: Beware the woman who wants to get drunk in the middle of the day in a department store, but don't deny her the drinks that will allow her to buy that three-thousand-dollar dress. Would Chandler come back if I started buying expensive gifts for myself on his credit? I wanted to use his money, and at the same time I didn't want a single penny. I felt both of these things because of his being American and the war in Vietnam. What kind of person was I to benefit when so many were hurt and at the same time, someone owed someone else, didn't they? I swallowed a large bite of my sandwich and imagined swallowing all my thoughts of him with it. Chandler did not matter.

The child next to me screamed. I watched the family out of the corner of my eye. The woman was rolling a stroller where a baby was sleeping, back and forth with her foot, while wiping the mouth of a toddler who had just smeared most of its lunch onto the table. The father, presumably, was looking at his phone. The woman kept telling the children's father about their schedule. Asking him questions about this or that, to which he responded with various versions of "you decide." I knew what she was doing. I'd read articles about it before. She was trying to share the labor and bring him into decisions so that she wasn't doing everything. So she could quiet the continuous list of to-dos running in the back of her mind.

A toy was pushed to the ground, and I watched her wait for a microsecond and then a full second to see if her husband would notice and pick it up. Even I wished he would do something useful in real time when she needed it and without her having to ask. I saw moments like these all the time when I watched families. It was one of the many reasons I couldn't bear to be around children and their mothers. I hated seeing how sexist men still were. Did this woman marry up? Did she stop working when the children were born? Did she work a full week while worrying about drop-offs, breakfasts, lunches, dinners, snacks, groceries, trash, laundry, cleaning, lawn care, and cooking?

I tried to guess their financial worth. Their stroller was a fancy contraption. If they had a nanny, wouldn't she be with them? Were they nice enough people to give their nanny time off? The woman picked up the toy, and the man put his phone in his pocket and stood up. He didn't even move to carry the bag of all the baby shit. I squinted at him. If I cut him out of the picture, he could be anywhere. His clothes were unwrinkled and unmarred by the sticky, grasping hands of children. It must be nice to be able to walk out and into anything without being responsible for any messes. *Good luck, lady.* I hoped she had women in her life who might catch her when enough was enough.

I finished my sandwich and stopped thinking about the family. It was no use worrying about the problems of strangers. I was enjoying my second glass of wine when Lauren dropped into the empty seat across from me.

"Hello, darling," Lauren said.

"Hi."

"Have you gotten my texts? Did you like the new phone Jessica sent you?"

"Oh, I forgot to activate it. You know, the holidays are so busy." When it had arrived, I had kicked the box into my apartment and left it next to my shoes.

"Fancy seeing you on this side of town. I almost didn't recognize you."

"Oh." I had forgotten about my fake hair. "I like wigs. It makes me feel like a different person."

If Lauren could recognize me, who was I kidding? I felt ashamed and stupid. Had it been that obvious all these months? A server dropped off a plate with grilled salmon and a glass of champagne for Lauren. When they turned from the table, I stuffed the wig into my coat pocket.

"That sounds like such fun. This is exactly why I need you in my life." Lauren raised her glass. "Cheers!"

I lifted and clinked my glass with Lauren's flute. Lauren drank all of it in two gulps.

"Are you okay?" I asked. "I mean, how are you?"

"Please always be honest with me. I need that from you. None of those tiptoeing niceties. All of that stupid bullshit."

Lauren waved at our server and motioned for a bottle and another glass.

"Did you drive here?" I asked.

"No, of course not. You did? But you can leave your car without being worried. They have the best security at this mall, as you might guess. I'm sure many expensive cars get forgotten overnight here."

"Thanks." I accepted the glass of champagne Lauren pushed to me. It tingled down my throat, and there wasn't an inkling of that vomit aftertaste cheap champagne usually had.

"What other wigs do you have? There must be others. Don't let me down, Linh."

I stiffened at the remark. Did Lauren see me as some Asian sidekick in her life?

"Did you want to be alone? I can leave," I said, reaching for my wallet.

"No, no, no. Don't leave. Please. Share this champagne with me. I'm sorry, I'm a bit of a mess, and the holiday was a disaster for my family. I just had to get out of the house, and then there you were, and I slipped into something else. Someone else."

"Do you want to talk about the family stuff or not?"

"No. Yes. It'll be fine or whatever. It's my mom. She was diagnosed with MS, and she's afraid. When she's afraid she tries to destroy everything around her. So, I just left my dad to deal with it. Isn't that cowardly? And I get why she's afraid. But we have all the money in the world. She'll get the best of everything."

"Most people want to die quickly and quietly."

"Yeah, I certainly do. Just give me a bottle of pills if it looks bad." Lauren refilled our glasses. I looked at Lauren more closely and saw the bags under her eyes and how the skin on the side of her left hand was chapped, like she picked at it.

"I follow my mother when she goes on dates. That's why I have wigs," I said. I didn't want to hold it anymore.

"I knew you had more than one." The sparkle had come back into Lauren's eyes.

"Have you gotten your dress for Jessica's wedding? It sounds like we both need a distraction. I have Chandler's credit card."

I'd decided everything was different if Lauren was shopping too.

"You're devious." Lauren clapped with excitement. "Oh, this will be fabulous."

Lauren picked up the champagne bottle in one hand and our glasses of wine in her other.

"C'mon," she said. "Let's take a look to see what they have here."

One bottle of champagne later, I settled on two dresses so that I could decide at the last minute. One was a dark red dress with a boat neck and a full skirt. It had an elastic waist and would be flexible. The other was a fitted rose-pink knee-length dress with an asymmetrical collar. The dresses were the most expensive things I'd ever worn. It gave me a thrill to charge them on Chandler's credit card. He could cancel the card if he had a problem with it. He could pick up his car anytime. If he really had a problem with it, well, he shouldn't have left his credit card with a practical stranger.

Lauren carried one of the bags of dresses for me, and we sat on a bench outside to wait for our rideshares. I was too drunk to drive home. The champagne gave us a buffer against the cold.

"Will you be okay to go back to your family now?" I asked. I'd forgotten everything she had told me up to that point.

"Yes. Well, there's nothing else to do, is there?"

"Family is family. You don't really have a choice."

"Not with my parents at least. There's my car. See you soon?"

"Sure." I gave her a wave because I'd already tucked my mouth behind the high neck of my coat.

My rideshare drove me past my father's old apartment. Traffic had died down as dark clouds swept over the sky. Would we get snow this early? Out of habit, I scanned the parking lot, but his car wouldn't be there. His car was long gone. I'd sold it. Its price had only covered a fraction of the funeral. I leaned back in the seat and shut my eyes.

♦ 29 ♦

THE DAYS WERE GETTING longer now that the winter solstice had passed. Between the time I'd taken off work for my father's death and the time the university had given us for winter break, work had become a mere footnote in my life. The sunlight that broke through the plastic blinds was the only light I lived by. I had always been a good sleeper, and the shortened days meant I could stay in bed for long unbroken periods. Getting enough sleep was healthy, after all, wasn't it?

On the floor of my bedroom were dirty socks and sweaters. I thought about doing laundry like I frequently had over the past few weeks, but didn't get out of bed. I wasn't sure what time it was. The feeling of freedom that I felt by not having a cell phone was so strong that I still didn't want to give it up. My computer was all the way in the living room. The light wasn't so bright.

I sat up. The comforter fell from my body. It was Christmas Eve, and that meant dinner with Peter. Peter and his whitened teeth. I felt the greasiness of my unwashed hair and got into the shower. I conditioned my hair and plucked my eyebrows, which had been growing freely for weeks. My eyes watered, but I muscled through so I wouldn't embarrass my mother. I kicked dirty clothes out of my way as I looked in my closet for something cheery to wear. There was a single green sweater somewhere. I knew I owned one.

My mother had put up Christmas lights on her house, with the help of Peter. I'd watched them from afar weeks ago, all the while fuming at Peter. His leg was still in its steel frame, which meant my mother was the one on the ladder. I would have never allowed her to do something so dangerous, and it had been a painful hour of watching through my fingers.

She'd put up a tree inside. We were sort of Buddhist, but she'd always put up a tree to be more American. It was a new tree. I could tell even through the curtained window. Of course, the old one must have stayed in the attic of the old house. It was probably home to a colony of mice by now. The multicolored lights flickered on and off. I could see my breath. As I weighed whether to ring the doorbell or go in, Mom opened the door.

"I keep telling you to just come in. I thought I saw you drive up." Mom pushed the door open wide.

I could tell she was nervous by the way she smiled and the way she kept looking back toward the kitchen, where Peter waited.

"Your decorations look nice. Happy." I took my time unzipping my boots. "I didn't bring presents."

"I said no presents. Those are from friends who wouldn't listen." Mom waved at the boxes under her tree.

She was walking toward the kitchen, but I couldn't follow. I knew Peter was there. I saw his car on the street. He'd changed to a Honda CRV after the accident. SUVs sat a little higher up. It probably had more safety features than his old sedan. No more broken legs after getting run off the street by a racist.

The living room light wasn't on, so the Christmas tree stood out. I had the urge to put my boots back on and leave. I'd stopped breathing and forced air into my lungs. The air in Mom's house was warm and humid. My lungs were dry from the cold air outside, and I started coughing.

And so it was because I couldn't stop coughing that Peter came out to me with a glass of water. Over my coughs, he looked at me twice and laughed, explaining to my mom that we had played tennis with each other for weeks and how we already knew each other.

I turned my coughs into something like laughter, and tears came out of my eyes. It was so funny that we knew each other before Peter started dating Mom. It was so funny that when we played tennis together, and I played with aggression, it wasn't just for the point. It was so funny that I had spent the last ten months following my mother around the metroplex.

Eventually, I stopped cough-laughing, and we sat down for dinner. Everything was ready, and I didn't have to lift a finger. Peter was the kind of man who helped set the table.

"Did you cook any of this?" I asked.

"Oh no, I'm still learning." Peter was passing my mom dishes instead of leaving them in the middle of the table where we could all reach them.

"He's a good cook. I'm just teaching him a little." My mom waved her hand like she should wipe away her contributions to Peter's life.

"You don't know how to cook?" Underneath Peter's nice surface, he was just another man who needed a woman to take care of his most basic but most necessary needs.

"I'm learning. I stopped cooking so much when my kids grew up, and I got busier at work."

"So then, what do you eat?" Under different circumstances, I would not talk to someone who was older than me like this. But we were speaking English. Since we were speaking English and I knew Peter from tennis, he was imbued with an Americanness that I used to my advantage. I didn't have to show him absolute deference.

"Mostly takeout or easy meals. You know, boiled noodles." Peter smiled after his reply, as if he had expected me to ask him things like this.

"You mean ramen. Do you know Mandarin? Or Cantonese?" I asked.

"Peter's going to try to learn Vietnamese," Mom said. She gave me a look.

"My family's been here so long, and there are so many new additions. We mostly speak English to one another," Peter said. "Sometimes there is a sprinkling of Spanish. Chinese when there are enough elders. Some of my nieces and nephews want their kids to learn."

"And your kids?" I asked, even though I knew. It would be a good opportunity to officially know everything I had researched about them. I pretended to be focused on getting the right amount of pickled daikon into my next bite.

"Felix, my son, just started college. Aurelia is a couple of years younger than you. She's twenty-five. You'll meet them soon, I hope. They only speak English. Their mom was American. She only spoke English."

Peter's assumption that I wanted to meet his kids annoyed me. They weren't like me, with their clean-cut, silver-plattered lives.

"Was?" I asked, even though I knew.

My mom put her chopsticks down. "Linh."

"It's okay," Peter said, putting his hand on my mom's forearm. "She passed away."

"You killed her?" As I voiced the words, I felt as though I was separate from my body, looking down at us. Their near perfect harmony. Their blossoming love. And then there was me. A stain on their perfect first holiday together.

"Linh." Mom raised her voice.

"It's okay," Peter said again. He patted my mom's arm. "Sometimes I do feel like that. I loved her, and I can't help but feel like I didn't love her enough. To keep the cancer from forming in her body. Enough to help her beat it."

I didn't look at my mom, and we ate in silence. The kind of silence that I'd learned best in childhood. Don't talk about things. Let them ride that silence. Things will work out eventually. You just had to let them sit long enough. Tough things could be like a fog that won't go away. A ghost that the household must host until it chooses to go away. Things might fester, and things will certainly break, but if you're strong enough to withstand it all in silence, you could survive.

When I did finally look at my mom and saw the crease in her brow, I saw how I'd brought all the shadows from our lives into this new life she was trying to start. She was angry, and I had made her angry.

"What will you do with your time off, Linh?" Peter asked. "Your mom said you worked at a university. You get the entire next week off, right?"

"I have a friend's wedding," I said. Peter had punctured the suffocation of silence with a completely normal question. Like the weight didn't bother him. Like he could swim through anything.

"Is this Hoa? Is Hoa getting married? You didn't tell me," Mom said. The light was back in her eyes. Her smile was a smile new to me. *Where and when did she get a whole new smile?*

"No, not Hoa. A friend from tennis. She's getting married on New Year's Day."

"That sounds like fun," Peter said. I remembered then that Aurelia had broken off her engagement, but I couldn't say anything. I shouldn't know that.

Peter kept the conversation going through the rest of dinner, and I said very little. As Peter and Mom put dinner away and then served slices of cake, I saw the future. It had always been my mom and me against my father. All of my life, it had felt that way. She had protected me from him as best she could, and now I was protecting her from the world as best I could. But watching Peter help clean up after dinner, watching them talk to each other and laugh, I could see how things would always be with them. It was them against the world. Hadn't I wanted this for my mom? I'd wanted her to be kept safe. I wanted her for myself. But had I wanted her to be happy?

"Do you want to watch a movie with us?" Mom asked.

"No, I'm tired. I'll just go home," I said. I didn't want to have to keep pretending to be cheery. My face would be sore from trying to smile enough at Peter.

"You've been working too hard." Mom looked me up and down. "You've lost weight and gotten paler."

"It's winter, and I haven't been playing as much tennis." I moved to the front door.

"It's been a rainy end of the year," Peter said. "Though I've been glad for it, so I don't feel like I'm missing out on much."

"It was good to meet you again." I wasn't sure what I was supposed to do. Did I bow and recite some goodbye like Mom used to make me do to relatives when I was younger? Did I shake hands like a business associate? Did he expect to be able to hug me whenever he wanted, like an American?

"Drive safe," Mom said.

I nodded, then put on my shoes and jacket. Peter said goodbye and didn't move in for a hug, which I was grateful for. I couldn't make eye contact with him. I wasn't against him. I wasn't fighting him. Still, I felt defeated. Mom didn't need me to help her with anything now that she had Peter. Peter would help with the dishes. He'd help her put things away and pick out a movie. He'd make her laugh like I could not.

When I got home, I stayed up petting Lollipop and staring through my patio door into the darkness. Christmas was tomorrow or later today, and I had not been invited to anything. I knew that Mom would go meet Peter's kids. I knew that I would watch.

♦ 30 ♦

THE COLD WIND BROUGHT tears to my eyes, and I tucked the binoculars into my jacket and stuck my gloved hands into the warmth of my pockets. A convenient park trail ran behind Peter's property. I had found a nice spot a few feet from the trail down the hill that swept into this backyard. A jogger crunched through the snow on the trail above me. What kind of person goes jogging in thirty-degree weather?

Once my hands were warm, I looked through the binoculars again. They hadn't sat down for dinner yet, and Peter was wringing his hands together. I'd never seen him like that. They all lifted their heads at something I couldn't hear, and Peter left the room.

He returned with my mom and held out his hand, presumably introducing his children to her. She smiled, and I could tell she was nervous too, by the way she held her shoulders. The kids got up, and instead of shaking her hand, they took turns hugging her. I could count the number of times I'd hugged my mom. Then everyone was smiling and laughing. They were picture-perfect. I put the binoculars down and quickly climbed back up to the trail. I ran all the way back to my car.

I kept my hands in my pockets and turned up the car heater. Peter and my mom were getting serious. They were already serious. And what would I bring to the family? Anxious silence. Monotone clothes. Unremarkable tennis ability. Mom deserved a normal family like Peter and his kids. Kids who would get married and had attended Ivy League universities.

I wasn't even really doing anything to protect my mom. I was only following her around like an obsessed child. The car heater had made all my windows fog up. I reached out and drew a line on the windshield. It was time to stop. I should have stopped after my car accident. I should have stopped after my father's death. I was stuck in a routine and where would it send me? How could I look at my mom if she knew? How could I explain it to her if she asked?

When I parked in front of my apartment, I was too distracted to notice that someone was at my front door until I was out of my car, and they walked out into the light. Was this it? I would be another dead woman in the world. I couldn't remember in which pocket I'd put my pepper spray.

"Hi, Linh," Chandler said.

"Chandler." I stopped. He looked like he usually did. Put together, even though it was late on Christmas. Under his wool jacket, he was probably wearing a sweater vest. I thought about the boxes and dirty laundry strewn about my apartment. There was so much more since the last time he had been there. He wouldn't be able to miss it. There was probably an odor.

"I've tried calling you." Chandler had his hands in his pockets and shifted from foot to foot, human language for "I'm cold." There was no way I was ever going to let him see my apartment, or maybe if I did, he would leave me alone. That Linh is a mess, he would finally find out.

"My phone fell into a lake." I bit off the sentence before I apologized.

"Would you like to come over to my mom's?"

"Now?"

"Yes. I mean, not just to meet her. I want you to, though. We always host a Christmas party. It might be hard to find her, but I was sitting there and thinking about you, so I thought I would go see if you wanted to join us."

I imagined a mansion full of sweater vests and drunk white people. I imagined sitting in my apartment alone again.

"Sure." I'd showered and dressed, so why not make a night of it?

I followed Chandler to an SUV he was driving and nodded for him to turn on the seat warmers. The heaters made it feel like I had wet myself but felt delicious at the same time. He drove toward the center of the metroplex as I knew he would. I watched the houses and trees grow larger. This was where neighborhood watch signs became noticeably newer, not aged like they had been put there in the eighties and forgotten. No, these neighborhood watches were healthy. This was where neighborhoods hired their own security, and even though I could probably get through without being pulled over, the cost of my blood pressure was too high.

For Chandler, those signs and those thoughts were far from his mind, that is, if they ever occurred to him at all. I could feel his ease and as much as I wished to feel what he felt, I couldn't let myself relax. It was dangerous for me to believe I could be like him. If I said something, all I would be doing would be destroying his peace. I'd remind him of things that he didn't want to think about at the moment. I practiced mindful breathing as he drove us deeper into the neighborhood. He belonged here.

The gate to a private drive automatically opened at the approach of Chandler's car. Scattered lights illuminated a large lawn with massive oak trees. Cars were parallel parked all along the lane.

"It's a pretty big party. Family and friends come from all over," Chandler said. "This is where the extended family always gathers."

"You're going to inherit all of this?" Around the next bend, I saw a three-story building. It was the standard-issue Texas plantation home and then some. There were more white columns than I could count.

"I guess, if my mom doesn't write me out of her will." Chandler pulled into a four-car garage and hit a button to close the garage door.

"Am I going to be the only person of color here?"

"Of course not."

Chandler replied so quickly, I doubted he'd registered the question. He turned to open his door, turning his face from mine, which made me think he'd answered without thinking. I'd kept finding myself in this position, walking into a group of wealthy white people as if I needed to be scared. I'd read somewhere that some people got to a place where their brains couldn't distinguish between pain and pleasure. Was this how it manifested for me?

There was jangly holiday music playing over speakers that were installed in the ceiling. It made the garage feel festive.

"Is the car you left me your backup car?" I stopped in front of a vintage blue sports car. I didn't recognize the make or model.

"The car you have is actually my favorite. This one is my late dad's favorite. Mom can't bear to sell it quite yet."

"I'm sorry. When did that happen?" I decided not to say anything about my own father's death. I didn't want to engage in some death competition.

"Oh, it's okay. He died when I was in the fifth grade. A long time ago. I have a hard time remembering him. I was so young. Mom's a good one."

I looked at Chandler, and I could see why the women in Barrick's held out for him. Despite his golden boy looks, his face was open and warm. He was either exceptional at acting, or maybe he was genuinely open. His money hadn't distanced him from the world. Or maybe that was all the rest of us being wishful about Chandler.

"That's how you ended up at my school? The rumors weren't true, were they? You didn't get kicked out of all the other schools. There was no need for that."

"No, I didn't get kicked out of school," Chandler held open the door. I took a deep breath and walked into the house. "I chose to go there. My father went to those schools. He didn't come from money. My mom couldn't say no to me."

I was surprised his mom had married a poorer man. I put the thought away as we walked down a hallway leading from the garage to the house. The music was getting louder, and to the tune of "Jingle Bells," the house opened up. Two of my apartments could fit into this kitchen. Like at most parties, people were standing around a long island, snacking and laughing. By the number of vents, I could see the kitchen was designed for one to three chefs to be able to work in the space. Plates and more plates of desserts and snacks were spread around. Opposite the stovetops, there was a breakfast nook that could easily fit six, in addition to a dining room table, also with six seats.

There were a few poinsettias, but not the kind in the garish foil from the grocery stores. These were set into enormous floral displays that sat in the center of the island and tabletops. No one glanced our way when we entered. There were easily thirty people in the kitchen.

"Do you want to be somewhere quiet or loud?" Chandler asked.

"I want to be somewhere beautiful," I said, and I meant it. If you had this much money, why would you waste your time with anything else?

There was a Christmas tree larger than any tree I had ever seen in the entryway. I imagined they'd had to put scaffolding up to decorate it. It put anything I'd seen in a mall to shame, and by the smell of it, it was real.

Chandler led me up the stairs that encircled the tree on one side. We had to weave around people scattered up and down the steps. There were so many people everywhere, and I could feel the adrenaline pumping into my blood. It wasn't the fear of making small talk. It was the fear of being surrounded by hundreds of people and not one of them wanting to talk to you. That you could walk from room to room, and no one knew you, and everyone could tell they didn't need to know who you were by some detail of your clothes or merely the color of your skin. I followed Chandler as if losing track of him would mean death.

"This is my favorite room," Chandler said, opening a heavy wooden door.

It was a study. With a real fire going and another Christmas tree, but this time one that I could see the top of without pulling a muscle in my neck. The decorations on it were subdued, and the lights were dimmed and twinkled slowly, like stars. It was beautiful. The music wasn't playing in this room, and maybe for that reason, there were only a handful of people there. A teenage girl, who was reading in an armchair set its own nook, looked up when we passed, then returned to her reading.

"Is this the silent room?" I asked.

"We can do whatever we want," Chandler said. "I meant talk or whatever."

I nodded and smiled at Chandler's accidental double entendre. What was I doing with this person?

"Whiskey? Wine?" a woman sitting in front of the fire asked.

There were three of Chandler's cousins. Florence, Mark, and Bea—short for Beatrice. Bea had dreadlocks, which I had really thought was no longer okay. Bea was back from a Peace Corps stint abroad, which was also no surprise. Mark was a senior-executive-vice something or another—I had stopped listening to his title—at a wealth management corporation. I assumed he got the job through connections because he looked like he was twenty-five. Florence was Florence and did not seem to have any obligations.

I sipped the wine Florence had passed over to me, and half listened to their conversation. How many years had passed since the last time I'd been at a Christmas gathering like this? Extended family sitting around talking or not talking. Kids underfoot and enough cookies to build a house. It would have been more then fifteen years ago. Before middle school, when my father's drinking became a problem to hide. I set the glass of wine on the side table and toed off my shoes so I could pull my knees to my chest.

Chandler adding more wood to the fire woke me up. The others had left, and he smiled when he noticed me watching him.

"Are you very tired? You can sleep here tonight if you want."

"I haven't been sleeping very well," I said. I didn't want to admit how sleeping was usually easy for me or how it was also an excellent way to excuse yourself from present company.

"Anxious about the end of the year? Haven't reached some goals?"

"I don't set resolutions."

"You really don't seem the type."

"Are you?"

Chandler sat down next to me, and I pushed the blanket someone had covered me with down to my lap.

"My resolution all year has been to slow down."

He brushed his fingers through the tasseled end of the throw blanket. I imagined a fast life with the sports car he left me and as many women as he wanted. He was that kind of man. He was too tall, too handsome, too wealthy. Yet somehow, he had turned out kind.

"What do you think about when you're with me?" Chandler asked. "You always seem to be working on some big thing in your mind."

"What you want. Whether you have a stash of Asian women porn."

"No, nothing like that. I told you, Linh, I wanted to get to know you better." Chandler smiled. "I'd like to see you in the clothes you bought on my credit card. Was that for a wedding by any chance? One that takes place on New Year's Day?"

"Perhaps."

"And are you going with someone?"

"I don't usually go to weddings at all."

"But this wedding?"

"I'll decide that day. You don't have to go to weddings just because you're invited."

"Despite RSVP-ing yes?"

"It's going to be a huge wedding."

"Going with someone would make it a lot more fun."

"We'll see. That's days away."

I stood and stretched. The firelight wasn't bright enough for me to read any book titles from my distance. I tried to picture sharing Christmas morning with Chandler's extended family. Was staying at this estate like being in an expensive hotel? No staticky hair, no pills on sweaters, no trace of anything slightly worn. They would be opening presents, and there would be none for me.

"I should probably go home," I said.

On the way through the house, I tried to remember all the details like it was a museum I'd never go back to. The plush rugs, the rich creak of wood floors. The ornate moldings and sconces. The painted accent walls and wallpaper. The kids had all gone to sleep, and the adults who remained were in different states of subdued sprawls across armchairs, sofas, and sometimes the floor.

When we entered the kitchen, a woman was leaning into the fridge. As she straightened, I could see a collection of bangles come out from under her cashmere cardigan; her big, blonde Texas hair; and her big smile.

"Mom, this is Linh," Chandler said.

I forced a smile when I felt like frowning. I had really wanted to go home and crawl into bed.

"Hi, Mrs. Lindquist," I said. She was too far to extend a hand. She looked like the hugging-but-not-touching type who would blow some random number of air kisses, and I was grateful for the distance.

"Linh, Chandler has told me about you. It's good to meet you." Mrs. Lindquist walked to me and wrapped me in a full-body embrace. I felt the softness of her breasts against my hard chest. "Please call me Babs."

"Thanks for having me over." There was no way in hell I was calling her Babs. She towered over me even without the extra inches her hair gave her. I could smell her perfume, which she had just blessed all my clothing with.

"I just made some tea. Chamomile—would you like a cup?"

"I was taking Linh home," Chandler said.

"You should feel free to stay." Babs pulled out three teacups. "We could make up a room if you wanted. There will be a full spread for breakfast by eight."

She poured tea into the cups, and Chandler helped carry them to the breakfast nook.

"Tell me about yourself, Linh." Babs cupped her mug with both hands like she was settling in for a long story.

"I know Chandler from school." I looked at Chandler, who was studying his teacup.

"He told me that. What do you do with your time? What are your hobbies?"

"I work at the university. I play tennis. That's about it." I shrugged. I never knew how to answer these kinds of questions.

"Chandler always lets me beat him when we play tennis. Ever since he was a kid. That's when I knew I raised him okay even through all the trouble he gave us. He should bring you to the club to play sometime. We can play two against one, and he'll still let us win."

"I'm pretty rusty," Chandler said.

"Because you work too hard." Babs poured more tea into our mugs. "Did you spend the holiday with your family, Linh? I hope Chandler didn't force you to skip out on obligations?"

"I don't celebrate." I brought the mug to my mouth, so I couldn't say more. Babs had laugh lines around her eyes that she didn't try to cover up with too much foundation. She radiated warmth, and I could tell if I spent more time with her, I would tell her anything. There was that mothering quality about her. Babs would take me under her wing like any other orphan she found across her path.

"Oh yes, Christmas isn't everyone's thing." Babs pulled a rose from the arrangement in the middle of the table and brought it to her nose. "We always have this huge party. I suppose it's hard to break with tradition, but sometimes I wish it was a smaller thing. Something that involved fewer floral arrangements."

"All this time, I thought you loved the flowers," Chandler said.

"As they say, if you love something, you should know when to let it go." She put the rose in someone's discarded water glass. "Christmas is a great day for clichés, isn't it? If no other time? This party! I've probably eaten my weight in one night alone. Off you two go. I'll be here cleaning up when you get back, Chandler. Drive safely, please."

Chandler hugged his mom goodbye. When I looked back to the kitchen, Babs was doing what Mom would be doing after a party: covering trays with plastic wrap and figuring out refrigerator Tetris.

"She doesn't want to fuss. My father died on Christmas," Chandler said. "She almost stopped the tradition after that, but I think having everyone around helps her get through the day. The preparations help her take the grief in more manageable pieces."

"I'm sorry. I didn't know. I should have said something?"

"Time makes it more manageable, I think. That's what they say anyway." Chandler opened the car door for me.

He drove straight to my apartment, and I was glad. It was three in the morning, and I fought the sleep that the seat warmers were pushing me toward. The scent of the fire was stuck on our clothes and filled the car. I felt guilty about being the reason why Chandler had to stay up late and be out driving. I remembered he had come to me, so it was only right that he had to take me back.

"I'll be around through New Year's, Linh," Chandler said when he stopped the car. "Will you call me? We can hang out?"

"Sure," I said as I got out of the car and let the door shut behind me. *Sure* always felt like a good way to answer a question the way the questioner wanted while giving me a way out. The word questioned who exactly was sure enough for something to happen. To me, sure wasn't a yes. It wasn't a no.

The air was so cold I thought it might snow. It was spiky on my face. I wasn't pretending as I hustled to my apartment. Like a good friend, he waited until I shut my apartment door before driving away. I stopped only to take my clothes off before climbing into the mess of blankets on my bed. Lollipop meowed at my disturbance.

31

I SLEPT PAST NOON. When I woke up, the smell of smoke reminded me of where I had gone last night. I thought about Chandler's family estate. Peter and Mom putting things away in the kitchen after dinner. Babs covering catering trays with tin foil like mothers all across the country. Babs had it all, but in her eyes, I could see that she still would have traded it all to have her husband back.

I thought about the exchanges in life, as if there was a scale keeping everything balanced. My father had so deftly ingrained that into my mind. If I kept our house clean, it meant that my father had fewer things to be angry about when he came home drunk. He couldn't scream at me.

If I stayed quiet at work, I would continue to get raises every year. Not extraordinary amounts, but they were dependable. Once someone like me appeared to be asking for too much, they would get pushed out. I'd watched it happen over and over. Someone like me, with grand ideas, was foolhardy enough to believe academia wasn't built on an old, sturdy foundation of white supremacist patriarchy.

If I stayed vigilant, then I could protect myself and my mom from anything bad.

What would I be exchanging for a life with Chandler?

I stared out the window as I drank my morning coffee. With all the blinds in my apartment open to the bright winter light, I saw how disarrayed I had let everything get. As if I expected some woman to come in and clean it for me. I finished my coffee and surveyed the mess.

It took the entire day for me to break down all the boxes. I barely fit them into the recycling bins. They mixed with wrapping paper from the holidays, and it looked like I had just had one big Christmas party with hundreds of gifts. It took me another day to dust and vacuum. I even managed to wipe off the blades of the ceiling fans. I spent the next morning at the grocery store to restock my kitchen. I bought fish sauce, red pepper paste, limes, sugar, and garlic so I could make nước chấm. I bought greens that I only knew by sight. I didn't know their English or Vietnamese names. I bought my favorite pastries and the largest bag of rice that I could carry. I planned out the kind of meals that took days to make. At the exit of the grocery store, they were already giving away calendars for the new lunar year. For the first time in my life, I took one and put it up on the wall of my living room.

I spent hours doing four loads of laundry. As I folded the clothes, I separated them into a pile to keep and a pile to give away. There wasn't a way for me to erase the last few months, and there were some good things that had come from it. There was the jacket with three-quarter sleeves, floral print on top of black, and deep pockets. The extra-long beige sweater with a mustard stain could go.

Then there were the wigs. I posted them online and met up with a woman who was throwing a themed New Year's party. She looked at me as if my looks could tell her how much to trust the wigs. Then she gave them a deep smell. I pocketed the cash she handed me.

★ ★ ★

When there was a knock on my apartment door, I planned to ignore it. I wasn't expecting anyone, but I got up to look because I wanted to see Hoa on my doorstep. Had she come home for the holidays? Would she consider this place home still? It took me a few seconds to shake off my disappointment when I recognized Lauren through my peephole. It was Jessica's wedding day. I stepped away from the door and leaned against the wall, exhaling the longing I'd had for Hoa. I'd been waiting for her to reach out to me, but that was a little selfish, wasn't it? She had been reaching out to me all her life. I resolved to call Hoa tomorrow. Lauren knocked again. I flinched at the sound.

"Linh?" Lauren said. "I've knocked on every single door of this apartment complex, so you'd better let me in."

I accidentally kicked the package I'd left on the floor and froze at the noise. The box contained the new phone Jessica had sent me weeks ago. I'd walked around it all this time, moving it out of my way as I cleaned, not quite ready to deal with the world to that extent. It was fitting that it would give me up like this.

"Linh, I heard you. Open up," Lauren said.

I sighed and opened the door. Lauren looked me up and down, then hugged me. She let go of me and walked into the apartment without asking. I watched her as if I were waiting for a cue. It had been so long since I'd talked to anyone. Even my mom. I'd let her drift from my mind, and apparently she was so busy that she hadn't given me another thought. Maybe she was angry with me for not being nicer to Peter. I would be too.

"You're still coming to Jessica's wedding, aren't you? She said you would, even though we haven't heard from you. You haven't been answering our messages or emails."

"How did you know where I lived?"

"We dropped you off after Jessica's bachelorette weekend. I couldn't remember how exactly to get here, but then I remembered Chandler. You know, he's worried too."

"I'm fine," I said. I looked around my clean apartment. If she'd popped by days before, she would have seen how fine I was.

"What happened?" Lauren sat on my couch and motioned for me to join her as if this were her apartment, and I was the visitor.

"Nothing happened. I just hadn't gotten around to turning on the phone Jessica sent."

"Linh." Lauren hugged me from the side. "I really have missed you. You're sure everything's okay?"

"It's the holidays. Everyone is busy with family," I said. I still didn't want to tell her about my father. I'd realized I wasn't sure who I considered as close friends and wanted to give myself time to figure it out.

"I lost track of the days," I said. "I'll be ready in a few minutes."

"All right." Lauren smoothed her dress. "Chandler will be there too. Just so you know."

I got up without saying anything. The dresses I had purchased with Chandler's credit card still had their tags on. I picked the one with the fuller skirt so I could pretend I was in a fairy tale. I cut the tags off carefully, so they didn't tear the fabric. Lollipop watched me from under the bed, where she had hidden upon Lauren's entrance.

The dress was looser on me than I remembered. I put on tights to guard against the cold and opened the drawer where

I'd put the costume jewelry I had chosen to keep. It was time to give the items new memories. I put on a chunky necklace of strands of fake pearls of varying sizes and then layered gold bangles on my wrists. The thin gold bangles were fake, so they didn't make the right sound. A sound that I remembered from before my father started drinking. I chose a pink lipstick that just barely changed the color of my lips and steadied my unpracticed hand by leaning my elbow against the mirror.

"Want to ride with me?" Lauren asked when I returned to the living room.

"No, I'll drive Chandler's car. I should return it to him."

I'd made the decision in that moment. He had said he wanted more, and he had also given me space. Did he know how much I'd needed that? Or had he changed his mind?

★   ★   ★

I locked Chandler's credit card in the glove compartment before I handed the keys to the valet. Lauren waited for me, and we entered the building together. As soon as we walked into the entryway, someone took our coats. The air was humid and warm.

"Remember that spring theme?" Lauren asked. "Even down to the humidity. You won't need your jacket. Even if you go outside to walk along the grounds. Don't ask me how. All I know is that money can get you anything. Let's go up to see Jessica. Unless you want to mingle?"

"No, let's see Jessica."

I wanted to stay hidden throughout the wedding and reception. I could feel my anxiety simmering in my blood. It felt like it had been too long since I'd spoken to Jessica or Tiffany. Was there an amount of time that would relegate you back into the acquaintance zone? I also didn't know what I wanted to say to Chandler. What if he was here with someone who made sense for him? I didn't need to be a witness to that. It annoyed me that I cared, and I focused on the annoyance instead of my anxiety.

Lauren led me upstairs and down one of three hallways. I could hear laughter and shouting. As we got closer, I could make out chanting. They were chanting *Raptor* again. Pushing through an ornate door, I was plunged into a room full of silk dresses in pinks, purples, blues, and greens. My dress, just a shade too dark, made me feel like I was the spring thunderstorm.

"Linh! We have been so worried," Jessica held her arms out to me.

The skirt of her dress was so large that she could only really tap me on my shoulders. I forced a smile.

"Congratulations," I said.

"Bless you. We have missed you and all of that sarcasm," Tiffany said, coming up to my side. "Obviously, Jessica sends hugs and kisses. Now stand up straight, Jessica, or you'll wrinkle your dress and make that wedding planner devil furious."

"How is everything going?" I asked Tiffany. There were two photographers that danced around us, their cameras clicking.

"Fine, oh, fine." Tiffany touched her perfect hair. "Once she walks down that aisle, I am going to chug a bottle of champagne. Our mother is already drunk."

"Drunk on happiness," Jessica said. She was standing on a pedestal and was a foot higher than usual.

"Where are the drinks?" I asked.

Tiffany pointed me to a side room that had a bar and buffet. After filling a plate, I tried a door on the other side and found that several rooms were connected by doorways, probably for the ease of servants. Since Jessica, Tiffany, and Lauren had seen me, was I free to leave? Finding an empty room, I swallowed tiny cubes of cheese whole. Out the window, I could see the light from the metroplex reflected in the night clouds. Music began to play overhead. I heard footsteps in the hallway, and I peeked out. Women were filtering from the room and going downstairs.

I left my plate on a table and fell into step with them. The crowd of women joined up with men coming from the other direction, and we mixed and mingled down the stairs. The stamp of our feet echoed down the hall. We filtered into a large ballroom, and I followed the crowd to the left. I couldn't remember if that was the bride's side, but I couldn't have changed direction if I'd wanted. It felt as though all the other guests had attended a rehearsal for every step they took, as they seemed so confident. I sat down and listened to the rustle of silk and the click of heels on the wood flooring.

The music was actually being performed by musicians above us. The strings soared and then quieted as the pianist took over. I looked around but did not see Chandler anywhere. There were too many people. I had never been to a wedding so large and remembered how Jessica had chosen New Year's Day as a way to reduce numbers. There were so many people that I doubted Jessica would have noticed if I hadn't attended.

Everyone stood up at some cue I missed, and I followed them a second later. The wedding party filtered through, and I watched Cor, Sandra, Tiffany, and the cousins walk down the aisle on the arms of men who looked like they had all stepped off some runway. They were all tall with broad shoulders. Jessica walked down the aisle after her parents, and I was still stunned at how picture-perfect she looked. She was always so manicured, and I had been under the impression that you couldn't look more polished. I was wrong.

The ceremony was amplified and played over speakers. Velvet bags of rose petals were attached to the backs of seats, and I took a petal and ran my thumb over its softness as I listened to the pastor say words that meant nothing to me.

Marriages ended in divorce or death. How would hers end? Her husband was blond with dimples. I could see the blue of his eyes from my distance, and bet there was a whole legion of women waiting for the news of a divorce. As I watched them, I thought of my mother and Peter. If Peter's wife had lived, would they still be married? I tore the petal into tiny pieces that I let fall to the ground.

Applause broke out, and Jessica and her new husband started down the aisle. People threw rose petals at them, but they didn't go far. It didn't matter because petals began to fall from the ceiling throughout the entire ballroom. As people stood and started to move around, I was stuck between chairs, dresses, and children, running underfoot, who gathered armful loads of petals. The flowers reminded me of my mother, who had gotten into the habit of having a vase of fresh flowers on her dining table. A luxury I'd never had throughout my childhood. The guests trampled the petals, and I could see the dark shades of bruising on the velvet surfaces.

Ushers directed everyone down a hall. In the distance, two doors opened into another ballroom. Massive chandeliers sparkled, drawing everyone toward them. I could see French doors, and I pushed my way toward them, moving at a forty-five-degree angle through the river of people. The crush of people made my heart beat faster. If I fell, would they trample me like they crushed the rose petals underfoot? Would I have time to bruise before I died?

The air outside was warm. I expected to be hit with cold air, but as Lauren had said, the gardens were heated. I walked across the patio to the stone balustrade like I knew where I was going. My heart was still beating too fast. At times like this, I wished I smoked, so I would have something to do.

The chatter of the guests inside sounded like a low rumble of thunder as the door opened and shut behind me. I expected to see Chandler when I turned. Instead, it was a woman coming toward me.

She was wearing a hat, but I could tell by the unyielding blackness of her hair that she was Asian. When she got close enough, I recognized Peter's daughter.

"Do you have a cigarette?" Aurelia asked.

"No, I was going to ask you."

"I should have brought some. I knew coming to this would make me sad." She stopped next to me, facing the gardens beneath us.

I turned in the same direction but didn't reply. What could I say? I shouldn't know anything about her life.

"Your mom is dating my dad," Aurelia said. "I've seen you before. You were at the hospital when my dad got hurt. But the accident was before they started really dating, wasn't it?"

"Around the same time," I said. It was the truth.

"I recognized you from some photos your mom posted online."

The lights spread around the landscaping changed from blue to pink.

"Do you have social accounts?" Aurelia asked. "What's your username? So I can follow you."

"I'm not really online." I thought Aurelia had deleted all her accounts.

"That can be freeing, can't it? Then no one can look at your life. Private accounts don't really cut it, do they? Then the corporations can follow you, and if someone works for those businesses." Aurelia shrugged.

Had that happened to her? Or did she know someone? I'd never gone as far as hiding my IP address. I thought about the false name I set up for new social media accounts and the separate email I used to set those up. I thought about how I put five filters over a stock photo to use as a profile picture. I thought I had been so smart, but I'm not a hacker.

"You know, there isn't much about you on the internet." Aurelia turned her body to mine, and I did the same. Was she going to push me over the stone railing? It was a fifteen-or-so-foot drop down into the landscaping. I couldn't die from that, could I? Was Aurelia trying to protect her father from me? Or maybe protect her inheritance from my mom?

"There isn't much to know about me," I said. "Are you looking for something?"

"I looked up your mom when my dad first mentioned her. Before he even asked her out on a date. But it's weird to see that side of people, don't you think? And different generations use social media so differently."

"How long ago was that? That you looked up my mom?"

Aurelia shrugged. "A couple of years ago? My dad doesn't usually mention people from work, you see. So I was curious. He's never dated anyone for a long time, but there was something different. Your parents' divorce seemed messy. But I was happy for your mom. It's best to get away when it doesn't feel right. I'm sorry if she suffered for a long time. She's strong."

I spread out my fingers as far as they could go on the stone in front of me. The stone was cold on my palm. The heaters couldn't heat the rock that brought up the coldness of the earth.

If Aurelia had been watching my mom two years ago, I would have still been online. What did she know about me?

"How come you're here? At this wedding?" I asked.

"Oh, I went to school with Jessica's husband. It's really a tiny place, the metroplex. I think the world is, really, once you open yourself to people. Then you see familiar faces everywhere. Like Chandler, you know—he's all right. I grew up with him too. I can see him over there now, but I don't think he'll interrupt us. He's got good intuition like that. He doesn't have a fetish, in case you wanted to make sure."

"Have you and he?" I turned to where she was looking, though I knew Chandler would notice and know that we were talking about him. He was the same as always. His tuxedo made him look like a model. He made me want to press myself against his side, under his arm, where I could rest. Where I wanted to rest.

"Oh no," Aurelia laughed. "We've always been friends. But I wanted to verify the non-fetish. If one day we're sisters by marriage or something, we'll look out for each other. Well, we don't even have to wait for that."

I watched as people started to wander into the garden and obscured Chandler from my view. In the past, I would have gotten away from Aurelia as quickly as possible. It was risky to stand together. Someone might think we were teaming up to cause trouble, and call the police and cause a stampede. But at that moment, I didn't care. So what if we were? I knew I could ask Aurelia to help me figure out how to get rid of my father's shotgun. I had pushed it into the back of my closet, frustrated that I had to deal with it. I had imagined carrying it around for years and years.

"We must be in the clear. They finished the first dances and all of that sappy stuff." Aurelia bumped my shoulder. "I thought it would make me cry. I was supposed to get married this year too. What's your excuse? Why are you hiding from the festivities?"

"I felt anxious."

"Do you want a beta blocker? Or to find the potheads or something else?" Aurelia spread her arms wide. "I bet we can find any number of things among this wedding party."

For the first time in what seemed like years, I really smiled.

32

THERE WAS A SMALL dent in my bumper to remind me of my mistake. I hadn't heard anything from my insurance company, so the woman who was not Eric Ryan, must have skipped filing a claim. I knew I should fix the bumper; otherwise, it would begin to rust, like a wound festering with infection. I would do it tomorrow. I would clean up all my messes before the Lunar New Year and start on a good foot.

The wind picked up, and I pulled the hood of my down jacket over my head and turned away from my car. With that kind of bulky jacket on, from afar I could be anyone. A green blob wandering through an ungated cemetery alone the day after New Year's Day. It was apt to come out here on January second. A nothing day. No ceremony or ritual about it.

The dirt over my father's coffin was sunken, bare, and cracked. Grass wouldn't be able to grow over it until the spring. The grave next to his was decorated with plastic flowers. I hadn't brought anything with me. I had driven to the cemetery without thinking. His death and the time around it were like walking into a dark room without turning on the light. I didn't want to see it all yet. I fumbled around in the dark for what I needed before leaving the memories tightly wound up.

I wondered if I should have sent my father's remains back to Vietnam. But there wasn't anyone there to receive them. His life had been torn from everything he knew when he was an adult. I sat down on the cold ground. Mom had wanted him to be buried, and so I had complied. I'd thought cremation would be easier to deal with, but she'd resisted for some religious reason, though our commitment to religion was questionably thin.

And what would I have done with his ashes anyway? There was no ceremony to be had. Would I have spread his ashes at the bars he frequented? Would I have put his ashes in my closet next to his gun? Carried both around with me until I died? I wondered if I was supposed to clean his grave every year now. Was that a Vietnamese tradition? Could I look it up on the internet and then adopt it as my own, just like that?

I felt like I should have at least brought incense, though I wasn't sure I would be able to light it in this wind. Could you use a lighter in American cemeteries, or was it against the rules? Was the incense to light the death's way to reincarnation? I'd read the Buddhist reasons for it once but had already forgotten. I felt like I should bow to my father's grave, and yet I could not. We were only two more humans damaged by the cruel systems of the world. I would do what I did. My father was dead. He wasn't going to come back and yell at me for my stubborn lack of respect.

An iciness was building in the air, as if it could be crinkled like foil wrapping paper. Like it might start snowing at any moment. But I was warm in my jacket. I'd put on a down vest over my sweater and wore a buttoned-up shirt under that and a T-shirt under that. I'd learned how to dress for warmth in the past year. I'd learned how to keep track of cars on the highway. I'd learned how to pass a car, then backtrack to it. I'd learned how to apply eyeliner, lip liner, and lipstick. I'd learned to layer necklaces in a way that would make that New York style lady proud. I'd learned a way to demonstrate my love for my mom. I'd have to relearn a new way. I'd buried my father. So what now?

I didn't hear my mom's steps. Only when she was standing next to me did I realize there was someone else in the cemetery. I jumped onto my knees and made a weird high-pitched noise.

Mom laughed.

"I'm sorry I scared you," she said.

"I wasn't paying attention."

"You didn't tell me you were coming here."

I shrugged. She hadn't messaged me since before the dinner with Peter.

"He protected me after the war. From other men." Mom had brought a bowl of uncooked rice, an orange, an apple, three sticks of incense, and a lighter. She set the bowl and fruit at the base of the tombstone.

I held my hands around the flame of the lighter so the incense would catch. Mom gave me one and kept two. I stood slightly behind her. I knew what to do. How to hold the incense between your hands in the international sign for prayer. How to bring your hands to your forehead or chest. I didn't know if it was a personal preference, if it meant something specific, or if it was nothing at all. I didn't know what one said in their mind when they went through the motions. If I had ever been taught, I'd forgotten.

I kept the incense near me as my mom bowed over and over. The scent was sacred to me, but not directly tied to religion. But it was not exactly comfort, not exactly home, but something of both of those things. The scent represented everything I associated with Vietnamese things, with the reverie of a Buddhist temple, with the mystery of ancestors, and with the motions of something older than I will ever know. I brought the incense to my forehead and bowed.

We watched the incense burn in silence until it went out. Three red sticks of charred wood stuck out from the rice. The gray ash had blown away but left a stain in the rice where it had fallen.

"It's better this way." Mom put her arm around me. At first I stiffened out of habit at the contact. "We shouldn't stand in the cold all day. You'll get sick. What are you doing today?"

"I don't have plans." I let Mom turn me around and lead me back to our cars.

"You can come shopping with me. I'm going to meet friends for lunch. We can leave your car at my house on the way. We'll drive together."

"Okay," I said. I nodded, even though I knew my mom couldn't see it. She was talking about something else; some plant seed she was searching for. How long had it been since I'd let my mom drive me anywhere? Since I'd been in a car with her instead of following her?

Something hit my face, and I stopped. Tiny Texas-sized snowflakes were falling.

"Or maybe we'll just go home and watch a movie with hot chocolate?" Mom said.

She laughed and opened her mouth to the snowflakes. Instead of telling her about the microplastics in rainwater, I opened my mouth and waited for a cold flake to hit my tongue.

ACKNOWLEDGMENTS

THIS BOOK CAME TO me in the moments before sleep, when countless worries were pinging around my mind. As I wrote, the COVID-19 pandemic was raging. As this book went out on submission, there was yet another shooting. In the face of a world so accepting of avoidable death, I write because I want to live. And so I want to thank you, reader, for spending your valuable time with my novel and giving it space within your heart.

Thank you to Amanda Orozco for finding my writing admirable and wading through things like contracts so that I could keep my mind focused. Your expertise made the entire process feel easy when it most certainly is not. Your edits and feedback were instrumental to getting this story into its best form.

Thank you to my editor, Toni Kirkpatrick, for advocating for me and this book, and to the entire team at Alcove Press/ Crooked Lane Books for shepherding me through the publication process with aplomb.

Thank you, me, for telling me you are proud of me despite my enduring disbelief.

Thank you to Lise Ragbir. Your encouragement and cheering, from a writer I hold in such high esteem, gives me strength in those moments of doubt. Our conversations over the last few years helped me feel so much less alone when I needed it most.

Elizabeth Schwaiger, you show me by example how to follow desire and ambition tenaciously. Thank you for giving the book an early read and confirming how it matches up to the sprawl we grew up in. Seth Orion Schwaiger, your perseverance and enduring kindness keep my faith in humanity from completely snuffing out. Thank you, Schwaigers, for over three years of weekly video calls. I don't know what would have become of me without our friendship as an anchor.

Thank you to Anabel Graff. You prompted a series of dominos that got me so very far! I benefit from and am so grateful for the energy you bring to those around you.

Thank you to current Super Fun Writing Group members, Christine Alvarez, Becky Liendo, and Jenny Mott, for reading an early draft and celebrating all the wins, no matter how small I try to pretend they are. Thank you three, and especially Becky, for holding me tightly through a white-out-rain kind of storm and not letting me forget my value.

Thank you to all the members I have the honor of sharing space with at Louis Place, including Steffani Jemison, Quincy Flowers, Naima Lowe, Laura August, Ginger Carlson, Jessica Harvey, Kristen Leigh, and the many writers in the daily writing room.

Maria Sanchez and Brandon Ross, thank you for welcoming us to a city and helping us create a sanctuary during a portion of the pandemic. I will never forget our time on the land of the Tohono O'odham and Yaqui, and how it was marked by an abundance of black widows, the grandeur of the clouds during the monsoon season, and the steadying presence of the saguaros.

Thank you to friends who have generously nourished me over the years by sharing their lives and listening to my fears and hopes: Milli Apelgren, Dalia Azim, Michu Benaim Steiner, Ana Esteve Llorens, Lope Gutierrez-Ruiz, Ronny Guye, Mark Lynch, Rebecca Marino, Desiree Morales, Shalini Ramanathan, Jill Schroeder, Elisa Sumner, Joel Sumner, and Chris Tomlinson. I am lucky to have many friends who also play tennis. Thank you for all the balls hit, lobbed, aced, mooned, volleyed, and walloped.

There aren't enough words to encompass my gratitude to Brian Willey for over a decade of support. You have seen me change, encouraged me in all of my pursuits, and loved me through it all. I could not do it without your belief and championing.